ALSO BY MARVIN COHEN

The Self-Devoted Friend

Dialogues

*The Monday Rhetoric of the
Love Club and Other Parables*

Fables at Life's Expense

Baseball the Beautiful: Decoding the Diamond

Others, Including Morstive Sternbump

The Inconvenience of Living

*How the Snake Emerged
from the Bamboo Pole but
Man Emerged from Both*

*Aesthetics in Life and Art:
Existence in Function and Essence
and Whatever Else Is Important, Too*

*How to Outthink a Wall:
An Anthology*

Baseball as Metaphysics

FIVE FICTIONS

FIVE FICTIONS

MARVIN COHEN

TOUGH POETS PRESS
ARLINGTON, MASSACHUSETTS

Cover design by Rick Schober.

ISBN 978-0-692-07904-1
Tough Poets Press
49 Churchill Avenue, Floor 2
Arlington, Massachusetts 02476
U.S.A.

www.toughpoets.com

To Darwin, who evolved me.
(No, he only described it, so I have
to withdraw most of the credit.)

CONTENTS

FOREWORD

I wrote these five fictions so long ago (around 1964, it now being 2018), that it feels like I've climbed meanwhile to the other end of this known world and found enough strangeness here to delete "known" and substitute "unknown."

What's happened? A major jolt of time, or a weird bolt. With expected bodily decrepitude (though I still play softball), I'm ready to fall off by losing track. The plunge awaits me.

P.S. Maybe the world has done the changing, more than mere me.

Marvin Cohen
New York City, 2018

HARVY'S FAILURE

1

Morning rose, dawn sunned over the horizon, light signified a new day. In a room crammed with dust, kept dark by nailed fabrics on the window posts, a sleeping mass named Harvy Furstwitz kicked half of a blanket off, smothered by the rising steam. His dream was unsatisfactory, and so, scorning its lack of realism, he succeeded in dismissing it. Had it been pleasant, and also unreal, he would have justified its function and tried to sustain it. His waking censor presided over sleep.

Never in his life had he been without a month, and today was no exception, being January. He felt out of place when unattended by the formalities of time. He kept Order for an ideal, by never practicing it. On his pillow was a crumb from two days before, on which several household insects were dining at leisure, confident that their human host, whose cheek breathed so closely by, would refrain from interrupting them, kept occupied by his slumbers. Instinct, tempered by habit, taught them this: though solitary, Harvy had been minutely studied and observed, such was his stationary disposition toward sloth, inertia, and other sedentary states of being. Movement itself was just a variation on sluggishness. Of his virtues, industry was not one, nor was Harvy avid to acquire it.

Outside, a city raged. People rose and prepared for work on a civilized American industrial Tuesday. The arts of commerce and communication, left over from last night, were tyrants over their practitioners, demanding to be resumed. Harvy benevolently included himself out, inside his dusty room. It was peaceful not to participate; he worked hard at his sleep, and kept jealous possession over its reward. Serenity, laziness, and boredom were his Three Graces. He wooed them assiduously.

His room was devoid of a clock, as an undesired alien influence. He preferred, instead, the more conservative refinements of a soft-contoured innocence, which his critics confused with ignorance. When awake, he sometimes read. Pages of strewn books were sprawled in the disarray of evidence, borrowed under pseudonym from random libraries whose shelves would not be honored by their return. This passive criminality served to improve his culture and to advance his education with a few consolidated fragments of stray unmemorized facts, whether literary or scientific. Freed from specialization, he remained liberally at large.

The reason he woke was to relieve bladder pressure. The sink was only a few feet away, but he couldn't negotiate the distance, in a painful stupor of lethargy, which imprisoned him to his bed. Two terrific needs were in combat, and finally one subsided, letting him deposit the joyful fluid within that makeshift lavatory, his sink. Thus, chemically restored to balance, he sought his bed again, blinded and groping. His loose pajama bottom, undisciplined by button or pin, fell to the floor as usual, displaying an embarrassed nudity from the waist down. The bachelor stepped out of the garment, returned to let the faucet run, then clogged it off, and stumbled back to bed. Reluctantly, sleep, with whom he shared his celibacy, had vanished for the day, leaving him miserable, and uncomfortable.

He mechanically closed his eyes and drew the blanket up, reclining in his softest semblance of mirrored slumber, from memory, yet energetic consciousness, like stinging bees, broke through the fortress, forcing thoughts upon his recumbent inaction. Hunger grumbled its requirements, and the abstract practicalities of life hindered his peaceful drowsiness from settling into lost oblivion's bliss. "No use being stubborn; I'll eat," he admonished himself. Still in bed, he reached far and wide, but encountered no food: no remnants of the crumb, no speck or spillover from those sated insects, now dozing in their happy cracks.

The core of a former apple drew dust to the bedtable, and Harvy was fastidious. Better fast than court some intestinal disease. Vaguely in a corner nested a banana, wholly unpeeled, but that would mean quitting the bed. Life spun out its web of obstacles that charitably littered his home. He glanced at the door, where at the bottom an ominous envelope had been slipped through. Difficulties were early encountered, and accumulated through the day; things were hectic, and distracted his soul from being its own object as an exercise for contemplation. Harvy knew the envelope was from the landlord, an eviction notice. It distressed him to be reminded, in that sneaky way, of his negligible possession of so material a thing as money. Morally, it put him at an unfair disadvantage, while rendering irrelevant his means of combatting it: dignity. "I hate this predicament I'm in!" Harvy commented, in a signal note of rage. The dust was stirred.

That self-made sound was followed (though not in the logic of cause and effect) by a door-knock; unanswered, the woody noise was repeated, with a more insistent tone; it was imperious, not to be unheeded.

"Who is it?" roared Harvy, by way of anticipating and obviating a third series of knocks, which he would have found unbearable. "It's me. Open up," he thought he heard, and was annoyed at this impudence, not knowing the identity of "me." "What a presumptuous friend I must have!" he assumed, sitting up on the bed but covered decently. "Well?" he heard, a rising note, definitely impatient. "It's deplorable, my lack of privacy," said Harvy self-pityingly, loud enough for the phantom behind the door to comment in a rude vein, using an unspeakable oath. Thus, the adversaries were at an impasse, a locked door dividing the reluctant host from an adamant guest, each determined in his stubbornness. Ten minutes passed, and each stood his post, as a bitterly shared silence passed between them, those foes of embattled obstinacy. The situation was not conducive to the development of a binding friendship, and though Harvy felt known by his intruder, the latter remained, for him, a mystery of obnoxious proportions. Harvy had no phone, so couldn't call for assistance. Behind the door, a lunchbag was opened, and the barred visitor, still apparently standing (and not on ceremony, either), started munching. Harvy salivated in response, and this removed him from his bed. On opening that most attractive refrigerator, he recoiled with mild electric shock, but discerned empty shelves: nothing but ice cubes, and the rind of what had once called itself a lemon. Then he slammed it, absorbing his second shock. His one-room apartment, by necessity, included both refrigerator and bed in the one room, not to mention other articles, less readily identified. The stranger concluded his repast, leaning against the door, and Harvy was ravaged by those familiar stomach pangs that so curtailed his aptitude for pleasure. He looked under the door for the landlord's note, but it had vanished, and the rustle of paper outside indicated that his unwarranted persecutor was casually perusing it, to wile the hours with a more absorbing diversion than can be afforded by gazing at the staircase. Harvy lived six flights up, so to jump out of the window into the blank back alley (there was no fire escape) would risk physical injury and insult bodily integrity. "I'm trapped," he concluded, and his observations terminated with dread. He blamed his precarious state on the need to urinate, which had caused him to wake up. It made him feel better, to place blame so impersonally, so cosmically, on so mechanical a factor. "I have an immediate worry," he analyzed, "to go with my standing, permanent ones." These words were carefully inaudible, so as not to provoke his outside visitor. The thought of that patient fellow, now seated with his back against the door and his legs sprawled into the abominable hall, scared Harvy, whom threat sorely distressed, afflicting his soul with quite acute agony. He had restored to his lower parts his pajama trousers, and now thought it wise to get dressed for the day. "I might be impelled into activity," he forewarned himself, and that set off, for reaction, a frazzled yawn, which he broke in the middle, so as not to antagonize the man who was waiting for him. Might he not yell out of the window? No, the neighbors would suspect him of being strange. So he endured his confinement, and grew more violently hungry.

"Shouldn't I face him?" he thought, though the courage to open the door was missing. "He sounded like he knew me, so what harm can come from that? At least, can't I question him?" No, he was timidly apprehensive, and hated to court danger. Thus ebbed off the afternoon, and except for a few absences of a couple of minutes, his unknown tormentor had remained steadfast, as though with some devout object in mind, sustained by a soul-consuming dedication. No words were spoken, in the quietude of evening. Harvy spotted the banana that he had seen in the corner from his morning's bed, and barely could sneak the skin off before devouring it wholly. At this moment, his life seemed intolerable. Might he not confront the man now, urged by desperation? He grew hearty, unlocked his portal of safety, and knobbed it open. Nothing but emptiness stared at him: one staircase leading to the roof (his was the top floor), and that well-traveled one that in diminishing steps descended to the street. Had it been a hoax? But the skylight was open, revealing a starpatched section of that detached particle of universality, the night. Its distance froze him, and the sharp local wind. Suddenly a leg hung down, then another; his adversary was descending from the roof!

Harvy banged shut the door, locking it twice (thus unlocking it). "Don't terrify me!" he yelled. The door opened, and a man's shadow loomed with stark immensity. The light was out, the room was dark. "Who are you?" Harvy asked, gently, and with humility; no sense being bold now, to offend a persistent guest, who had condescended to visit him, taking time off from a busy life. There was nothing to offer; his stock of hospitality was insanely inadequate; but at least Harvy struck on the light, with its symbolic implications of warmth and the absence of suspicion. It was welcome, right now, to have faith. The man before him he had never seen before. "Am I known by you?" he asked, puzzling his grammar. "It's hot. I'll take my coat off," said the other in reply. Thus, Harvy had company that evening.

2

The visitor coughed, and complained that the room was dusty. Harvy's apology was pathetic, for it implied that he could never remedy it. They sat on the only two chairs, and were rapidly getting cozy. Ease warded off awkwardness, and Harvy confidentially discussed his landlord's action of eviction; contrite, the guest returned the note he had stolen, with its legal stamp of notarization; and offered Harvy his most sympathetic condolences, which Harvy was at once eager and forward to accept, assuring a closer bond with this now apparently harmless stranger. Harvy studied him; the face described itself, and the dress was a further telltale. But the only conspicuous characteristics were the nondescript ones. "He scared me all day, and now I find he's ordinary," Harvy non-articulated to himself, scarcely moving his lips. Harvy himself was gazed at, without insolence, but out of perhaps clinical curiosity. "Why'd you come, and announce yourself as though you'd known me?" asked the proprietor of the room, his habitual cowardice startled by this abrupt, undiplomatic audacity. "I *have* known you," assured the stranger, "though you never saw me." "Why were you rude, why did you wait outside all day, like a haunting specter? What was your game?" These forthright questions amazed their mouther, whose own courage struck him as incredibly unprecedented. He looked gratefully at the guest for having provoked it, and felt more warmly kinder as he grew more aggressive. "He makes me brave," thought Harvy; and the visitor's aspect was indeed mild, inclining more to the meek than to what had been imagined to be ferocious. Nevertheless, he chose to ignore what Harvy asked and, in turn said, "Why do you live like a bum? Can't you get a job?" "You have no right to ask me that," warned Harvy. "Now get out!" He was heeded, obeyed; Harvy was in sole possession of his own room, and as the stranger's steps grew inaudible down the staircase, his mystery, as a discarded keepsake or memento, a remnant of the strange experience, enlarged itself grotesquely. "Wait!" shouted Harvy, and ran down after him.

The moonless midnight approached, with nothing in sight but Wednesday. So many buildings, and not one stranger! Where had he run?

"That guy left his overcoat behind," Harvy remembered. "That's maybe a clue, for what needs a lot of explaining. And I don't have a proper one myself, so I can keep it. That leaves a profit for the day."

Shivering, he went back up, but the door had been left ajar, and the visitor's overcoat was gone. But Harvy himself had heard him descend; had there been an accomplice? Or was reality on a holiday, paid for generously by his diminishing sanity? "Ouch! I'm hungry!" Harvy said. Putting on a warm jacket, he locked the door and went out. The streets were abandoned, but an all-night cafeteria stood open. He located it, and found his stranger in there, and on the rack—it was undeniable—hung that very coat! "Hey you!" said Harvy, and strolled over.

The stranger got up. "Pardon, I don't know you," he said, looking puzzled. "I don't understand your approach. Have I done something wrong?"

"Yes, you were in my apartment, or hanging outside all day; you're crazy, aren't you?" The food-server, an old man with a waiter's apron, told them to shut up; he ran a respectable joint. No other customers were around, but the cook emerged. "Cut it out, you guys," he sagely advised. "Come out with me," Harvy asked his stranger. Then a cop on a night beat happened along, saw trouble from outside the window, and entered. "Okay, what's going on?" he said. "I don't know him," volunteered the stranger, "but he's bothering me. I have no idea why."

The cop instantly believed him, but took them both to the station, where they were booked for disturbing the peace. In adjacent cells, they spent the night.

Harvy remained sleepless, calling out for food; the warden plainly ignored him, hinting at sadism. The stranger's cell was in shadow, but no movement was heard. "Don't be so restless," the warden shouted at Harvy's pacing. "Well," said the confused victim for his own interior ear, "I had an eventful day, and tomorrow promises much the same. Perhaps my reason has crashed. If so, I'll know."

At dawn the prisoners were examined, told off by rote in a droning voice that reeked of standard procedure, and dismissed, jointly, to a hard city street. "I'll buy you breakfast," offered the stranger, and in sooner time than immediately, with quick promptitude, in sudden alacrity, Harvy, at once, accepted. He barely gulped down his thanks, already tasting the food.

It was before the business hour. They entered an unpretentious joint just as it was opening. The stranger ordered for them both, indifferent to aversions or preferences in Harvy's captive taste; it was disrespectful, as though Harvy had deserved no dignity and, precisely as to his merits, was accorded none. Now the stranger was host, Harvy the guest; their relationship entered another baffling plane, or kept its broken progress of continuity. The eggs were too flabby and underdone, and Harvy spilled almost all of his coffee in the repressed anger of his nervous tiredness. Neither had removed their outer winter protective garment. From afar, a seductive apathy swooned over Harvy, costing him his vigilance and wiping out that keen discernment which would have served to assess the situation and study its unresolved factors. "I'm too sleepy to discuss what I'm curious about, but can we meet when I've rested? Frankly, I can't focus sense on the real, and you're washed out in the general blur," Harvy said, in the face of his companion's polite and almost ironic alertness. This request, and speech, brought out, at most, a smile; the listener possessed the most inflexible features Harvy had ever seen: an immobile squadron of responses, a lax coolness that dipped into the diabolical and seemed to play at life. Yet, in the apartment, this person had "surrendered" to Harvy, and fled. To reconcile piece to piece and pierce the whole together was too formidable a task for Harvy's indolent will. As his waves of sleepiness increased, futility came on to drench him. Wordless, he stood up, hardly dropped a thank you, and went home, unfollowed. The apparition would plague him forever, when his consciousness resurged.

At home, he let his clothing fade off him, sag or crumble with a dying moan on the floor, while the escaped portion of his unclad body found a dead warmth under the blanket, washed in the stale waters from time's ceaseless backdrift. No dream complicated his Wednesday, and the facts preceding had been forgotten. Dullness throbbed to the cure, and painted blank the day before. His ordeal had been officially "unlived," though unofficially its credentials were valid enough to plague and worry through his peace, in regions of doubt and God. It left him, permanently, a mystic.

3

At five-thirty Wednesday was dark. That was when Joe Candrov knocked, calling on his friend after work. The knock was friendly, but Harvy started. It evoked, by association, dreadfully unpleasant echoes. But within this similarity, a welcome note of difference was heard in Joe's familiar yell. Admitting the visitor, Harvy returned to bed, to bake his twelfth doze. Joe Candrov, in business attire, had come to convert Harvy to his own respectable routine. "There's an opening in my firm, and you need work. The vacancy will be filled if you wait too long. Tomorrow morning be sure to report, so this opportunity won't go to waste. Hey! Are you awake, or what? I don't like to talk idle." Joe took the nearest chair to Harvy's bed, and prodded his friend. The more resistance, the more he was irritated, so he stroked harder. Along one of the light bulb's rays, some motes or specks of dust arose, and a dank odor ensued. "You disgust me," said Joe, as though completing a formality. Here and there, unreturned library books added to the litter. Joe fingered one, and found it six months overdue. He was furious that Harvy should be hopeless, and this determined him on a crusade to reform his friend and set him on the right path. "Let's see your best suit for the interview tomorrow," Joe requested, and Harvy sullenly pointed to the closet. Joe couldn't see one thing wearable, though he examined the contents on every hanger. "You're a case!" he concluded, and stripped his own suit off for Harvy to try on. What he'd begun would be carried through, to Harvy's peril or to his salvation. The bedsmitten host, mumbling from the recesses of a pillow, warned Joe of the penalties of energetic excess; then, clasped by the ankles, was dragged violently off the bed. "On your feet, and see if this fits you," Joe commanded. Their height and general dimensions blending lumpishly into vague sameness, Joe's suit felt at second home on Harvy, though wrinkled into postures of stooping. From his underwear, Joe saw that all was right. He put on Harvy's rags, which he'd replace later at his own wardrobe. His act of mercy to Harvy disposed him even more kindly to the man he had vowed to help. He envisaged another's transformation, to justify his own drastic intervention in that case. "He's my clay," he thought, quickened by the creative impulse. But his suit was being crumbled and creased; its borrower, in his slovenly fidelity to the horizontal, had reverted to an archaic semblance of sleep.

At that instant, a soft pressure sounded outside the door. As deputy host, empowered with delegated responsibilities, Joe Candrov stepped to the breach and admitted some stooping ancient male with a foreign cackle, who demanded the rights and privileges of a landlord. "That sluggard over there, he's evicted," he indicated. Joe grimaced, and realized he'd have to move Harvy into his own apartment, but this step would facilitate his friend's rehabilitation, with his own constant example set before him: haste and upward propulsion, industry accompanied by the mobility of external rewards, a pride of the self as part of society. "I'll wake him up, literally," Joe promised. Turning, he saw the landlord spitting, with guttural despite and aversion, at the sleeping innocent. "He cost me money, he didn't work. Who's going to pay me my rent? … You,

you owe it to me," said the landlord, selecting Joe as immediately handy. "I'm only a bill collector," Joe explained. "That's some sales uniform you have on!" he was told. "I recognize Furstwitz used to wear that. Don't fool me. Hand it over. I want a check. Here, I show you the total," and Joe was treated to an exact account. "I'm not his relative," he protested. "It's not my responsibility; you can't charge me for him. His affairs is his, but I have my own worries. I'm not connected with your problem; you can't hold me to blame for what he was negligent. I have nothing to do with you or him. I prove it now," and Joe Candrov left, having renounced his scheme for Harvy's reformation as an impractical whim. In shame, he kept away, for he feared he had behaved ignominiously. For consolation, he reckoned having partly propitiated his deed by leaving behind a good suit, his own sacrifice towards Harvy's eventual welfare. "It was a material contribution," he calculated, salving a benefit for the resumption of his conscience. The vacant post at his firm was filled next day, and to Joe was entrusted the job of initiating the newcomer. Once, showing the latter his round of duties, he slipped and called him "Harvy." But by putting in active overtime to burden his memory with tedium, he ejected his friend from guilt's overworked consideration. "Harvy will be better off learning from his hard lumps," he rationalized. "And anyway, what does he mean to me? Is my life that settled, that I can afford time off to put his in place? No; maybe later, when success gives me greater assurance; then what I bestow will have more effective power to do him good, instead of us both floundering." With that, he dismissed Harvy from the vacillating field of his concern. His extra industry, the week after, resulted in promotion and a good word from the boss, who had complimented him for being "attentive." This confirmed him, in retrospect, for the rigor of deserting Harvy. "I'm awarding myself my due justice," he said encouragingly, and from him oozed ever more difficult application, as though he wanted the business to expand. Due to his efforts, it did.

Unprotected, confronting a landlord's vindictive wrath, Harvy had the misfortune to be awake. "And I'm taking your clothes in security," concluded the angry investor in real estate. "By the way, what time is it?" he asked, being engaged to a dinner appointment. "No clock here," Harvy shrugged, looking every image of what apathy should be, and generating a healthy air of complete helplessness. "You've got no use," informed the landlord, looking under his own wrist sleeves, to encounter no watch. He piled up Harvy's clothes and wrapped them in a string. The apartment being furnished, he couldn't confiscate what he already possessed. But what belonged to Harvy he bulged into the parcel, which he'd remove into storage and later auction off. (He had no sense of values, despite his proprietory career in dealing with spatial and actual goods. For that reason, he remained ambitiously poor, which he partially offset by also being a merciless tyrant.) "Mr. Furstwitz, pay me tomorrow, or I prove you to be arrested and give you a police record. You aren't going to be pampered no more, Mr. Furstwitz, so I hope today you were instructed a lesson. Good day." Then the door shut, leaving Harvy clothesless except for Joe Candrov's suit he was wearing and the shoes he still had on. This enforced economy seemed sparsely inadequate, as January could be humanly cruel for an impersonal month, while February was humanely endowed with a lack of warmth. While these reflections occurred, the utilities company shut off Harvy's gas and electricity, as a stern measure against non-payment. His next thoughts, then, were clad in darkness. Then the radiator hissed off, the steam pipes stopped functioning, and the water supply was cut. This compounded violation of his comfort brought home to Harvy the notion that his circumstances were none the best; conditions at present were intolerable; improvement was sure to bring relief. This decision appeased his faculties, and averted their protest. Obviously, he must carry out this resolute plan of action. But first, in preparation, he me must rest. Sinking back, he waited. Sleep swooped down, and rescued him.

4

There he strove to remain, his alarmed instinct armed to ward off the world by dreaming it down. As he changed positions, Joe Candrov's suit became worthless as an adornment to job hunting. He had to keep it on, as the landlord had removed pajamas and other clothes, as well as sheets and blankets. With the steam off, he had scant protection against January's interior blasts; the domestic scene was not cozy. Sleep, weary of him as a lover, repulsed his ardors. There was too much back rent to pay, so he would change his residence. Hunger, his most traditional enemy, found a gap in his defenses and charged to the assault, inflicting an untimely wound. His parents were not accessible as sources of temporary financial respite. Whom could he call a friend? Joe Candrov, evidently, had betrayed him in a time of need. Former companions had drifted to stray winds. But love had an insight. What of Lydia Swick, with whom he had conducted his life's most scorching passion? They broke up two years ago, but he had heard word that she was still unmarried. Her apartment would do, if compassion kept its maternal residence yet, in the snug harbors afforded by her bosom. How lovely to snuggle up there, to live on and off her, and drain her ample resources. It would proudly restore his manhood.

She was only a working girl, with no private income. But why fuss, at a time like this?

He made kissing motions, in anticipation of the enormous gratitude he'd owe her, in debt to her cheery protection. It was a warm proposition, kindling thereby the rising devil lurking at his groin. He conceived how their evenings would pant and growl, and how saturation would be burned away in renewed inflammations. What steaming conflagrations, what unquenchable amours! Ah, would it were it not a daydream, but the fact itself. Was he empowered to manufacture that fact? He stood up, and quit that bed for the last time. He'd take leave forever of this miserable apartment—what was it but a rented room?—and restore his fortunes to a better fate elsewhere. He looked around, to see what the landlord had left, or missed swiping. But with the electric juice off, there was no seeing-power to locate dusty articles scattered among debris. He opened the door to let in the hall light from a flickering cheap dimness. All he owned was what he had on, so he slid the key in a dripping refrigerator tray, where a stinking puddle of defrost had accumulated. He sought his toothbrush, but its holder at the sink was bare. The landlord had false teeth, but a true sense of vindictive evil. "Goodbye to this," the departing tenant said, slammed shut the door, and furtively, with a light-heavy step, sneaked out six flights and down to the street. "At one a.m., Lydia wouldn't be receptive," he computed, after helping himself to the tower clock of an immense insurance company, with its all-night lit numerals for stray prowlers. It stood half a mile away, unfurling a frosty visibility. Harvy shivered, devoid of the fare for a local telephone call.

To wake Lydia up would create a bad atmosphere for their resumption of festivities; he would tread easily, and initiate a casual re-originating from where they had left off. Then survival warned him how cold it was, so he let a tremor spread in waves down his back. Seeking warmth, he reentered his old building he had so newly quit. This instantly delayed the imminence of his future, and it was but briefly postponed.

He huddled against the mail boxes, remembering that the heat had been turned off. Far overhead was his room, and just above it was that skylight. He thought of the mysterious visiting stranger, the unaccountable account of his intruder's coat, and other muffled circumstances surrounding it. It had crippled him into mysticism.

And Joe Candrov's abortive attempt to help, and the gruesome spectacle of the landlord, returned to his trembling mind. He'd wait for the dawn, and catch Lydia preparing for work. She lived only a few miles off: a deliciously stimulating walk, to invigorate his circulation and send some icicles sailing into his arteries. It was admirable to be so sleepless. His indolence was but a figment of the past. His eerie somnambulism was behind him quite. If only he didn't freeze, a life of living off Lydia called out to him with imploring arms. Harvy was aroused. "I'll not trade my destiny for anyone's!" he almost shouted. But now it must be three a.m. He slumbered, standing.

He was startled, later, to be awakened by the landlord. "Do you escape like a coward, Mr. Furstwitz? That's not nice. Come with me to court."

"But it's not even dawn yet!" Harvy screamed. The landlord gripped him, and made him a moral prisoner. Thus was his future further delayed; patience replaced freedom, for the next several lively minutes. "I'm stronger than this old crank," he realized, and he bolted away. He ran, in Lydia's direction.

5

Out of wind, but safe in shadows of gloom, he paused at a three-block distance from the site of his retreat. Drawing breath in and out, he poured forth puffs of fog to defile the crispness of the night's deadly air. Not one moon was visible, at any height, to so unseasonably clad a mortal city dweller as Harvy Furstwitz was. Temporarily, he was between abodes: a transient.

Walking on Lydiawards, he suddenly exclaimed, "What if she moved?" Two years ago is some time. So he entered an outdoor telephone booth to consult the directory for her latest address. It would be listed under "Swick, Lydia." "Why not under first names?" he pondered, momentarily impractical. There, he found her; she had moved!

Moved next door—the adjacent building to his own recent one he had just barely vacated. And, he knew, it was owned by the same landlord! How precariously near, so tightly close, his escape would prove to be! And always the danger nearby, of being apprehended. He'd be hidden at risk, and would have to enter and leave the building furtively. There was no honor in so concealed, so subterfugal, a life. Ah, but what recourse had he? Only Lydia would put him up.

Now there were signs of dawn. Any late—or early—stroller made him start; his landlord was omnipresent, disguised into all other people! *Any*one might be his henchman or agent. Life sagged sadly, and hope sank. With belated recognition, he'd visit, in logic's deceitful circuit, his very neighbor herself. How dreadful was this appalling return to a scene so barely escaped from, cast in so morbid a pall of familiarity! He walked stealthily along the buildings, avoiding everyone. Then, in sight of his destination, he made a brisk run. In the hall he sought her apartment number along the row of mailboxes and found it to be street level, first door to the right. His knock was carefree; only a man whose desperation was constantly renewed could have so practiced a boldness, so to-hell-with-it a disdain. Plunged so low, he could only rise.

6

The knock was unheeded, with no stirring within. It was much too early.

Today would be a working day. "Thursday," Harvy calculated. He was a recharged man, so indifferent formerly to the day of year, or the year itself, now his mental faculties made shift to speed their pace around the clock itself, pursuing the motions of time. It was cold, so he knocked again.

Not even the hint, the least hush, of some response. Lydia had not been that solid a sleeper. Harvy wearied of his nocturnal adventures. He longed for oblivion's assumed song of warmth.

The street poured more light into the hall. Not owning an overcoat was monstrous. He reviewed that Lydia portion of his sad past: three years together, beginning five years ago. She had quit on him, but in the throb of tenderness. Might her sentiment have endured this long?

A stab revealed how hungry he was. All his life through, needs never stopped plaguing him. He had sought the retreat, and dabbled in methods of freedom from need. The lazy inclination to sleep, a sloth based on inertia, the craft of refined apathy, had slowed up life's onslaught and dug a self-fitting little plot of artificial death. Now the body renewed its demands for comfort, on more active terms that upturned his system's internal pace. A vision of Lydia stimulated his whole force. Vehemently, he knocked.

Not a pulse of reply, not the slightest impediment to silence's unbroken rhythm within. Sustenance and shelter were required badly; the threshold of relief unnerved his most palpitating tissue. He violently assaulted the door, weeping bitterly as he damaged his fists. It was evident that there would continue—the despair of desire to the contrary—to be no answer. Lydia's apartment, which he had peopled with her image, was humanly bare, deplete of her warm surprise. It might be coldly furnished, but no welcome or recognition greeted him. A dweller from an upstairs apartment passed him, gravely suited on his mission to work.

Then others, deep in warm overcoats, passed by to leave the building. The hall was a regular boulevard. Harvy glanced to ascertain no threat of a landlord. But was his clutched fragile freedom that precious? What did it demonstrate, as a deed for his welfare? He possessed the emptiness, where the solid objects of fulfillment would not reside. Then how poor was his wealth?

It was no good to just stand there and risk the landlord's presence any minute. He slipped out of the building and decided where to go: to Lydia's former business office, to see if she was still working there. It meant another mile or two of walk, but a slanting sun would pave a partially golden path for him, and cheer the lighted journey. With what stupendous value did he contemplate a breakfast! Then he hoped Lydia would advance him the money.

As he went along, people stared in pity at his want of the minimal overcoat to keep January at a safe distance. To be skimpily clad was the prerequisite for begging, so he held out a palm. It collected nothing but frostbite, for its empty pain.

The subway stations ejected workward passengers. The streets were flooded with the morning hustle of humanity.

The discernible boundary, where the residential district stopped and the commercial zone obtruded against a white sky its wild shoot of skyscrapers, went by at Harvy's rapid rate, he straining with famished eagerness toward his showdown meeting with Lydia, an event immensely distant from her own anticipations. He rode up the elevator to the fortieth floor, adjusting his hair and smoothing his suit against the shining metal. His ears went dim in crazy sound.

At the receptionist's desk he asked to see Lydia Swick. "Not in our firm anymore," he was told, by that dyed glamour villain. "What company is she presently working for?" he intoned. The girl buzzed one of the interior offices from her switchboard apparatus, and repeated the information: "It's not known, sir." The disappointment was so huge, it surged with the pressure of relief. "Not an ounce of luck," Harvy summed up, in a terrifically descending elevator. New shoots of pain went up from his stomach, signing not merely the breakfast signal, but the call for lunch. Unless he acted, his strength for normal units of energy per working quota would summarily collapse, letting him publicly faint into private fatigue. The efficiency of his health would be held under vast suspicion, and he might be ambulanced to a hospital ward. There, he would be well fed. That decided him, so in a crowded thoroughfare, near the honking traffic, he picked an isolated spot and started his downward momentum. But a businessman and his secretary rushed to the gap, jostling past in a panic of hurry, to the inadvertent effect of uprighting him. He needed a premium of available space. Haste went everywhere about him; wherever some sidewalk air offered itself for his falling act, some busy person would emerge from the mass and fill the breach. Thus was the ground a dense mass of squirming shadows, with but lone linear wisps of retarded sunlight to represent day's protest against sprawling swarms. "If only I had a place to fall in peace!" Harvy offered, as a devout aside to God. It was not granted him; the city enveloped him. His isolation was crowded into a trap of intense human wilderness, where it resided in bewildered fury. The festivity of a commercial lunch hour agonized his hunger. "I would simply crave to eat," Harvy dreamed, pouring his thwarted power into that acute verbal wish. Anyway, numbers protected him from the landlord. He was safe, to pursue his misery.

7

He wandered out the day, and took his post of waiting, for Lydia's homeward return across the street. It was his old neighborhood, with his own former residence next door. His helpless dependence was a terrible state. It humiliated dignity and debased pride. Human contact was so immeasurably difficult. What of his past friends? In a pinch, wouldn't they assist? Lydia might *never* come home. Thus, what alternate emergency would avail itself? Harvy was not a self-starter, nor could he finish what others started. In a word, he was a leech, a parasitical sponge. These occupations afforded him little time to promote self-reliance as one of his outstanding virtues. As an American, he lacked a steady devotion to the mechanism of success, as a standard business formula. Even as one single human being, he was devoid of an independent instinct for survival by means of his own two-handed pluck and enterprising audacity. His taste was too retired to admit of competitive greed. Failure was his most constant consequence, whatever he undertook. This bit huge chunks away from his self-confidence, until he no longer believed in himself. To beautifully rationalize his deplorable earthly condition, he referred to mysticism, with its haunting refrains, cosmic overtones, and serenity of worldly renunciation. "I'm spiritually superior to my material superiors," he consoled himself. But mysticism is heady, and the stomach gnawed away. Physically, his system howled in protest. It wanted food, rest, and comfort; warmth also. "Wait a while," he adjured it. But even his patience developed symptoms of remarkable impatience. "When will I have relief?" was a question that assaulted his integrity and reminded him that, just then, he wasn't quite well off. It would be wise to have a change in store, and admit it readily. It would be foolish to provide conservatism as a means for sustaining his immensely ungratified state of being. So he embraced radicalism, as a personal necessity, not as a political obligation. Radicalism did not return the embrace, so he had to endure a while. "To prolong suffering is merely to aggravate it," he meditated, resorting to philosophy as a potential portal to the magic glitter of indifference. It didn't work. Life, inside and out, frustrated him. Then, in the gloom of the dark, he spied Lydia's shadow. The lamppost lighted her to the doorway.

He sprung alive, and shouted, "Hello!" She turned, so startled that she dropped her handbag. The expression playing dearly on her face revealed a tone of displeasure. That staggered him; it was the most crushing blow.

8

He crossed the street and drew closer. "It's me," he pleaded, with the most tender tribulation his voice could carry. "So I see," she retorted, grossly matter of fact. Her beauty was heightened in the falsifying dark. Her dress outfit and her smart coat were sedately indicative of conspicuous business brashness, yet she lived in a low-rent building. Why wasn't she pleased to see him?

"I knocked this morning, but no answer," he explained. "Early. You didn't come home?" "I slept elsewhere last night, but how can it concern you?" she delivered. "Honey, I love you," he said. "When?" she asked, implying how uncertain the tense was, in time's complex web of ambiguity. "Now," suggested Harvy, who could practically smell her home cooking. She smiled, disdainfully. "It's not the same," she said, and sadly shrugged her head. "But do come in," she added, while Harvy wilted in total delight; his interminable reign of deprivation had soared fruitfully to a climactic change, a chemical recompounding along new required lines. His saliva danced in splashes of mirth, so he kept firm his mouth, to compress and conceal throngs of budding sensations spawned in a manic fertility of image. "But there's nothing to eat," she cautioned.

9

"I'm not particular," he gasped, his soul fortified in intense prayer. "No, you tend to generalize," she agreed. "I can't eat philosophy," he thought, as she unlocked her door. She led him to a chair. "You're not dressed warmly," she scolded, somewhat coldly. She didn't care.

"I'm weak," he said. "Yes, you always were a hard worker," she commiserated, withholding sympathy to the extent that her maternal constitution could withstand. It cost her effort. The past competed with her *new* love, and the present won out.

"You see, I have someone now," she informed him. "Look," he bolted out, "feed me something or I might die on your hands, and that wouldn't be romantic for your new boyfriend. Not that he deserves to be. Once you were mine; it was signed forever."

Lydia laughed, while filling some pots and pans. But on low heat. Then she retired, out of Harvy's once possessive sight, to strip and put on casuals: rather slinky slacks. She had filled out a bit. Knowing Harvy's habits, she could provoke him, easily, to want more than food. But would that be fair to her current lover? The latter, Mercer Barwegan, had remained a stranger for two years, in her arms and out. His aloof reserve was inviolate with mystery. At least, Harvy had been personable, with particular features; you knew who he was, however inconsequential were those honestly displayed characteristics. This reverie was broken when Harvy asked, "It was with your new guy that you stayed away last night? Is that why you didn't come home?"

"You can get out, if you pry like that," Lydia threatened, "and not eat here, either." That shut Harvy up, with resounding force. His mouth would open for another purpose.

"Is dinner ready?" he meekly supposed. Odors of cooking, imaginative and actual, were galloping down his taste. Delayed pleasure is magnified by pain's stalling duration. She set the food before him and, before she herself had been seated, his dinner had been wolfed down. His head puffed up like an adder's, for his sensation had been violently altered. It made a bad impression on Lydia. "I still prefer Mercer," she assured herself. Harvy's successor was due, later that evening, on a casual basis, tuned down to the minute of his care. Should she flaunt Harvy, and so whet Mercer's much retarded jealousy? She'd prefer her unknown new lover to stake more exacting pains, lavish more attentively his claim on her continued favors. To set Harvy off as a pawn and maneuver Mercer from the plodding routine of his complacency would arrest the somewhat sliding momentum of her feminine acquisitive ego. She ate, while Harvy slumped. He had had three helpings, and now was beyond help. The chair fell backwards, and he with it. A leg of the former broke, while his dozes grew bolder in his unconscious hurt. Lydia looked at her former lover, and hardly regretted the exchange for the new one. Her friends had mocked her, Harvy being an encumbering disgrace. She waited, at ease, on a large sofa in the sitting room. She was hoping to expect Mercer Barwegan, but defending the possibility of his not arriving. How complicated her life had been made by men, whose own inadequate imperfections, characteristically as to each case, became the impediments of her very personality! She'd better marry a safe one, and seek safety in a solitary lack of numbers. How many more reserves of endurance had she left? Her wearied meditation listened for Mercer's rap on her ever-opening door. She invented the sound, when it wasn't heard.

This was futility itself. Harvy was asleep below the kitchen table. How could she proudly boast of him, to catch Mercer's elusive jealousy? She'd been a fool, and was one again. Harvy was no rival, and Mercer would detect that at once. Lydia waited, willing Mercer's knock. Her mind heard the noise. Then reality repeated it.

10

But it was the landlord, instead. "I'm looking for Mr. Furstwitz," he said. "He's there," she betrayed him, pointing him out. "Good, now he can be arrested," said the landlord, doting in glee. He had somehow deducted that Harvy would resort to Lydia, having known of an alliance between them before. He borrowed Lydia's phone, to notify the police. In danger, Harvy woke. "No escape," insisted the landlord who, though old, kicked Harvy vigorously on the back. Lydia enjoyed the process; her love for Harvy was now complete, as an item totally of past duration. Besides, she felt wicked. It was Mercer's doing, who had instructed her in foul practices. "I've avenged you!" Lydia said to Harvy, who was in pain. "What took you so long?" Harvy asked, wincing. An alerted policeman came in, and handcuffed Harvy. "Follow me," he directed the landlord, who was only too willing to comply. Lydia was left by herself, and needed Mercer all the more. Her desperation sighed, and even emitted a pant.

Her sexuality was aroused as by an internal steam bath that plunged her into a perspired stimulation. Then midnight closed the scene, and she retired, fumbling after a lost sleep. "Poor Harvy," she dreamed. "So helpless; won't anyone fend for his fate, if not myself?" With that, she entered that region of sleep forbidden to the insistent banality of analysis. And Harvy retreated far away, while Mercer was so close that their bodies overlapped, thronged in the wild private hall of intimacy. Had she been yet a maiden, a blush might have been required. Nocturnal desire violated the ease of her sleep, and disarranged the pillow. The twin pillow was being unused, by a phantom of conspicuous absence. Mercer was bright as an image. And, in reality, Harvy, uncared for, rested restlessly in his cell. He was sad, but remembered a nice meal. It had been so quick, and he craved another. Why these sensual longings? He was battered by them, and was moreover bruised by the thought of Lydia's hips, now so adroitly withheld. For every desire there was a corresponding inconvenience. The satisfactions were exceptional rarities, very sparse. They were never enough. If only he had Lydia, food, and freedom of shelter, his respectability would be liberated and his manhood emerge. The remoteness of this thought tired him deeply, and he dreamt lust after Lydia. There she was, and he deep inside. That was the place to be; it was superior lodgings.

11

His cell was the same as the other night. But no stranger this time, to accompany him in the adjoining one. The landlord had registered his complaint, and Harvy was condemned officially. Lydia had abandoned him, after feeding him. Hadn't Joe Candrov, whose suit he was still wearing in a disheveled state markedly advanced, also let him down? Through the night long, and feebly as the dawn came up, Harvy lapsed into self-pity. It was a luxurious indulgence, somewhat sensuous. Lydia came back to his mind, and he wanted to crush her. Then he dreamed that she was the landlord, their features merged. He hated them both, one for persecuting him successfully, and the other for being feminine. He wept, and the warden stopped by. "Ain't you a baby," was his astute comment. Harvy didn't hear, and sobbed rapturously, as far as his laziness could permit. It constituted a relief. Then he thought: Who could be Lydia's boyfriend? By intuition, he associated that unseen person with the haunting stranger who had kept vigil outside his door the other day. Were they one and the same? Hard to say. Then the cell opened, and he was escorted out. The examination and the punishment lasted all day. He was called no credit to the city, a civic waste. Well, he was *some*thing, anyway.

He was humiliated, and tortured practically. It was inconvenient to be subject to so concentrated a malice. The detectives, the landlord in their midst, gathered about him, pelting him cruelly. "This has got to not keep up!" he shouted, and stealthily, the weakness of hunger invaded him, familiar but unwanted. He took this series of opportunities to pamper an unconscious need to faint. This he did, until revived. A week he lasted in jail. And the others, what had happened?

12

"I'm sorry I didn't pay the rent," he at last confessed. This somewhat assuaged the judge's wrath. "Get him a job to pay me my money back," ordered the landlord, who was ignoring his other enterprises to pursue the case. So Harvy was given a vocational test, which he failed. His aptitude was declared negative, and unsuitable for work. At last, he had a calling!

"The only thing you're good for is to be unemployed," he was told. There he was, still in jail, feeding regularly and sleeping well. But he missed Lydia, whose thighs, that enlarged as they diverged upward, obsessed his mental faculty to think, and his emotional capacity to feel. As in the old days, he would have liked to enter her, pay a brief call, and scatter his compliments. But in jail or out, he knew her to be inaccessible now. Someone else—his antagonist who had violated his privacy the other week?—was indulging her dear favors. Harvy was envious, and acquitted. He was employed by his landlord, on a servile basis, as an office boy in a real estate chain that was reeking gradually no profit. Business staggered to a loss, which Harvy proceeded to increase. The landlord became mad, and even insulted Harvy; his new worker had this habit of sleeping at inopportune moments. Harvy loved oblivion, to escape. He dreamed of revenging himself on faithless Joe Candrov, fickle Lydia Swick, his landlord boss, and his previous tormentor who had succeeded him in Lydia's affections, named Mercer Barwegan, but for Harvy nameless, nominally the devil's unknown self. March arrived, with its wind. Then April, and a song of flowers.

13

It was the big city, and the flowers were unseen. They hid in the park, but children recognized them. Harvy had paid the landlord back, in kind, and was released from captivity. Again, he was homeless. The landlord had chained him to the bathroom, during his term of employ there, when "work" was over. Now, having evacuated his lease, Harvy ranged free, wearing spring hand-me-downs, and looking for sordid trouble everywhere he went. He found out where Joe Candrov worked, and visited him there; and he was hired, miraculously, by Joe himself, who in apology was vindicating the desertion of Harvy at a critical moment. Harvy's duties were at first vague, and continued so. This extended his progress on a maximum footing, as a thoroughly useless member of the firm. One evening, when work ended, he asked Joe, "What can I do to hurt Lydia?" "By harming her lover," Joe's answer was. Joe was his roommate, and confidante; Harvy had moved into Joe's apartment, on permanent invitation. There, he slept more than necessary, and gave way to dreams. He reported to work daily where, in fits, he slept on a couch in Joe Candrov's office. His title was that of "secretary." Joe tired of him, added a bonus to the payoff, and fired Harvy on some flimsy pretext. Harvy was also dismissed from Joe Candrov's apartment, with but a minor ceremony of farewell. However, he now had dollars in his wallet, and some safely secured in the bank. He paid a call, without phoning, on Lydia. Mercer Barwegan answered, since Lydia was inside nude. "You recognize me?" Mercer asked, smiling. "You're the mysterious stranger," recalled Harvy, pushing past him and sitting on the sofa. Lydia rushed a gown on, to join them.

The three incessantly spoke. They drank whiskey, and became drunk. Harvy was given free run of the refrigerator, accelerating his keen, responsive joy. Lydia and Mercer seemed friendly, the latter's features turning flexible, contrary to his immobile frozen face before. Harvy wanted to ask him about the incident of the coat, the staircase, the skylight, and all the whys and wherefores by which his gnarled curiosity was stunted of other subjects, comparatively. But Mercer was now incoherent, while Lydia clung to his lap, hoping to erect him. He was inflamed, where she sat on him, so they left Harvy sitting alone while they retired to "bed." Their grunts were disgusting, and Harvy was appalled by their morals. Abstinence had converted him to a puritan, but resumed lay activity would reawaken his toleration of bluntly physical acts. Thus, from the *personal* point of view, he surveyed an alien world, dragging from his observations those random pieces of philosophy, like unreturned library books that littered the discarded remnants of what in casual formlessness became his mind. When Lydia and Mercer had concluded their joy, those drunken beasts grossly broke out in slumber, sprawled in nude obscenity. Harvy peeped in, shocked and aroused by their joint double nakedness. He felt ashamed to be a member on the outskirts of the once famous human race. Should he withdraw, and belong to a more favored group? Life stooped well below his ideal, and he rose to sink with it. It was late Friday night, or Saturday morning. How lovely would the spring day be tomorrow.

14

He slept on the couch, so long that they woke him. "Get off the sofa," they said next morning. It was a cheerful atmosphere, and light darkened the window. Mercer looked stolid again. Inscrutable, yielding only mechanical humanity. Harvy wanted to hate him effectively, and spoil Lydia's union with him. Lydia, in an unkempt, wild-flowing gown, was another ambiguous object. She deserved punishment for having betrayed him to the landlord. Other people Harvy intended to hurt were the landlord and Joe Candrov. So he had lots to do, and would have to set aside inertia until such a time that would best fulfill apathy's yawning demands. Before being evicted, Harvy had left library books behind. The landlord had sold them at original retail prices to second-hand dealers in stolen effects. But why call him a landlord, when Harvy was virtually homeless? He ate the breakfast Lydia served him and Mercer. The toast was too overcooked, and the muffin baked too well. And the coffee was effete, as well as tepid. However, the napkin was delicious, had it been an article for chewing. Mercer stared at Harvy with insolence and contempt. Lydia was eager to have sex again, only Mercer wouldn't buy that idea. What a peaceful Saturday morn. The birds were on the trees, miles away. There was no work that day. Mercer dressed, and left. Lydia protested, but he availed. There was love forthcoming to her, which had not been delivered. Harvy remained, trifling and indolent. Lydia saw him, briefly, as Mercer. Then they coupled.

The pleasure afforded to Harvy was acute. His loins glowed in giddy tingling of sensation. However, Lydia didn't love him. He was being used. To fill up the absence of Mercer. Thus his rival triumphed, even while Harvy possessed, in his turn, that shifting perishable piece of consumer merchandise. He waited a while, then went in again. It took longer the second time, and was twice as lovely.

15

Lydia had decided to keep him. She had a job as a department store buyer, with a slick knack of shop talk. She was hardened, business-brassy. She measured wares at wholesale outlets, and sometimes purchased a whole inventory for her big chain store. She could also shop well, when going out for groceries. In cooking, though, she hardly excelled.

Mercer didn't return. Harvy was trained to look and appear like Mercer, to freeze his features accordingly. Because of food, sex, and shelter, he learned rapidly.

Summer had arrived. The landlord had flopped in business. And Joe Candrov had soared, was now executive Vice President. He commanded a room of suites, for an office palace, equipped with private stenographer. He entered into secret matters with her. For the purpose, she wore a slip-off dress in a jiffy. To waste time is a business sin, and Joe had instructed her well. She was his nine-to-five wife, those being her informal hours of disarray. Tiring of her, he hired another. Thus, his business underwent a turnover, with a sharp upswing of invigoration. He never thought of Harvy, being elsewhere occupied. He had already discharged the debt, by assuming Harvy as a burden, in office and house. They were quits. Joe

Candrov continued to rise. Magazines of commerce and industry featured him in lead articles. Success had become his most assured domain.

As for Harvy, he had no incentive. As Mercer didn't return, Harvy was guised in the role of Mercer. Lydia went to work, and supported him. Then she had a two-week holiday, and went off. Harvy was left behind, minding their apartment. His was an empty, do-nothing vacation. Ownership of the building changed hands. The landlord had been proven bankrupt, and sold his liquid assets. Thus, for a while, the water supply was cut off.

Dog days were on. August glittered in the streets; sidewalks were kissed by the sun from an insane, chaste astrological distance. A blue sky proved an exceptional rule. Once in a while, Harvy pondered on Mercer Barwegan. It mystified him. Then he missed Lydia, until she returned.

"I'm back!" she shouted. It was a hot day. Stupidly, they increased the heat with bodily warmth. Their organs were animated, trading sweat for sweat. Only then would they decide to cool down.

One day, the "landlord" knocked. He no longer owned the territory. "Is there work for me to do?" he asked. He was poorly down-and-out, debased, decrepit, and sorely fond of the money he lacked. Lydia made him wash the dishes, for a few cents. Then, out of charity, she fed him a bone. He accepted it humbly, and bit his teeth out. They were false, so he grinned and inserted them back in. How miserably had he come down.

Joe Candrov remembered Labor Day. It was when his ascension had so perfected itself; he led the whole industry! So far had he risen, Harvy Furstwitz would never be his friend again. Joe was eminent, and strutting. He had become king, a great mogul. Everything he had wanted was now his. With such power, it was easy to forget Harvy, and not bother to reclaim the suit his friend had once borrowed. How magnificent his charity was, so viciously virtuous; he had climbed to where he could do good, at his own benefit. He ruled an empire, and his reign was mild. No terror, merely dominance: great control from above.

Lydia saw that Harvy really wasn't Mercer. The resemblance was inadequate, so she kicked him out. That was at October. He had money saved, but nowhere to go. So he applied to his old friend, now so newly famous, that economic wizard of finance, loyal old Joe Candrov. (His name had been changed to Candy, since his fortune had become sugar-sweet, and syrupy-ripe. The first name, Joe, remained as a concession to tradition, and the homely origin of the low.)

"Mr. Candy is in a bitter mood, and can't see you," said the startling receptionist. October blew cold, but Harvy was well attired. He walked about the city aimlessly. Never had he had less ambition, now that today was now. Upstairs, where gods are said to dwell, a cloud roamed about the sky. The cloud drifted, with a specific indifference to direction. Bored, it crossed the sun. That was a hot path of adventure, but the shadows lengthened. Autumn was approaching night.

Harvy rented a room. He littered his arms and legs on the bed, and let sleep gather them up. As for Lydia, she was the subject of no dream. Harvy dismissed her. Lust had been plentiful, but pent up into the confined precincts of a past. Harvy was, momentarily, content. He lay straight back, looking up. He sneezed, sensitively responding to dust. He just didn't care, and was fired by no passion. Idleness consumed him. He drowsed. His life moved, while he stagnated as a rotting consumer of time. Like this, November arrived. Then, even December came. He looked for a New Year's party, to celebrate the final eve. Horrible to spend it alone.

He made phone calls, wasting dimes at a time. His old acquaintances didn't respond. Then he even rang Lydia, and she told him of one. Mercer Barwegan would be there, and Joe Candy would put in an impressive appearance. Not to be outmentioned, the landless landlord was expected to crash. Other gatecrashers were due to arrive. And Lydia was sure to be there. It was to be held in a loft, belonging to a painter named Frank Gambra. The host had been exhibited recently, and the show had sold out. His canvases were a sensation. And the areas of paint on them became a fashionable subject of conversation. How enlightening it would be. Culture would abound. And plenty of whiskey to splash. Harvy put on a good suit, like a negligible bohemian. Maybe he'd pick up a girl, and bring her home for fireworks. How dandy that would be.

He was given Frank Gambra's studio address. The year's last day brought a swirl of snow. Did the loft have pipe-stove heat? Harvy hoped so, for comfort's homely sake. But why would rich Joe Candy be there? Hadn't he loftier-level friends to be amused by, and formidable men from the world of business? Or was he slumming, and had a later engagement?

Another problem-mystery was the case of the "landlord." Why had he been invited?—Oh no, he was one of the crash guests. How informal of him, to abuse the host's liberty. Still another question mark was that of Mercer Barwegan. What did he do? Who was he? Had Lydia and he reunited? If so, in what pose? Indeed, the world was a guessing game. If he could avoid being drunk, Harvy would search for answers. There would be loads of people, and hot jazz served live. Even a poet would attend, it was rumored. Such an unnecessary honor. Harvy could barely breathe, so intent he was on the splendid occasion. He arrived early. The door was locked. Even the host had not been present. It was the downtown part of town. Snowflakes flew from the sky, round and furious. Harvy waited outside. He wondered would there be food. This interested him immensely. His appetite felt fantastically huge.

Still no sign of anyone. He huddled outside the door, defending his internal system from pneumonia, or such allied evils. Then it came to be ten o'clock. Only two more hours, and where would the year be? In the past, lost somewhere.

Then a guy showed up. It was Frank Gambra. "Hello, I'm a guest," Harvy said, delicately introductory. Gambra focused both visual graphic eyes on him. "He's abstract enough to paint," concluded one of modernity's artists. "Come up," he said, and they climbed rickety stairs. Inside was a palette and easel, and many cases of whiskey. Yes, there'd be a feast. Some sumptuous turkeys stood on a table, dead to all intent. "Can I eat them?" asked Harvy. "Wait for the others," he was told. Thus began his long vigil.

In a few seconds, everyone else arrived. They were in a rowdy mood. Wow, what gala festivity, what pure hell to be loosed! They drank, and Harvy ate. He kept sober.

Eleven o'clock struck. Only an hour more, and the replacing years would exchange past to future, while deadness would penetrate birth. Frank Gambra shouted laughing. His was a good time.

Lydia was there, and she giggled. Mercer Barwegan flirted with another. Joe Candy was surrounded by gold diggers. The "landlord" tried to slip a turkey in his pocket. Frank Gambra tossed a babe on his lap. Many men boozled, including an odd poet. A Negro sang out jazz. Harvy ate, stuffing. He was feeling gay. The heady atmosphere went to his head. Bubbles sparkled, and balloons burst. Already, a smile was arrested for speeding on the one-way street of his face. Yes, he felt good.

It got crowded. Then a clock gave indication: a quarter hour more, and what was will be, or is was. Time will have turned over, and done a yearly trick.

16

Harvy danced with Lydia, bumping bellies. They both drank a lot. The pervading emotion of this loud and beefy occasion was a spiritual depthlessness, the despair of negatives. Joe Candy spoke of money, which he knew well. A girl who heard him wanted him to propose; therefore she passed her hand, carelessly, to the trousered seat of his manhood, until its hardness rose to meet her. With the other hand, she pointed down her bosom. This double-quick act, a one-two stroke, captivated Joe Candy. He went nuts, made a grab, and was accused of rape. Abjectly, he apologized.

The landlord was trampled underfoot. In the confusion, he might have died, only didn't. His survival met this foremost test.

Who understood Mercer Barwegan? He was that inexplicable quantity, known to algebraists as X. A psychologist was in attendance, and studied Mercer. His stunned response, on the spot, converted him to a fit of mysticism. He never practiced psychology again, without invoking heaven's source. This was the impression Mercer made, most mercilessly. His features were stoical, unmoved. Had this man a signal destiny? Or was he but a legend personified? Harvy was too ignorant to guess. The other guests abstained; the puzzle was too perturbing.

Five minutes away, the New Year waited. Time was on its side. It had no need of that ancient virtue, Patience. Merely to exist with joy was its immediate aim.

17

Bang! It was the New Year! Then the excitement subsided, a subdued murmur went around. It was last year, only repeated.

What an awful climax! Yes, there they were, still bound to a stale dimension. Solid units of flesh, wearing an empty heart where the soul should have been. Melancholy hounded them, so they resorted, that partying crew, to fun and alcohol. A total stupor prevailed, in each contributory case. Lydia was out. Excess had ousted Mercer Barwegan even, from the proud ranks of that calm sanctity, Sobriety. Joe Candy was on top of a girl. They writhed. But the lights were dim; no one attended. It was the same hussy who had so overtly tempted him, by provoking his ready member. The "landlord," old as he was, was absurdly drunk, like a young man. He mumbled something, but no intelligence plucked it into available cognizance. Frank Gambra, whose party it was, was in an excessive state. Few could describe him. Somewhere, in all that fog, a discernible poet roved. Perhaps he was composing, if not decomposing. His lines of verse were as remote from sense as is the night from the day, in separate spheres. Harvy Furstwitz was not well. He had ate and drunk too much. He, too, had avoided the mean. It cost him, that immoderate disciple of chaos, and anarchy's favorite. Lost in his own puddle, his dominion was sleep's, in the faraway. Dawn moved in; no one moved out. The studio was empty, being humanly full.

Hardly a stir. Groans, as from an inferno, were uttered in ghastly misery. Such hedonistic pagans, and now they suffered!

Sleep couldn't remove Harvy from his hell. Lydia was far from her best. Mercer Barwegan, the mystery man, was quite abnormal. The "landlord" was close in the way of death, only to be ejected from the door as an unwelcome intruder. Joe Candy, whose lechery almost rivaled his business acumen, had vanished from his professional dignity, and arrived as a low bum. A debased scale presented itself. Judgment rated humanity poor, just then; the horror of a void had sucked up all morals. This was the element in which Harvy was gracefully immersed, to his total incomprehension.

18

Throughout January, Harvy reverted to his old self. He found a dusty cornered room, strewn about with books and pieces of food, and there withered a fitful variety around the clock of sleep. The most dynamic drive to awaken him to motivation and stimulate his zest for life was lethargy; stupor and apathy were his other vital forces. His money eked out, and so deprivation stuffed his appetite. He displayed an amazing capacity for sloth.

Lydia took on a new boyfriend, as Mercer's disappearance stretched out a lengthy absence. Since the party, he was unheard of. His substitute was Joe Candy, who seduced Lydia to drop her job for a position as his interior secretary, private and intimately personal. This worked out well, and they enjoyed a mutual rhapsody. Its nature, however, was short-lived. Actually, Joe was succeeding, not Mercer, but Harvy—in chronology, that is. Lydia, so much a woman, loved a dancing male end squirming inside her depth. Iit rendered her that much more "complete" and compensated for the birth-mistake of her femininity. It was interesting to observe the *other* party at work, with herself so interestingly involved. It reduced philosophy to its most certain sensation, and embellished pleasure with the virtue of a profound principle. It was truly delightful contact, and proved how sensitive some areas of the skin could be. As an idleness-cure, it throbbed in resounding excellence, affording intricate entertainment to the passing of a simple matter of time. It was Lydia's central balance of life, the longest straight line between herself and death. Nor would she shorten it one bit.

Joe Candy's business rise, culminating on an apex, toppled from its farmost pinnacle. There was something fluky about his success; it was a hoax of speed, and lacked maintenance-power. A scandal was exposed, an embezzlement, a stock fraud, with Joe the central culprit. This dimmed his popularity, and his greatness waned.

The "landlord" was now a bum. But he was still too genteel, too phonily elegant, to be a guzzling alcoholic. So quietly, he dwindled.

Mercer was away, somewhere. All other facts were bound in foggy mystery, layer upon layer of inmost confusion. Had he been the stranger who waited outside Harvy's door, and trapped him, a year ago? Yes, in the sluggishness of identity. His behavior was not clear. Too dense and muddied, it couldn't be explained. Nor was Harvy curious: he, the marathon sleeper, the dark dreamer of dooms of himself. He deteriorated, and wasted the spark of his only youth, entangled in the comfort of death-mirroring life, deceptively at ease. It was a morbid cycle in his career.

Frank Gambra hardly survived his party. The alcohol was drained out of him, and whiffs of oil paint substituted instead. Then his painting entered a new phase, so criminally abstract that even non-representationalism looked illustrative, pictorial, and concrete. Frank Gambra, evidently, was a painter of the future. The future wasn't there to say "I'm not flattered." Otherwise it would have confiscated Frank's paintbrush and burnt his easel. Time is fussy about its appearance. As a subject for Frank's portrait, it would have turned into space and lost its dimension forever.

Harvy became hungry. Joe Candy, Lydia's latest lover, was arrested. Harvy stepped out of bed. He dressed, and called on Lydia personally. She was home. Then they kissed and necked. Then the action took place below. Organs turned red. They churned, and secreted. In gratitude, Lydia made Harvy a meal. It was mighty tasty, and very good. Harvy ate to his most immense and fullest capacity. He asked for more. It was given him. He *ate* more, too. Finally, he could hold no more. He sought relief. His was a chemical imbalance. The sight was vulgar. Lydia was slobbering, herself. They were not at their dignified best. In fact, they were disgraceful.

No word from Mercer. He was far away by this time.

19

Frank Garnbra was getting money for his paintings. They were hardly realistic. They were the abstract abstractions based on abstract points of departure from abstracted abstractions. They didn't look like anything. Yet, they were visual. This property—being visual—prevented Frank's paintings from being condemned as fakes. He was called "a genuine natural primitive." His personal life was sexually shady. He was known to cohabit with women, in notorious bouts of indecency. But it didn't interfere with his painting, except to augment it. As a bohemian immoralist, he spurned society. He was one of those wrecks on which the culture of civilization is founded.

The loft had survived the party. It was still high up, in that downtown "building." Frank put paint on the canvas. It was too wet, and dripped. This happy accident helped to achieve a magnificent masterpiece—or so the critics said. Frank, being implicated as the creator, bravely desisted from disbelieving them. He merely went on painting, while the applause grew. He let all drips fall; they were his chief stroke.

What he produced was remunerative. So he set up a mistress: Lydia Swick. She abandoned her street-level apartment in a crappy district, and moved down—or up—with him. She became his "model." She no longer had the job in Joe Candy's firm, which had disbanded. How could she be the secretary of a jailbird? Frank Gambra, an actual real-life painter, applied his brush to her. She responded with a blush. They went at it on the studio couch. Art was blessed to have such happy imitators.

Harvy had again been abandoned. Where could he go? What was he to do? He went back to his "room" and did what came easily to his nature: sleep. The only sense perceptors of oblivion were those inverted eyes of hazy dreams, rehashing a splash of sensation-confusion drawn from an out-of-order past whose composite particles shifted and shaded into ever-renewing compounds, varieties of shapeless newness. His dreams made Harvy sick. Yet the world was ugly, and easily disappointing. The choice was slim, in a meager narrowness of value. Negatives were exchangeable, and made a most worthless barter. Harvy would have loved money, if only as a distraction. Life supremely bored him, almost with gusto. The zeal of his ennui was extravagant, almost rash. But Harvy was not a moderate person.

Lydia made a gorgeous model. She was so true-to-life, Frank Gambra preferred her to any canvas. Wherever her legs parted, there Frank Gambra was sure to be; the painter was fastidious and prompt, and left part of himself in her for a few minutes. When he withdrew, he was indeed but part of himself; Lydia had stolen that artistic passion for which, notably, his paintings stood in no fame. Frank the artist and Frank the man were one and the same, but Lydia detected some subtle discriminations, by which the ardor of her body profited. She extracted a man's best self, and returned it but as a butt, and a burned-out one at that.

The weather outside belonged to February, and showed it. Then March pulled along, and took over. Thus had time an effect on dim Harvy Furstwitz, distant Mercer Barwegan, Lydia Swick the nymph, the brought-low outlaw Joe Candy (now Candrov), a derelict "landlord," and that painting lecher, Frank Gambra. Others were affected, in numerous quantities everywhere. After March came painted April, then sweet-scented May. Gorgeous June bloomed. July drooped, while August wilted. September seemed more pleasant. October, somehow, was sad.

November was too cold, and December even colder. But after Christmas belonged a New Year party. Traditionally, Gambra's studio was the scene. In what framepost of similarity would his guests show their alterations? Lots of scotch, this time. He was exhibited in galleries and museums, as a contemporary light beaconing an aesthetic darkness: the glow-lamp of the ages.

The art of Frank Gambra depended on understatedness, on toned-down absence of flashy sparkle. His note was "blue," the scheme was "cool." Predominantly, it was a harmony of slightness, not of muchness. The less he "painted" a painting, the more it was liked. Semi-emptiness was considered his major artistic virtue; "restraint" became the enraging fashion; and Gambra's had the most convincing authority, a brilliant assurance of terrifically disciplined negatives. The greater be became, the prouder his virility, and Lydia was often seen under him, by the angelic eyes of invisibility. He went so far into her, he feared himself permanently lost; then, anticlimactically, came his "Paradise Regained."

That was where the New Year's party would be: the colossally huge loft, near the cool front of a river. Harvy was first to show up. He made for the ham, and proceeded to dispatch it. "Leave some for others," Frank warned him. "Do, you scrum," Lydia seconded. Harvy felt belittled. His humiliation found some relief in a burning bottle of scotch. "You freeloader!" Frank shouted. The more he drank, the bolder Harvy became. The timorous guest was now arrogantly wrathful; "You're mine," he beckoned Lydia, while punching the host. "You punk!" scorned Frank, ducked away, and delivered a blow on Harvy's jaw that thrust a nerve pressure on the victim's crumbling system. Harvy fell flat, and was left there, more for scenery than for decoration.

The other party-goers arrived. They were mildly shocked. "Why did he drink so early, and miss out on the later fun?" was the consensus of their stunned and sympathetic curiosity. Then they shook their heads, and proceeded to get drunk. They joined Harvy, and all fell down.

When the next year arrived, they were out flat. Including host and hostess, down to the least invited guest. The "landlord," scarcely a skeleton of his former self, was there, and his foul-smelling inconspicuous attire was lost, but for his age, among that decadent set of wayward Bohemia. Joe Candrov was absent, behind bars. Another man who wasn't there was Mercer Barwegan. His absence was less formidable than most of the others' presence. Dawn was soon near. Harvy stirred. Frank Gambra, at another corner of the loft from his dear Lydia, was folded out unconscious. Lydia, sprawled in a most unwomanly fashion, looked out of a half-open vacancy of what romantics call her eyes. In general, the setting was one of inebriation. It was not conducive to a studious contemplation of great Man's nobility and nature-driven seat of heroism. Decadence was more descriptive of such an un-self-conscious assemblage, whose casual disorder would not be a theme upon which the epic or grandly dramatic is exalted to inspiration. Harvy stood up, on shaky pinions. He surveyed the scene. A brutal disgust, a physical repulsion, swallowed itself down his bitter throat, only to be sent tumbling up again in dire loathing by his corruption-wasted, dignity-assailed assimilative organs, where the bile freely flowed. "What vile beastliness!" he said, affecting English. He'd reform the whole lot, or be a martyr to their scoundrely scorn. Thus was the new Harvy Furstwitz born, from the decline and death of the morals of his "friends." He vowed to be less dissolute, more resolute, and aspire higher. His goal wafted in lofty heights, and pierced the chandelier of ideals. "I'll force God on them, and divine Love," he fanaticized, with an irrational glow insanely bulging from either of his nether eyes, those soul-mirrors unsteadily dilating to his revolt, his murder-bent rebellion, from the overhumanized real. Now, selfproclaimed, he had diabolically become an angel, and an immortal saint if necessary. He'd cleanse the soul of human sin and evil. It was obvious that Lydia was ever so naturally his first project in this reformation. He'd cure God of man's affliction, or go to rot.

20

He delivered a rousing lecture to the debilitated party guests when, all as one, they revived and rose. "He's crazy," each of them thought while listening. Undaunted, Harvy sermonized with righteous fervor, like an evangelist. "Don't drink, and beware of sexual opposites," were two points he preached. He was roundly booed.

Morning invaded the studio. But the stove wasn't burning, the pipes were unheated, a hung-over audience trembled to a barrage of internal shivers. "Go home, you bum!" they shouted.

And started taking the advice themselves. They thanked Frank Gambra, who smiled wanly. Lydia stayed, living illicitly with him. Harvy, to drive his message home, also stayed. He'd administer a dressing-down to that obscene though handsome couple. And deliver them unto the Lord's hands, in whose safe harbor or snug haven the wayfaring young pair would mend their sinward ways and repair. In the sanctity of piety, they'd be saved.

"Repent!" demanded Harvy of them. They munched on something for breakfast, feeling bleary. "Go away," they dismissed him. "I'll not," retorted Harvy, "till you give up abstract painting" (addressing the painter) "as a foremost insult or indecent sign to God; and till both of you forget the carnal pleasures of the bed." They wanted to disobey him right there, but lacked the strength or energy. But they'd muster a resistance to his appeal, and knock the holy pedestal from under him. The year was new; their bodily delights and joys of vanity trod the ancient and unrelenting path, a tradition resplendent with earliest ancestry. "Be good!" admonished Harvy. "Abjure folly." Lydia and Frank jointly disregarded him; each turned the cheek of his other ear.

"What a tedious moralist!" they complained, for Harvy was far from stopping his harangue. "Shut him up!" Lydia requested, so Frank Gambra slugged Harvy, who immediately desisted. With his tongue still hung out, the victim of this intrusion lapsed backward, and gently followed gravity down. Once gravity stopped, so did he. Why exceed nature, whose economy is rarely false? Frank wanted to hit him again, with the injured pride of guilt, but Lydia, surging in a tide of gentleness, held him back. Mercy had redounded to her grace.

Blood trickled from Harvy's mouth. Lydia stooped to wipe it, but Frank prevented her. "Stop showing tenderness!" he ordered, while she shrank. She bowed, and her master had won. The first day of the new year had demonstrated a critical turn in the progress of Harvy's spirit. He cited God's authority, and could never lose.

Thus he lay, oblivious. Religion cruised in his veins, with white blood of the Lamb. Innocence had been installed, where ignorance lately dwelled. A halo sprouted, and fair Harvy slept on.

21

"Don't wake him!" pleaded Lydia. But Frank did, brutally. "If you martyr me," Harvy instantly threatened, "then, irretrievably, watch your soul fry damned." "You god-damn freak or phony!" sneered Frank with fury. "I'll break your stupid bones." "Don't!" implored Lydia. By then, it was evening. They were tired, but Frank, stirred up, took her, and did violence to her, in carnal possession. Bound as a captive witness, Harvy helplessly looked on. He berated himself for being stimulated, feeling a groin glow, in emulation of the act of beatification that transpired before him. Thus, his resolutions were confused, and the physical confounded his soul. He'd have to practice more severity, with harsher discipline on himself and others. The devil had delegated all human souls, who were working for him. God alone, and Harvy, those twins in isolation, defended the True and Just cause. Wouldn't anyone help?

Frank Gambra exhausted himself in Lydia, and face-downward on her chest he was suddenly still. Concentric spasms still echoed rhythmically, like the wider circles in a lake where the ripple still vibrates an hour after the pebble had been thrown plunk in the center. "You did an evil deed," muttered Harvy, "and defied chastity's sacred code. It was a defiling act of impurity. It was pleasure for the moment, but pain in a bad lifetime. I must pronounce it wrong." Lydia was still pressed to the floor by her inert lover, her legs spread in the ultimate of indignity. She appealed to Harvy for forgiveness, with a wild signal from her eyes. But Harvy was stern, and would not redeem her sin. Absolution would be, relatively, too lax, and undeserved. "Believe in the Lord," he recommended, and Lydia hung her head in shame. She tried to get up, but the dead weight over her was too much. Frank had collapsed, in a compact heap or sag. Their position was a dead giveaway, as if their crime required evidence. Harvy felt infinitely above. He was empowered to distribute justice, and exact propitiation. It was a role that suited him.

Frank Gambra, make no mistake, was ill. Harvy rescued Lydia and fitted her in raiment. She would be a reclaimed virgin.

There were others to rehabilitate, once they would be found. That "landlord" would pose a knotty salvation problem, so far had he strayed on an errant path. Joe Candrov was being punished in jail. But was his soul cared for? Police were negligent in that department. Harvy would assume the burden.

Then Mercer Barwegan, who was gone. What category did he fit? Morally, enigma protected his culpability, to an extent. Yet Harvy knew that Lydia had received his pierces; unflinching, even. How busy God was, to properly populate His sparse Kingdom! Harvy would be a recruiter, and set up, within convenient access to the daily vulgar marketplace, a popularly centralized and well-located booth for personal salvation and incidental confession. It was shrewd business sense, a cash-procuring idea theoretically practicable. Why not try it, and sell religion as a useful doctrine for redemption? He would provide a money-back guarantee unless immediately satisfied in the hereafter. The bargain was downright irresistible, from all hard-boiled estimates. Ideally, it combined reality with ethereal dreams, and sold passage from earth at excursion rates. Should a profit be attached, it would be cleanly non-taxable, nor would metaphysical dirt cling. Thus Harvy, the man, a mortal, set God up in business as a broker or agent. Having chosen a profession, Harvy knew it was a fine one. Was ever man's work enriched by a loftier goal? Not likely, as lifetimes go. Beyond death, Harvy wouldn't contemplate. Why anticipate, when Now seemed to outfuture the glory of all ambition? Spiritually content, Harvy relaxed, yet Lydia was rubbing his genitals, and fired his resolution to the test.

22

"Stop tempting me," begged the would-be saint. But Lydia was adroit in her vindictive fury, determined to be less low by inducing Harvy to succumb in abject passionate lowliness to her own shiftless level. This was easier done than said; Harvy was grappling with holiness on an unlikely bed. The fervor of his adoration for God had been converted to an earthier goal, transformed in rapture, upon this *accessible* divinity, who had inflamed his devotion. The more coarsely they tightened in snug twist, the more purged Harvy was of God's roaming ideal; consumed in fire, he was purified of thought and, in the end, was a tired beast. Lydia rose in triumph, smiled in glee, and watched the ashes of Harvy's piety grow cold. Frank Gambra regained his self, scattered oils on a glassy table, and made a creative rape upon an unsuspecting white canvas. The result was a few putrid colors, arbitrarily joined together through coincidental accident of an eye taking them all in. "That's art," Frank boasted, and Harvy, with broken spirit, was unable to contradict. Lydia made a meal, and they all ate.

THE SPRING THAT
NEVER SAW PRINT

When Gerald Folkdale was extraordinarily young, he was fascinated by newspapers. Print seemed permanent, if not final. Throughout high school, he failed in love. He had been, with poetic liberality, granted a lyrical temperament, and a romanticized constitution. He took to words, as a sea takes to fish. Though poor, his parents sent him to college. They figured it would pay off later. Gerald was a scholarship pupil, majoring in journalism. On campus one spring, he conceived love. She for whom it was conceived was stern in not requiting it. She preferred, much by far, the then reigning football hero. That she gained him indicated the extent of her glamour. Gerald had aimed too high, himself lacking in handsome looks and wearing glasses that betrayed his intellectual obsession. It was out of fashion to be brainy. Especially inappropriate, in a college student. But he attained to the dean's list, and graduated amid honors. His parents were rewarded, but not richly, for their investment to reap the adequate returns of fruit, their Gerald was doomed to a professional career of work. An evening newspaper had an opening, which Gerald closed once he entered. Now would his childhood ambition be idealized.

Most of his salary went to his parents, in the bosom of whose parental home he was yet still a resident. His first assignment was in the ranking role of a sports reporter—he went to spring training and covered baseball. (The regular veteran writer had been overly alcoholic, and even was known, on occasion, to drink too much. So the newspaper made him a society editor, for in nightclubs his talent might attract gossip and fantasize authoritative scoops, short of libel suits, and improve circulation in the scarlet printing hotbed of scandal.) But Gerald caused the local home team to lose, merely by interviewing its last-place players and watching them make errors on the field, strike out or hit double-play balls at the bat, and pitch home runs or wild walks on the mound. Someone was a responsible scapegoat, so at midseason the manager told the sports editor to remove Gerald from the beat and leave his team in peace. It proved effectual, for soon the club, unhexed by Gerald's presence, tore the league apart, and won the pennant with lordly ease. Thus, newspapers closely influence events, not only in the sports stratosphere, but in the political arena as well. Public opinion, being periodically fed, knows what to look for and democratically, it turns out in print to have happened.

Despite the success of the major baseball team of that immense city, and despite the improving literacy rate compounded by an expanding population, newspaper circulation fell. To arrest this disturbing tide, policy changes were inculcated, the format was untraditionalized, and sensationalism frankly exploited: sex was invented as an unsavory pastime of the famous. War news was played down, primarily because it was a time of peace. The newspaper by which Gerald was employed, corrupting his journalism aptitude, was known by every newsvendor as *The Evening Star*. It cost a dime. But it was worth much more, for it afforded hours of pleasure. Later, fish could be wrapped in it, to take to work for lunch the next day; it was an incredible preservative, since its stink was highly perfumed. In cultivated circles, it was known to be a "rag," and a coarsely-grained one, at that. The publisher, chairmen of the board, and editors conferred. It was decided to stress "features." Imaginative writing, in a popular vein, became a new explosive campaign. For example, the sun was exposed, as being a hot, torrid issue. Scientifically, it was said to cause all sex. When readers read this, they took more sunbaths. That created more babies, indirectly affecting the circulation. Newsstands were stampeded, by eager buyers, who wanted vividly to know what the sun was up to next. And they were told, illustrated by photographs. (One of the photographers, closely attentive to his work, studying his subject at close hand with blinding zeal, lost credit in both eyes, and was pensioned off. But such tragedies do not often occur. They're the daily hazards of newspaper work, whose ideal is to make the people glitteringly *see*. Thus, it was an educational device.)

But the news value of the sun became, gradually, eclipsed. No longer a hot item, it was gently shrouded in clouds; *other* subjects came in for extensive publicity. This variety kept readers on their toes, ready to trip, in nimble alertness, over the next stumbling tidbit, with its temporarily popular appeal. Gerald Folkdale, serving his apprenticeship as a cub office boy with delated demotion, was given orders by the night editor to haunt the morgue files for ancient news that might be freshly reapplied, told in today's outstanding new vigor. He exhumed timeworn articles of which all currency of interest had since faded. Glancing down the proverb column of an archaically dated edition back in the horse-and-buggy era, he read this phrase: "Nothing is new under the sun." "But if I tell the boss that, I'll be fired," Gerald noted in a self-aside of sage caution and saddening restraint. Then the door to the catacomb tombs opened, and the editor, wearing a green nightshade, floated in like a phantom wisp of vapor particled partly in spirits of alcohol. "We need to spike up the paper," said that gruffled veteran, who had survived several divorces in which he had somehow managed not to participate. "Yes, sir," Gerald alertly snapped, ever ready. "Gerry, have you lived?" tenderly solicited that paternally prone boss, whose soft side proverbially revealed a generous heart and humane impulse. Bob Bantam, he was known among his set, consisting of carousing buddies of immoderate early-morning habits shocking to the Protestant ethics of any virtuous old maid. "That I have done, sir," replied Gerald softly. "Call me Bob," he was told. It was the most exhilarating command that Gerald had yet heard; he obeyed it instantly, repeating the name Bob five hundred times, like a punishment exercise in school. Such eloquence endeared him even more to the rough, grizzled Bob Bantam, a boss if there ever was one. "See any juicy idea in the morgue files?" the latter imperiously hinted. "Yeah, boss, we gotta appeal to the emotions, see? Because people are softies, see? Yeah, and I'm your man, boss." "We'll have a feature series," said Bantam, "under your byline. Me and the City Editor want you to expose

spring—debunk it of its sentimentality, show it's only a decorative interlude so there won't be no abrupt transition between embattled winter,
that caravan of icicles, and summer, that tree-season city. I want terrific
rhetoric on this assignment. Research botany, if necessary, and scoop
out the inside of plants, if you see a scandal brewing in their chromo-
cells. And be blatantly scientific, see? I ain't no hard-boiled editor talkin'
to no sappy cub reporter. You're *The Evening Star*'s star, or my name
is mud. Ever write poetry, kid?" "Yeah," Gerald assured him. "Well,
put it in prose this time. I want the real story about spring, and make
it as metaphysic as hell. At any cost, and spare no detail! Our readers
must feel spring in their bones. It's winter now, but your features will be
appearing in April—a masterpiece of timing, don't you see? You'll need
all the information you can get; it's a topic of annual significance, so
your readers will bring familiarity to assist in comprehending you. Well,
don't go wastin' my time listenin'. Make a move, man! At it!" Thus spoke
Bob Bantam, and Gerald Folkdale had been handed a tremendously cosmic opportunity to make good as a great columnist, the star of *The Star*.
That winter, there was a dearth in current events. Readers demanded
news and soon. Wouldn't spring absorb their fascination to the utmost?
It was an earthshaking event, the cradle of juvenile tradition in romance
and love. Women readers, regardless of political affiliation, would really
eat this stuff up. Gerald hid away, and wrote. He conjured up every living memory, not to mention not a few dead, but equally vivid, ones.
He reviewed his past sad romances, and his intolerable bachelor lone-
liness at the moment. Spring would breed new hope, as the nocturnal
sap would rise. How darkly moonlit is lovelorn emoting over any girl's
absence, the pang of the lone tragic self at the season of beauty's miracle.
Oh, why not company at that hour!

ROMANTIC SPRING STROKED MY HAIR. IT WAS A BLEND
OF NIGHT. Quite caught in black, a moon scattered back her rays
and with tinsel imitation mocked out the absent sun from the shining darkness. I wished I had a girl. All alone, she was without me. I
sharply felt the sting, until numbness plucked the terror of her poison
and consigned me to a field of melancholy, where the small grass grew
into a new smell. How tragic, to be alone. And the arms, so rich with

their full emptiness, like angelic dreams that mask the nightmare. Oh, my potential. And ah, my sad waste. Get behind me, moon. Perhaps you can escort the spring, marry her away, and let my solitude ripen in the density of my thought. Dear melancholy, don't brood. We are ourselves alone, and beautifully together. The deep world gathers, and dawn will betray our lust. Sleep still, and be my guide. I'll despair, and give in. Be my bride.

"But we can't print this!" shouted Bob Bantam, after Gerald had handed him the copy. "It's too subjective, it's such a personal rhapsody, and over the readers' head. No, it's too mushy, and the essayist is obviously the victim of self-pity. And where are your facts? That's just a moonstruck reverie, and the corny imploring for a mate to share the mood. And the subject is not spring, but yourself. This is not a poetry magazine for hazy pinings after lost sentiment and moony meanings—this is an evening newspaper, for ordinary folks to read and want to buy again. We serve a business community, and people are too busy for thoughts like this. What you need is a wife, and to settle down."

"But boss, you told me to write well." "Yes, but journalistically, not creatively. And make fun of spring, don't exalt it. Don't give me a religious sermon of the soul. You're too slushy and soft. Get out, and try another!"

Gerald wept, and defiantly set about a defense of his subjectivity-matter style. His pride had been piqued, and his manhood lowered into doubt. He'd impose his own personal taste, and protect the integrity of his aesthetics; sure, and what though he were fired, so long as the inmost principles of his belief were unsullied by vile defilement and impure prostitution. Even as a baseball writer last spring he'd been faulted, and acidly brought to criticism, for his metaphoric literary flair in reporting how games were won and lost on a field of professional entertainment. But he'd sacrifice his job, in his one-man mission as culture's minister, his crusade on art's behalf against philistine vulgarity and the lowly worship of the common. Yes, he'd reform taste.

He sat at his tiny desk, and composed another "lyric." His window was smoked frozen by February snow. The whir of the presses could be heard, and the harsh pierces of newsmongers. This time, he wouldn't mention spring at all, nor would he condescend to the masses. He felt alive, and told of the human night. In a deeply sentimantic mood, elated out of recognition, he wrote in the fullness of his heart, a passion of dedication to the nocturnally stagestruck moon. It was for himself, and hang all the readers of *The Evening Star*, along with the mundane Night Editor, Bob Bantam, for whom drink was sleep's substitute, with spirit subservient to the hectic bickerings of his responsible career post. Gerald Folkdale swooned, and on his clattering rackety typewriter melted out, in his most unnewspaperlike manner, these un-matter-of-fact words, that smudged in vain contradiction his extensive journalistic training. The words grew, and found the pattern of this rhythm:

> While the moon prepares to shine, dabbing itself with brilliantine and grease, and pouring smooth oil in the pox mark craters to cover up an unfortunate childhood disease, night scares the clouds away and blackens the reputation of the sky, erasing the beauty spots left behind by a recent sunset chased down the drain of the horizon by the lateness of the hour, according to season. Tonight a special feeling has invaded my life, the air in my breath catches a real minute, as though, by thinking, I create my newest destruction, and live all over again, with a power to tear down age and advance youth and stand out of time, beyond my human self. Buildings hardly hear me, and traffic barely registers a scratch. People walk in outside circles, mere shapes filled with blood and outlined, for normal reasons, like me. My loneliness sharpens its self-sufficiency, and exhales a happy solitude, in the deepened splendor of a used-up new world.

Trembling with cowardly courage, the author of that "prose poem" dared timidly to submit his latest masterpiece to his prosaic master, Bob Bantam. "I was inspired," Gerald apologized, standing over his editor's desk while Bantam slouched back and read himself into malice, while his facial contours wore an aggrieved surliness, the look of a martyred bully. He looked up, and said, "You're fired." "But I must support my parents, who in their aging dotage have no other means; I'm an only child," wailed Gerald bitterly. "Don't try the sob approach," warned Bantam, whose soft heart, however, relented. He was fond of the boy.

Bob Bantam was childless, despite several divorce-prone marriages of ambiguous duration and vaguely bigamous simultaneity, founded on the domestic principle of disorderliness. "Well, we'll print that," he decided, in a weak moment, "and your first 'article,' too. Now, we'll plan your next sequel. Follow my directives, Gerry. You're an ace on my staff, and a gutsy writer. You've got it up here [pointing to his own heart, in a gesture of late nineteenth century melodrama]. Kid, you'll make us famous, and revolutionize the newspaper industry. And sneak good literature down the unsuspecting throats of the populace. Here, have a drink," and Bantam produced from a lower drawer an attractive one-hundred-proof bottle. Gerald closed the door, and secretly they became drunk. This was Gerald's complete baptism as a veteran newspaper reporter. It signified the end of a petty "hunting" for words; with hearty confidence, he wrote first drafts only, proudly uncorrected. Boldly, he was now a great scribe. In celebration of this token, a pay raise went into effect. The salary would much augment the living standards of his aging parents; his filial duty had been consumed.

Gerald loved his work in the great daily journal. Words were in his blood, and not unremuneratively, either. It was an occupation he was eagerly suited for. Soon, he'd start dating again, forget his sore past loves, and march a winning bride down the altar. Then his virility could play free, and be powerfully proven. Ah, life wasn't too bad after all, with luck and Bob Bantam for a boss. Then February desisted, only to be succeeded by March. Soon, his feature sequence would be printed, serialized in special columns, and decorated by broad print. Then, fame would publicize him, and girls swoon in glee should he cast them a side glance. He was moderately tall, though he wore glasses. His complexion was sandy, inclined to be fair. There was a poetical glint shading his eyes, and a talented but eccentric insanity. His figure wasn't bad, though slightly portly. No, his build wasn't too robust.

His suits were sedately discreet, down to his fine tapering shoes. His voice was more heard than seen, provided he talked at all; being loquacious, this was no problem.

In religion, he belonged to one of the major sects, though not in a practicing capacity. Politically, he was slanted along the editorial lines prescribed by the public vehicle for which he worked. It was an allegiance of loyalty, on the part of a steady employee. Why bite the ink-stained hand that fed food into his mouth and into the doddering slits or facial orifices, frequently opened, through which his parents prolonged their nutrition? So Gerald was well off, and in good favor. He had skill, flair, and style. And for Bob Bantam, he was a prince, with perfection inscribed in each sentence. Gerald's ego cast off worry, and found vanity attractive; it wooed vanity with impressive credentials, and accredited authenticity. He was accepted, and they were secretly married.

Bob Bantam was pudgy, and small. He had a pugnacious temper, kindling a heart of latent gold, by which, in turn, his temper's wrath was tempered and controlled. Bob had black hair in the former sense, and gray in the present tense. Prophetically, his future was bald.

Jauntily dressed, Bob belied his years. He was known as an old pro. In all the intricacy of his behavior, he was ever the newspaper professional, abstractly fleshed. Asthma somewhat interfered with his breath; he took his whiskey straight, and neat. In the art of lechery, he displayed an admirable versatility; *any* woman would do, with this abiding qualification: she must be endowed with a depression, or recession at the very least, at the place where the torso stopped and, on either side, the legs started. These demands were easily fulfilled, and happily candidates were found to include fully half of the known globe's inhabitants, at a cautious guess in roundly democratic estimate. Thus, Bob Bantam had his fun; the inertia of time alone would erase his momentum and reverse his profound vigor that had piled up an increasing crescendo of conquests. In Gerald, Bob Bantam detected a "son," a fledgling under his paternal wing. Whatever Gerald was pleased, in his youthful heady audacity, to write, would find its way to the light of print, under obliging Bantam's protection. Thus was Gerald fortunately blessed, such favor had been conceded to him, such unprecedented latitude; the other stars in the organ's galaxy envied Gerald his rich prerogative to be leisurely poetic and strike any note that fancy decreed; but Gerald was immune to protest, due to Bantam's fabled might in the organizational setup: the boss's ward was an untouchable, set outside the raging arena of competitive criticism and professional animosity reserved to wear colleagues down in survival's hectic pace. Subject only to Bantam's authority and benevolent intervention, and to no one else's jurisdiction; liberated from the hostility of rivals; Gerald merely had to write, according to his free fancy. What more conducive compromise, to art's advantage, was in life's province to dictate, in the accidental fortunes of luck? Gerald became insufferable, soon, and more melancholy, as past springs rose with nostalgia of lost loves. He was ready for his next "article," but consulted Bantam first, as an after-forethought. His proud confidence was so haughty, he would reduce his swaggering by meekly begging for a little "advice." Bantam was swiggering from a bottle, but recovered in the warmth of generous poise, as the afternoon reclined. He sat on the desk, to be ever closer to the vastly favorite Gerry. "Here's what to do," began Bantam tentatively, hoping not to offend. Gerald encouraged that tone, so the note of discord was struck out. "Obey these precepts," Bantam said, outlining what he had in mind. Appreciatively, Gerald determined, even to the letter of the spirit, to follow the words of his chosen father. It would frame and define the heady flight his Muse was prepared to take. The greatest artist must condescend to some outward discipline, at least. And in years alone, Gerald Folkdale was, in terms strictly chronological, young, to be exact. Why not heed the kindly old wise voice that experience had carved to a squeak? A fine vigor remained, as an indomitable trait in Bob Bantam's unimpaired personality. Age and youth spoke softly together.

"Your next tale," said the editor, "should have a title, as a brief commentary on the text beneath. Also, please divide your piece into paragraphs: it won't frighten the reader away, for he has gaps, knowing when to end and to begin again. These divisions may be pursued at his own rhythm; ordinarily, readers have other things to do. A paragraph signals 'time-out,' unless the suspense is intolerable, in which case he'll continue on. Play up the love bit, please. But have a 'point of view'—looking out of the window, for example. Compare the new spring with the old ones, showing how each year we fade and lose, removed from the old great triumph or loss. If you feel sad, be sad; I'll not shackle my author. There, Gerald, can you add these compromises and still keep your inspiration whole?" "I promise," said Gerald Folkdale, who then retired to his own small office, with its dull opacity from an unwashed window. The evening came on apace; Gerald felt alone, while nature stirred. Then darkness lit up the bare room, relieved only by the single lamp. A small Spring entered his brain, minor against dreams of deep and faded past realities. Words came, and he wrote this:

A NEW GREETING FOR AN OLD SPRING
IN INFERIOR RENEWAL

Sometimes, when the sky is clear, I wish for spring to be here—and it is. Generally, the hour is evening, in its pre-dark glow. Ghosts of nostalgia romp, in gowns of sad grayness: a wist of past pervades this mental scene, and a tree hangs limp, dragging stray branches through the air; how serene is the heavy pressure of melancholy! Then, how solitary is a lone bird: a lifted statue in a tiny dash of motion. I long for lonely things; gaiety is unthinkable. My festivity is one of gloom. I like it. I know how close distractions are, and soon I must resort to them, when this unbearable window darkens in a tragic tone, to an unheard sound of the blues. Soon, I will be happy.

Have you arrived, spring? On you hangs a former love. Where is she now?, though you be here. You are incomplete without her, no matter how many flowers you may bring. May I blame you? You phantom season of vanished mirth.

Thank God there's no moon. It would revive romantic notions, and be too heavy. Perhaps, I will take in a movie. That would be suitable and light.

No. I must remain here. The blackest window for my soul's eye. When summer is ready, revive me.

Spring, goodbye. Already, you are mingled with the past, so recent though you have been. Again, farewell.

After Gerald wrote this, he cried. Sure, he should be tough-boiled. But somewhere in him God had planted birthseeds of sensitivity, now sprouting in a newspaper office. Spring would be next week, if today stood March in its middle. Tenderly, the final snow of winter's tardy exit fell in big batches outside, with all the density of a block of wood. Gerald thought about his life; it scared him. So he vowed to be merry, and knocked on Boss Bantam's busily centralized office door that divided up the newspaper plant. Twilight or night was unbearably intense. "Here's the copy," said Gerald, though Bantam had been in conference. The bigwigs were told to leave, giving Gerald the floor of priority, a gesture that basked him in as honor's golden ring. Boss Bantam read, and pronounced it good. "You're a marvel, Gerry," he remarked, combining a friendly appraisal with the affirmative mark of the critic. Gerald was not displeased; the comment was itself praiseworthy, and reflected well on the good taste of the speaker. "I'm proud of you, Bob," Gerald tossed. His relations with his employer could hardly be excelled.

Soon, his first feature would be printed; the frequency would depend on reader reaction, but he expected an article every two days as a not too rapid installment rate. Next afternoon he reported to work, invigorated by the sunned-upon snow. He thought of spring with jaded smugness; his success, of recent, had deprived his responses of their direct primitive simplicity; something precious in him had been dimmed. Could he regain it, and rejoice in truer emotion? Pretending that spring was there, he expressed his past-plagued feelings with these not-quite-despairing words that deplored a reduction in time's vibrating thrill at spring (He wrote in longhand, in grand sweeping strokes full of stately majesty and eternal regret.):

SPRING VIOLENTLY EMOTIONAL

It's interesting that spring should reappear—as though it had never been away! Here are the same old flowers, living out their past lives in new glory. However, my eye is less enthusiastic, and lacks lyrical support from that source of romance, the heart. So I calmly note that spring is here, with restraint borrowed from indifference; which is a sad loss. Can the emotions go bad, slackened in apathy? That is evidently the case. I mourn it; I regret. But what in hell can I do about it, now that I am calmly the master of such complete wisdom? I can't send away the spring; only time can achieve that feat. So I'll endure its aging glory, with one of those smiles that God can't possibly reward. Why should He?—I seem so tired. I most definitely have lived, and am suffering an after-effect, in what must be my apparent prime, when all my powers are organized with grand and solid concentration. On what? On love and spring, found in their fading loss to revive an out-burst of bitter hope, an extension of ambition. Let tomorrow decide.

The writer sat sagging at his desk. Evening droned in clutters about him, and the newspaper plant was wild with motion, preparing the next day's edition. The din was continuous; *The Evening Star* actually came out at noon. Later, from midnight on, the organized insanity would intensify its process at a screaming pitch of madness. In contrast, Gerald partook nothing of the untoward scene; immobile, he sat transfixed, bent inward, outside the living struggle of men locked in their daily conflict. He picked up his pen, and applied it to a clean sheet of stationary. "Spring is about here," he anticipated; the image grew like a bud. Then, desolate, he realized how much more lonely less is this from those immortal springs that were its glorious predecessors. So much more was Gerald now, in the success of illusion's dear loss. Spring could never claim his immediacy any more. It was seen, only, through an aging filter. Nature's annual fairy tale was gone; instead, the heart made bold to show its more cautious wisdom, on a darkened field that dimmed the scent of new colors. In his shadowed imagination, Gerald roamed forlornly, plucking these blooms of tarnished hope, until the conversion of his mood gave melting flow to such words as eased his fainting flames:

SPRING SUNG SADLY

Spring has come on time, comforting us with its seasonal despair. The gardens have brought their cemeteries to life, in the similar new past; witness the unchanged daffodil, as though there never had been such intervening winters in their dull muddy snow as mark time in continual interruptions. We know how enduring is the temporary, but we mourn its passing: so sad, a sun-darkened heart, the lonely cell of freedom. And so we greet another spring. Illusions are increasingly difficult, for weeping is such a childish act. We only have imaginary tears now, but they run swiftly. In time, they will drown us; imagine that. It will be comforting, soul-consoling, to have a slippery bondage to an element of real wet—water, where we were made. And so, let spring reign: the kingdom of the lyrical heart, love's aching prime, and finally just another dismal show, flashing on the calendar. Sweet is spring, when the birds sing. Then would lovers be, and do as they are romantically bid, and of such exquisite ecstasy create their mortal agony—should requital grant such splendid, ideal, opportunity. It doesn't, generally. No, hence our gloom, and a sentimental indifference to the brave ornaments we call spring, a more mellow breeze, and lifting skies. How studied our calculations are, to disturb hope in the bud and settle for shallow consolations, not the dreamy melodrama that spring would be. We are perishing, to dwindle so far. Who can reclaim us, or redeem? The past is fixed, while the heart turns, and seeks new things, to thaw the frozen old. How we would delight! No good. Can anyone sing to us? A song wouldn't hurt. The ear would understand, for the deeper faculties have diminished, or are in disrepair; forever, it would seem. Isn't death tantalizing! Pity is undignified when directed to the self; true nobility would scorn it. But heroes weren't made for this age; we are degraded, and in human pain.

As Bob Bantam read, and Gerald stood over him, morose woe overtook them both. "These last two articles you wrote lack the anti-negative note; they're so somber, as to be pessimistic." "What would you suggest, boss?" "That you should personally become flowers, using an editorial 'we.' Engage yourself. Enter the garden as a cemetery—a concept in the second sentence of your last piece that brought home the nature of time as a binder, linking consecutively the annual repetition of a single season. Make believe you're on field study. Obtain full empathy with the subject. Use concrete details. Pretend that you, as narrator, and someone else, as partner, underwent a flowery metamorphosis in a time-filled garden among real objects. Make it a convincing fantasy, a triumph of literal imagination. Come now, how flush is this garden with spring, and you're in it. Isolate yourself, and write in your heart's deep power. Then come back, and show it to me. I'll be here all night, getting drunk occasionally. The spring blues are afflicting me; memory and desire are too poignant, in their deadly mixture. Away, Gerald, dear boy; leave me, and be a flower. Then bring back your testimony, with its rich breath of conviction. Go and grow, and rot, in spring's garden, so breaking even of time's ever-human heart, representing our tragic life in the sun. Then appear again, that I may know it's you. Or else I'll weep an April of rain, to heap an ocean over your flowerless grave. Leave me, my youth. Ah, how suicidal is life's simplest vision, its process of beautiful death. Oh, how can I go on? Restore me, and let me fade into your revival."

Touched by Bob Bantam's speech, Gerald retired and, dutifully, wrote this:

> The garden hurled its types of flowers, growing as we acknowledged them, continually into our vase-like minds, arranging themselves as bouquets. As we walked the garden, we fell and turned into struggling leaf, our noses the gay target of a frisky mosquito. Then we knew the garden more, but not as spectators; we had no more humanity than true humans are flowery. We had put on a new smell, had lost the ability to converse, and fell idly in love with the yellow divinity of sun. As for "hours," we surprisingly gave them no regard, since we had arrived young at our own burial place, and expected not a change of view, seeing the cemetery was full of neighbors in the mature of life.

"Good enough," Bob Bantam murmured, reading the copy at the late roar of night, silenced in by the enormous din, absorbed in the outburst of spring. "Now, do it over again, using other words. Pack your details with symbolism, employing the same concept. Keeping to the theme of before, dress it now differently, so that we may compare the two versions. But work in harmony with the original, almost paraphrase it. Now, go show your stuff, and come back again soon. I'm depressed as never before, in a most maddening misery as ever blackened a soul's native innocence. Leave me, Gerry; spring kills more harshly than autumn can; and write it quick, unless by being too late you return and find me—no, not dead, I promise. As I drink, kid, go ahead. Render nature's tragedy, by articulating our only human skill: Art, reporting our place in the world and God's swift will in replacing us, in the seasonal ceremony of renewal. Ah, my life is dark. Light me, Gerry, and enlighten *The Evening Star*'s group of motley readers, that anonymous band that pays us our living. Ah, if only I had your gift! Then would your words be mine, under general authorship. See, it's already dawn now. Come, before spring ousts us from our small circle of life. Time is more by you and less with me; mine is consumed, and yours yet to be."

As Bob Bantam wept, Gerald was moved with insane sympathy. He withdrew and, with careful haste, dedicated to his beloved boss, produced this rendition of life's tragic garden scene, transformed from his human identity to that of a plant, with exposed fragility in the murderous face of time. These words cost him his saddest pain. Will Bob Bantam still live, when their order had been composed? He wrote, against fear, investing such power in a flower as to subdue the breathing violence of the hour. When he had done, he slumped into a daze, and from his paper sported these words, borrowed from the lesson spring teaches to the soul's grim madness in its zest to arrest life's retreating pace and all-but-disappearing presence, here today, and gone in time to empty the garden for the next spring, trampling the ground bare for a succeeding batch to erupt with vanity and sprightliness:

Uprooted from a windy garden, purple and red flowers embroidered our eyes, and fitted like bouquets into our vase-hearts.

We fell and turned into struggling leaf; our feet were bound by roots, our skin divided into petals. We had both become stalk-waisted. Bees browsed in our nostrils; we no longer needed handkerchiefs.

Our wristwatches were peeled when the sun infused us, through our pores, with rays of patient infinity.

We were youthfully arrived, in the prime hue of May, at the same earth due to house our death. The cemetery was crowded with neighbors—odd petals and variations of our species, all sap-served, a brief summer on each stalk.

Gerald snapped awake, as the morning poured in. "Bob is waiting," he realized, and dashed with the manuscript to his boss-father's office. Bantam was in conference, giving last-minute commands. The early edition was soon to press, and the news kept slipping in: a war, a murder, a sex crime, and other noteworthy items. "Here's about spring," exclaimed Gerald, and Bantam dismissed the rest, citing urgency. He glanced over what Gerald had so lately done, and blessed it. Orders had been carried out—by his own young superior! He embraced Gerald, and said, "Not April but March twenty first—that's when your first article appears. Then every two or three days thereafter, a serial in the interest of impressing the public with that solemn event, spring. You'll be in print! Glory be, you joyful guy. Here, take a sip. Let's go home—I'll buy you breakfast. I'll get a sub to make decisions in my stead and worry over today's paper. I'm all buoyant with your rhetoric. Your garden was a swell idea, what with you turnin' into a flower. Would that all our reporters could equally *become* their subject! First-hand liveliness—that's the spirit of news scooping. Yeah, what you want to do is *identify* yourself with the thing you're telling about, no matter how complex or abstract. Then you're with it, in it, by it, of it. Sure, to imitate the thing itself, and apply style directly. Yeah, Gerald, you'll go far. A new star has been born, and the night ain't so dark. You explain cycles of nature, and clarify our diurnal course. Sure, you're a great guy." By then, they'd slipped out the elevator, and were entering a coffee joint. The morning was radiant; snow had melted. The air seemed to echo spring, from the printed word. "You're prophetic, kid," Bantam said. "What you write has *got* to come true, or the calendar is out of date. Yeah, what you comment on, becomes said; and being said, it's got to exist; that's the way we communicate. Words come first, and things later. Right?" "You said it, Bob," rejoiced Gerald Folkdale, and they throbbed in mutual elation. Wasn't spring wonderful? They ate a hearty breakfast: pancakes, sausages, toast, eggs, bacon, beans, tomatoes, cake, coffee, juice—and syrup, indiscriminately applied. They were at one, the older and the younger, joining experience with talent. This combination was bound, boundlessly, to prevail, and whip failure, and create the glories of their wish. Spring assented, seasonally, its mildness sustaining their brisk wind. Ah, life was fine, in each of their two bodies. Time alone could cheat so flowing a mental vigor, so physical a joint soul stripping infinity of its mysteries. They reduced all that's visible in the universe to its invisible components; and fascinated by mere difficulty, they converted impossibilities to divine everyday banalities for unrestricted consumption and grandiose feasting, as though man's appetite measured to gargantuan ecstasies. "Go home and sleep," Bantam ordered, as drowsiness deepened on him. "Wait, I'm just identifying with spring," panted Gerald, who had been scribbling on one napkin with an undependable pen, and had gone on to page two on a ripped-off half of a coarse and raggy tablecloth, so imperative were his pen's needs. Bantam knew well not to interrupt.

Bantam drowsed, and the sun's reflection flickered on his face, through the cafeteria's plated window. He lightly dreamed, to the tune of the grating in Gerald's rough pen-course as it frantically went from idea to word and back to the moving hand. Gerald's quest was to accord spring the proper response from all the tides of feeling latent in the dormant dawn of recognition. One perceives by memory's prime agency; that which one perceives, primarily, evokes; and what's evoked carries the key to what's to be seen.

Gerald wrote, fearing this predicament: craving the union of season and self, what of the absurdity of discrepancy? Wouldn't he realize the right response, before the source of his stimulation shifted its radiance beyond the interior scope of reality's evasive expectations? Wouldn't spring concur, to authenticate what he sees? Where is the soul of coincidental harmony, the seen expressive of the seer, an outside intimately one with the inside, and he who lives is in character with that through which he lives, as his journey is matched on nature's path by its own excellent fruit, in a blending of essence's equal sides, showing truth everywhere? How might an ideal fare, in its precarious intrusion on the real? Was spring in him, or was he foreign to the invitations spread in friendly snare to join that aspect of himself which, inwardly, he would call spring? Ah, how crudely primitive can simple belonging be:

One day, spring came. Of course, I wasn't prepared. There was no time to lose. What could I do? I remembered last spring, and applied its emotions. Still, they weren't appropriate. So at the risk of nostalgia, I went back to all my participating springs, to suck their memory dry. It even cost me tears. At last, spring was over. By then, I grew accustomed. How too late. I was in a spring mood, but all the plants were so far advanced—and their acclimating admirers, the people—that autumn had staked its season, while I was freshly awaiting spring, with a responsive willingness. Truly I lacked ripeness, and was untimely the victim of inconvenience. What a wasted emotion. How it would have welcomed spring. Can I save it? No. I'll lose it soon. The world and I can't agree. How tediously difficult, I felt, to get along. When will I ever be spring, and spring take the occasion to become me? All at once, or both at all. Or has my opportunity failed, and I prove myself supremely unfit? Spring, warn me, give me a little chance. I like you, if at all possible. Let's conform. Grant me my expectations, and I'll grow into you, absorb your masterful example, and arrive as your prime student, the sampling disciple at one with the great lesson. Then let heaven blend, blessing our union in the practical passion of peace, the internal spring conceived at the hour of bloom, the seed working quietly until explosive color matures, and a terrible completeness reigns in its true season.

"Is it spring yet?" asked Bob Bantam, recovering from his little nap. The day was glowing in March's windy beauty, with a startling sun. "Boss, I just done this. The writing is crude on these stray materials that came to hand, but do you think I achieved identification?" Bantam read, and said, "Sure. Even your confusion is harmonious, and spring is well stated as a state of mind. The inward-outward battle has long been our predicament. What you've written represents my own point of view; in effect, you say what we both feel, and express the joint attitude of the total reading audience of our humble rag, *The Evening Star*. Gerry, you've done superlatively well."

"Boss, I love your appreciation. Before we go home, can't you assign me another piece? And extend its scope, for I want my coverage to be large."

"Yes, prepare it at home, and you may come in late, or else tomorrow. Or better still, do field research. Perhaps a photographer should accompany you? In a few days' time, the first of your articles will be printed. So why stint, in your case, expense and thoroughness? Your whole series will edify the public immensely. You'll be a smash sensation, as though *you* caused spring, by publicizing its promotion. Then, kid, the earth is yours."

"Yeah, but there's not even any bud in bloom yet. And the season won't be official till publishing date. Where can I observe the effects? Can you send me south?"

"No, that's costly expenditure. Our paper is rapidly losing money.

You're expected to save it, with your eye-popping exposés and highbrow poeticizings in moods any lowbrow can understand. You'll pull us out of the hole, kid. That is, if we don't fold first. I hear that a competitor paper wants to buy us out. The financial board of directors and other top managerial officials will put together their heads, and perhaps contemplate a deal. Maybe we'll increase the price, charging fifteen cents. Can the man in the street afford it? He's avid for news, and we've got it."

"Those are top-level decisions that I'm exempt from being qualified to consider. I'm just a wage-slave, churning out words. Boss, spring is in my blood. Can you describe what should follow what I've already done, in nature's inevitable line of order and sequence? You must admit, I've a hot pen. Can you keep it going?"

"Yeah, but will the paper endure so well? Increasing costs and deepening overhead require a substantial cutdown, per fiscal budget per yearly annum. These are organizational terms, incorporated in the charter our executive trustees have drawn us. Gerry, this is a business. Circulation is the life blood of every newspaper. If not enough copies are sold, then our vital arterial connections are cut, the veins dry up, and the pumping heart ceases, in its special functionary role. You know what it means? Death. Death never did life any good, and never will. Can you accuse me of being dramatic? Well, life is emotional, isn't it? Not to mention all the glands and organs brought into play, as stop-gaps to boredom. Yes, consider the organism as an integrated unity, while …" "Boss, you're raving," Gerald interrupted. "We've got to separate and get some sleep. Your position is so inclusive, many worries must burden you, in putting out the paper as an entirety. While as for me, I'm consigned only to spring. I mean to write a broad essay. It would have even subdivisions—three chapters, plus one overall heading. You've told me that recently advertising has abated, leaving more space. And not much news is going on, of interest to such variegated literate humanity as consume our evening rag. So I'll write something large—a complete exposition, running through all of spring's gamuts. For consistency's sake, I'll centralize a viewpoint. I'll rage philosophical, and not be tempted toward easy cynicism. Spring, being a part of life, is itself composed of more than life. I'll bring it to life, and shove death aside. What a stupendous essay it intends to be! Both personal and objective at the same time.

Such range and scope will run up art's credit to a sublime flagpost. Boss, shake my hand, and say goodbye. Tonight or tomorrow it'll be ready, you'll see. Your duty is to keep the paper alive; otherwise my precious prose will shine unseen, for lack of an impressive showcase. How can my words look well, when printed on the defunct body of a bankrupt black corpse? It would be a most unsuitable conveyance of my urgent poetic messages. Keep our head afloat, and don't shake our unsteady boat. Else, dear boss, will rival journals find us sunk, whereby they gloat. And so, I leave you. We part, to sleep. May fortune bind us in equal destiny, the younger to the old. It's still winter, as yet. When will all icicles be prey to the friendly thaw? On what fruitful results will our elaborate beginnings pose? I'll pretend it's May, and submit you a wonderful work of prose. Guard your asthma, and avoid too many more divorces. Control your whiskey temper, and be the presiding paternal spirit on which my flying hopes rest. And while you're gone, what I write will be yours as well."

Then hours were donated to sleep. Gerald woke in a restive state of apprehension. The night would be his. He greeted his parents, dressed, and went on a date. The girl wasn't cooperative, nor were their souls steadily mated. Gerald dropped her off, and went back home to sleep again. He rose in the full consciousness of spring, and went to a public park. The morning was gray, with clouds. The barren trees belonged to winter, but Gerald pretended May. He found a bench in a "rustic" spot and wrote in creaking pencil on a pocket pad. He saw two months ahead, and from that advanced seeing, helped by hindsight, he carved out the following lengthy piece, prompted by an extravagant complexity of mood and some foreboding of disaster (He wrote hastily, but in clean-cut strokes simply hewn from his befuddled ambiguity.):

LITTLE DASH OF SPRING: AN AGREEABLE INTERLUDE

I

Spring is one of the major events of nature. It occurs with annual regularity, on a yearly basis of repetition. Is this good? Yes.

How can it be recognized? Through overt habit, and covert uniformity within the mood of growth, giving instinct to seed, and transpiring in flower. It certainly is hectic. Birds donate their services free, and just simply adore the climate. Oh, it's magnificent. Just think: spring.

It has its bad points, too. It literally destroys winter, and forestalls the free abrupt honesty in suddenly it being summer. It passes by in a pause of transition, linking extremes. Which has nature to recommend it, and perhaps philosophers agree.

Of course, spring is lyrical, too. There's a pastoral sentiment, difficult to ignore. It's a season of love, whether resulting in babies or heartbreak. Sin is licensed, and inhibition slumbers, with one fitful eye open to select the bawdy and obscene, which it must officially condemn, if not thoroughly ban.

Spring is ripe for suicide, promising resurrection. As for business, seasonal industries gain, or are typically reversed. Employees think about vacation, and the clock has a feeling it is looked at on the office wall, and papers on the desk have a blank, often dismal, expression. Of course, we must celebrate.

Now, May is here. Which, all things considering, has a fitness, a propriety, which swells the hearts in policemen and promotes the impulse of an emotion in our earliest infants, still damp in the dawn of their simplicity. This is no time for cynics. No, it isn't.

II

As for the weather, it's hopeful. So often the weather just appears, and does nothing but that. In these days, we require action, and we want to be convinced. We want, at least, strong weather. We have petitioned the sun. The matter is referred to cloudy bureaucracy, where the forecast of an earliest rainy decision is being conspired in the smoke-filled rooms that party to the traffic of politics, on a scale almost hopelessly above us. So, we wait. Which is what we're expected to do, until the blood boils over and dawn kisses dusk in the privilege of noon, damning the tides and swelling the flow. Oh, I feel like romance now. Such a lyrical sentiment. Spring is the occasion. We must not frustrate it. I've made a treaty with nature, promising mutual alliance. It shouldn't back out. I sit here, waiting. My window crowds with flowers. Which one, among them, is the hidden girl on whose cheek the stamp of my personal dream is at once bare and evident? Come to me, in the night. My heart is intricate, but may include you. Why not? You satisfy.

III

Hey, spring is crumbled up. Time messed it up, that's why. It sort of outgrew itself, collapsed flat, and folded into summer. Isn't that always the way. Too bad. My dreams lay crushed. The flower was not a girl, after all. It was only a flower. That was very limiting.

My plans? None, so far. I think I'll grow melancholy, and develop it like an art or a child. Explore its possibilities. Sing in tune and rhythm. The heart is badly hurt. It was cruel of spring, to promise, and not fulfill. Hereafter, I'll ignore it. Out of season, in. My time grows nigh. I've had one too much spring, and my hangover drags. All those useless leaves, on so many scoundrel trees. The grass, where feet fell free to romp. And those ugly birds, to scan the sky. What was it all about? Even weather was incorporated, to serve the general purpose. It was a conspiracy and, as I die, I'm glad to know it. A stab, and I'm dead. Spring did it. That fatal cancer, striking from within, and flooding the senses from without. As for sleep, riot will prohibit that. My stone is subject to spring, and the running grave shall wake me. Ah, my nice blood. It flows all over nature, and sucks on some beautiful tits. I revive, and now it's winter. Hello. I'm cold. It's chilly. How about a little fire for some cheerfulness, and forget an angry spring? God does it all over again. Let's wait.

It was cold in the park. Gerald felt forlorn, and must report to work that night. What good was all this writing? Had it any influence over events? At least, it would consume newspaper space. And be read, by people he'd never see. But would spring itself be affected? It grew from some majestic independence, beyond men's comment. Gerald went home, and let his mother prepare him a meal. Then he dressed in his business suit, but left without his latest article. He returned, and folded it in his careful breast pocket. Such words were his source of income, and were, as well, his and Bantam's spiritual resource. Only spring reared its head indifferently, with illiterate grandeur.

"Look what I did," he showed Bantam. "Lengthy, isn't it?" he was greeted. Bantam read it through twice. "It's nice, I like it," he said, without much conviction. "What's wrong, boss?" Gerald asked. "*The Evening Star* might be waning," the editor reported with lackluster spirit. "To be bought out?" asked Gerald, in a disheartened tone. "Some deal or other. It looks bad. Circulation fell. What could we do?" "But don't my stuff get printed?" asserted Gerald in protective despair. "It shouldn't be wasted. I'll see to it," resolved his senior friend. Rain fell outside. And inside, tears drizzled, weeping for words and their precious fate. Can't poetry be sacred, despite business collapses? Hasn't the fine word the right to endure, in the face of commercial ruin? "Quick, go to your room—you've already written nine pieces—and write your tenth. Speak, somehow, of words. Have a dialogue between a bird and a tree. Also mention money, in its worldly context. Of course, stick to spring. That's your theme, whether the ship of print will sink or not. Then runs away the season, so shut up the bird and tree. It should be allegorical, and show how what we write scares nature into its vigorous spring reality, with flowers in abundance. Delve into the nature of a bird and tree, and dope out what contribution they make to creating spring as a living word. And when humans speak, is spring the same? Communication is partially your subject. Write. It's certain to be printed." "But what if our journal merges with a rival whose policy is unfriendly to my inspired features? Where will spring go, and I?" "Ah, who can say?" sadly answered Bob Bantam, whose phone rang, and who, hanging up, excused himself to hastily make haste. An editorial meeting had been summoned for a minute ago. He was already late. He flew away. Gerald poked about, then went to his small room, where he puttered some more, meditating on ephemeral mortality, the transience of all living things and artificial projects. What's here is ever brief, and fatal doom brings it down. He put down words to arrest spring's brevity, on the wings of a tree-faring bird. Stick around, nature. Words create and uncreate you, in your dumb ring of seasons. Life grows on the seeds of silence.

"Spring is here," the bird said. "Nonsense, you can't talk," a tree answered. So the bird chirped, as all birds do, as a matter of traditional habit and not just as a flighty afterthought. "Speaking English. Imagine!" the tree said. But the bird was right. Though it shouldn't have spoken, it had uttered a communicable truth. Spring was impressed. It came on, and flowered. Everywhere, the bird's truth echoed. It was impressive. Furthermore, it was true. Now the bird never speaks. It merely chirps. But the word of spring came alive, and spring is all realism. The buds, sweet and sticky, can be touched. That's what the bird meant. Before silenced. And now only a human tree can speak. But what tree is ever human? They merely obey spring, and change their leaves. So the tree was wrong, having spoken. Words are human property, whether spring comes or no. The tree had silenced a bird, but itself had erred in using the same vehicle of mistake. The tree apologizes, and can't speak. So nature is dumb. It goes on existing, while humans trade words. Shilling words, mark words, dollar words. Even franc words, whether inflation or deflation. The winds change, and words alter, but meanings are always never the same. Now, for example, it's not spring. The bird, in all its glory, has flown away. The tree stands still, but looks bare. Waiting for a word. And the word can only come from a human mouth. We open it cautiously, and falsehoods fly out. We pursue them and, when captured, the falsehoods have become true. This truth becomes a mirror, reflecting another bird, and the same tree. And in the background, as always, picturesque spring.

Later on, Bantam returned to his office to find Gerald's latest article waiting on the desk. Bantam was all but jobless, unseated by the new setup. He had pleaded to retain the idea of Gerald's series of spring features, as a seasonal tribute. This was vetoed, and now he was depressed.

He opened a secret drawer for a decanter of his prime whiskey. He drank a few gurgling slurps straight, as a testimony to his manhood. He buzzed for Gerald to come in, and was seen reading the bird-tree episode with evident relish. "Gerald, why do we need spring, when we have your prose? So we'll skip the reality this year, and keep your personalized studies of it. This proves that art is strong, while life is all but faint. Here, take a sniff." Gerald imbibed from the decanter, and asked, "Is the paper saved? Will my work find the light of print?" "Well, kid, no. We're doomed. It's unlucky, just when spring was near. I'm ousted in the new regime. I retain only an advisory capacity, with but nominal powers. You, I'm afraid, must go. They don't like your pieces, and have overruled me. Can you write only one more, for friendship's sake? Then, privately, maybe, we'll get up some kind of edition, even if from my own pocket, at expense ruinous to my debts and commitments of alimony. Kid, don't ever get divorced. It puts marriage at a sour end, and makes a guy bitter. I'm gonna be retired. I'm through. You, I'll refer you, and recommend you to another job. You ought to make a crack reporter somewhere, and expose the periodical scandals that brew in nature. Sure, even your superpowered, highly condensed prose will find a welcome niche in the human interest realm that appeals to emotions. I notice, in your most recent 'fable,' that just before the end spring had faded into autumn. Weren't you anticipating just a little bit? Buck up, kid. It's spring tomorrow. I've got to pack away my belongings, and remove my desk. Tomorrow, my successor takes over, and our paper over which we lavished such care has officially changed hands. All good things end, Gerry. A sentimentalist like you ought to know that. Believe me, I'm sorry. Whose fault could it be, but an ill-omened star? Do your last farewell article. Make it, somehow, symbolic. A rose has ever been traditional. Say goodbye to it, to show that nothing lasts. Don't worry about your parents; you'll get a dismissal bonus, as a payoff. All your labors will be reimbursed, and the discharge will terminate your employment with all honors respecting your post. Behind you, a clean record glows to the career ahead. Consider this but a beginning; the most impeccable spring resides with certainty on your horizon's eminent future, in the distinguished dawn. We spend these tears to fertilize a greater tomorrow: yours, for mine has declined."

Bantam sobbed, heaving his breast. Twilight filtered in, and ancient nightfall. They were bound, the exiting editor and his departing writer, in the solidarity of their lonelily linked solitudes. It was their last night "on the job." To ease it and relieve the drama, they drank fitfully, and let the excess pour out of their eyes. Bright dreams lost, imperishable ideals flagrantly perished! A wash of overflow couldn't clean the joined knot of their holy woe.

They couldn't leave the office. They slept on cots, Gerry awaking first. He would do his last article. It was already the early pre-dawn of the day of spring itself. The day they would both have to leave.

Gerry started to write, but couldn't. His boss awoke, and mumbled advice: "Spring has begun, though we've ended. Later comes the rose, flush into summer. It bears both birth and death. Immortalize it, which it is already, deathless; but add your two scents, to buy what you're sold on."

"Boss, your obscure references to money impoverish my comprehension. Directly, will you explain?"

"The crown of spring is a rose; it arrives late, preluding summer. Show how annual it is, and indicate time that way. After all, the rose began a long time ago, and is cherished by yearly tradition. Let this idea reflect on proverbially human mortality, in deep nature's scheme."

"Yes, that's enough. I'll write it now."

The boss went back to sleep. Gerald was sad, sadly old, and old beyond his means. In all its immensity, the tragedy of life claimed him for its own. What would happen to his precious articles? His paper had folded, merged with another, and the changeover had united in a policy alien to any such spring series that Gerald had starred in in advance. Bob Bantam was finished, with only nominal power but actually shorn of influence. Gerald shut down his mind, and the image of a rose came up. Time surrounded it, in a setting of season. Gerald followed its motion, through the unending human mind. For each trace it left, Gerald dealt a word in return, until his sentiment had been accomplished, through his last essay:

A perfect rose is a true flower. Only deep spring reveals it. By then, impure summer molests it, the lavish ripening decay. Goodbye, fair rose. Your glamor was only brief, and will enjoy the long and fruitful memory inhaled in fragrant leisure by the comfortable human. That nose endures, and you are survived by your smeller. In your flowerhood's midget hour, you repeated last year's scent. How annually your inventiveness has dulled! Discovery indeed dwindles you. You are how old? Since the rise of the vegetable kingdom? What an ancient lineage! Such ancestral bliss, to console your many deaths. We pause, and take breath.

Goodbye, rose. Next year's edition will renew you. And with such freshness, in the morning dew! Then be immortal, till we die.

Spring dawn glowed through the window. Gerald left the office, holding an official note of dismissal. The manuscript copies of his eleven articles were arranged in order in an envelope and put with Bob Bantam's things. Gerald kept carbons for himself, and walked out with his briefcase in which were contained his newspaper effects. He went home. A big check momentarily consoled his parents. Yet they wept.

Instead of waking, Bob Bantam became sick. He was removed to a hospital, where at present his state is weakened. Should he recover, there's no doubt that his old self will never return. Combined infirmities have pooled all their evils to reduce his crowing spirit. Gerald visits him, at bedside. Bob now calls him "son."

Gerald has married. He never writes like he once did. He has a good job, as a conventional journalist. Secretly, he considers that he has "sold out."

Spring, in some ways, remains his favorite season. His wife is hardboiled, and calls him sentimental. She wishes he'd visit Bob Bantam at hospital less. She doesn't like his former boss's effect on her new property. Gerald earns enough to have set up his parents in a suitable old age home. He visits them on Sunday.

The news comes in that Bob Bantam is dead. The day is bitterly cold, and snowy. Gerald is distressed. His wife scolds him, for he has stayed home from work. Inside of her, their child is brewing. It's due for spring delivery, should the weather ever relent. Meanwhile, climate and the calendar collaborate. And Gerald is up to date. At Bob Bantam's funeral, Gerald is sedate in black. There goes his father, home to the earth. May the Lord strew spring ashes on him, and memory complete in perfection all the excesses that roughened up his character. Gerald is now supremely sad. In his will, Bob left Gerald the eleven essays. Now he's hawking them, peddling them around. The paper for which he works absolutely won't hear of it; the style won't fit. Somewhere in him, Gerald supposes, is the unburied poet. Will spring, that delivers his wife of their child, free him as well? No, his duties are too stiff, and imagination is no longer verbal. Goodbye youth, and farewell to that unlikely muse, Bob Bantam, whose legend sparks his soul occasionally. Time manufactures more springs. Each new edition of that honored season seems dim, compared to what imagination had wrought. Spring was once a magic of words. Now, green reality is plain indeed.

In spring, the child is born. Not a new Bob Bantam, for she's a girl. Gerald's wife has become prettier, now that her maturity is fulfilled. The couple, moderately happy, expect an even course of life from here on in. Eventually, spring will be the same as the other seasons, save for some surplus growth on the surface. It will be brightly decorative, and will have the sun's full sanction.

THE DON JUAN OF EAST EIGHTY-NINTH STREET

1

Donald J. Gervasi lived on East Eighty-Ninth Street of the enormous city, in a high-floor apartment of an above-middle-income apartment building. To say that he lived alone, unmarried, is semi-accurate. He was hardly ever alone, in those prime years. The women wouldn't let him be; and he let them not let him be.

Financially, he did all right too. He worked for an advertising company by arrangement that let him come to the office irregularly, while still pulling down the ample pay of others who strained and sweated putting in full regular lengthy office hours of stress and hustle. This arrangement, that softened and eased his life by affording him the luxury of free time for himself, came because he was so efficiently facile at his work that it was not necessary for him to be an office drudge plugging along all day at a weary pace. He fairly earned his privilege as a part-timer because, ultimately, despite seemingly little effort and apparently minimum input, he came up with impressive output. The executive supervisory administrators knew, on the cold balance of productivity rate, his quality value, and paid him not just in good money but in the liberal allowance of leisurely free time, which he requested and, on sheer merit alone, was granted. Some of his colleagues envied this seeming favoritism, but learned not to begrudge Gervasi's "luck," because, darn it, the work that he "effortlessly" did showed that he hadn't stinted, that he had pulled his weight, and done his proper required share despite not being seen toiling away at the desk, or harassed on the coils and hoops of telephone entrapment.

The extra time was filled by women.

The same efficient effortless facility with which he did his advertising work to the extent of his being rewarded on a part-time full-pay basis, characterized his notorious notable knack with women.

The first two initials of Donald J. Gervasi, by coincidence, were D.J., which could stand for "Don Juan." And the usual nickname for Donald was Don anyway.

Gossip circles alluded to him as "D.J." But "D.J." was his impersonal legendary public reputation reference. If a woman was closing in to get close and personal with him, hoping to be his one-and-only, she certainly wouldn't call him by the public and impersonal "D.J." For her, who aspired to pluck him away from the jostling social herds for her own exclusive consumption by the earnest hope of fantasy as her dearly own in cozy privacy, he'd be called "Don," which had the stamp of tender familiarity and a privileged intimacy suggestive of being engaged.

He was used to lots of hopefuls calling him "Don," each endeavoring to stake the claim of unique proprietory exclusivity.

He juggled his schedule to fit in as many of those specially favored women as he could on a flexible engagement appointment calendar program, rotating and renewed, updated, phasing out the used-up ones he wearied of—who pressed him too far with hysterical bluster, frantic pleading, forceful innuendoes and claustrophobic possessiveness that urged upon him in an unsubtle manner the approved custom of marriage as a convention sweetly applicable by the covenants of usage to the particular case enclosing like a balloon that woman and her "Don." Don would then puncture that dream balloon, and become merely a "D.J." to his latest outcast.

The turnover rate was ruthlessly frequent. The appointment calendar had to be ever continually revised and updated. The need for a social secretary to manage his busy, ever-changing schedule, grew imperative. Someone emerged, like a blast of appropriate magic, to fill the bill: a Leporello who would manage the Don's "affairs." He proved to be a colleague in the advertising firm, who worked full-time as an office drudge and pulled down less pay than the aristocratically part-time Don. Al Lehman was found, enlisted, and pressed into service, as a willing volunteer. He'd reorganize appointment bookings for trysts and assignations, permitting maximum action on a wide scale of many "fronts" with maneuvers and twists of strategy, while alleviating the hazards of embarrassing "overlap" by careful planning timed down to the thrilling minute in the turnstile whir of succession. Streamlined efficiency with this campaign allowed the Don to multiply the disciplined swarms of his lovely women.

2

"Al, do you mind my asking what is in it for *you*, acting as my social secretary in your hard-earned spare time away from your office grind? It's not as if you're getting paid."

"D.J., you've observed all along that I'm a bungler with women."

"Yes, your reputation with them stands diametrically opposite to my own. Are you serving me in order to get a voyeur's sublimation, as well as vicariously identifying with my fabulous success as an amorist?"

"Currently you've been my so-to-speak proxy; I've been only a sidelines spectator to your on-the-field participations as a prolific contestant performing your athletic feats, your marathon relays."

"Is being my spectator, my manager, my secretary, my apologist, of sufficient consolation for your being such a non-performer in your own right?"

"I hope to learn from you, as your disciple. Your veteran know-how may rub off on me; I may pick up a few pointers and, if not precisely imitate you, then approximately emulate you, with the lovely creatures we call women."

"But you seem utterly to lack the knack. You're just not cut out, genetically by nature or lifelong force of habit, to be anywhere in my league whatever."

"Don't bother to apologize for your bluntness. But you needn't caricaturize me in the stereotype of abject feckless total hopelessness in the realm of womanizing, of which you're the princely paragon of your time—the Don Juan of East Eighty-Ninth Street including the environing areas extending for a radius of miles around beyond the bounds of your usual haunts."

"Al, you're a sly one. You're withholding an aspect of your incentive motivation in volunteering your free services in your hard-earned leisure time as my social valet, so to speak. What's your game?"

"D.J., on my own, all my adolescent and so-far-adult life, I've failed, with steady humiliation, to get anywhere with the fair sex."

"You're not telling me anything new."

"But now I've cast myself within the umbrella and auspices of your aura. Some of your magic may rub off on me: a romantic spell, an enchantment, that—in your wake, hanging to your coattails—I can so partake of, as to dazzle a few beauties myself."

"You don't seem to be the type. But good luck anyway."

"Don't cynically disparage me. In return for my serving you, be so generous as to admit that in your service a few of your discards and rejects may, on the rebound, drop into my ever-ready but chronically deprived lap, which waits all erect for whatever openings may occur."

"A noble ambition—to be a scavenger!"

"At a whirlwind rate you phase out women into becoming eventually rejects. In their numb despair, some may fall easy prey to me, especially once I've picked up some of your wiles."

"To make it worth your whiles. I see. You damn parasite!"

"But you use me. Why can't I in turn use you?"

"Then it Is not parasitical, but symbiotic, in our mutual double-leveled usefulness. That's how I pay you."

"It's not as cold as that in tit-for-tat merely, but what's additionally in it for me is—!"

"Yes?"

"—I love the atmospheric aura you've set up for yourself, of being a winner a man of conquests. I admire you, D.J."

"Your hat's off to me—showing a bald spot. Well, in all due modesty—just short of humility—I hereby accept your admiration."

"Women will *associate* me with you. So if some can't have or can't retain you—you yourself directly—, they may get consolation by the next best thing: resorting to *me*, who will, by association with you as in a way your 'team-mate,' partner, or colleague, remind them of you. I'd partake of, smack of, that fabulous aura of your supreme inaccessibility, unattainability."

"I'm not inaccessible or unattainable to *all* of them."

"Not *at first* to all of them, but *ultimately* to all of them."

"Sure. I have to leave myself open to newcomers."

"So noble and generous you are with your favors."

"And you want me to cut you in on a little of my action, parasite?"

"I de*serve* it for I *serve* you."

"Our exchange. A business arrangement that suits me fine."

"Shake, partner."

They shake hands. Neither is the fool or dupe of the other. They're both open eyed, in their partitioning of functions, roles, services, influences, and assistances.

But will Al Lehman be thought of as an acceptable substitute for the real thing? He's almost comically different from his "master." Or will some rejected or dropped woman be so drowned blind in her despair as to overlook in her miserable distracted dejection that Al Lehman is no Don? Will her tears blur them together?

Al is taking self-taught lessons in trying to dress, look, and act like the inimitable D.J. He mimes gesture, mimics accent. But he fools no one—certainly not the women—except his own deluded and foolish self.

3

Al Lehman helped to facilitate and regulate Donald J. Gervasi's amorous swirl. After a while, they held a "business meeting" together, at Al's instigation.

"D.J., as your secretary-manager—"

"By the way, how have *you* been doing, chasing after my rejects and discards once I've either phased them out or cut them off at the start?"

"We'll go into that delicate matter later. First I want to talk about *you*."

"Me? Now, *that*'s a subject I can *relate* to! It's close to my own interests, and dear to my very heart."

"Facetiousness apart, D.J. Now listen. Just like you're so overqualified at the firm that the work is simple-as-pie for you and so the hours you put in are aristocratically diminutive and dainty, compared to *my* having to plug away like a bonded wage slave—"

"Yes?"

"So too, just as your working life is an easy cinch, a snap, a lark—so is your cushiony life with the lady folks."

"Too true. What's your point?"

"You're spoiled and overqualified both in your work life and your love life."

"That's good—I'm not complaining."

"D.J., stop patronizing me.'"

"You're my earnest apprentice. Why *shouldn't* I patronize you?"

"D.J., you're passive."

"I am?"

"You don't *go after* the women—you let them go to you."

"I find that a very effective method—though in *your* case it would fail, of course. ... Not only effective, but economical. I don't *have* to go after them—there's no need to—when all I have to do is—"

"But it's too easy, D.J.!"

"Are you jealous or envious?'"

"Of course I am. How could I not be?"

"Well, don't begrudge me. Better *one* of us should have the knack than that *both* should lack it!"

"D.J., you're spoiled rotten. You're turning soft. You don't have to pursue any dame—"

"Being pursued, of course not."

"But you're non-assertive. You let yourself be picked, chosen, and selected."

"Not by *every* woman. And not by any woman for too long. In those departments, that's where *you* come in: helping to control the traffic, regulate the driving permits, parceling out short-term licenses, shifting parking zones—"

"I know—I know only too well. Well, where's the *challenge*?"

"Huh?"

"Difficulty, challenge. Resistance. That's what you need. To toughen you up."

"Why do I *need* toughening up? Being soft is nice. I'll keep it that way. Wouldn't *you* like my soft way of being hard on the women?"

"Don't rub it in."

"I *do* rub it in—the women. Don't you wish they'd let *you* rub it in?"

"The women go for you in droves of accessibility and willing availability."

"Yes, they're open to me—arms and all."

"Legs too, lucky for you."

"How qualified are you to advise me, being admittedly so jealous and envious as you are?"

"It's not petty, self-serving advice; it's for your own good."

"*Why* would it be good for me to break up a winning combination, a formula proven and re-proven to work—just to make things hard for myself? That would be only perverse, self-destructive. You do me wrong to recommend it."

But Al, adamant, went on to get his way with his "master." He pointed out that true mastery must undertake worthy challenges, tussles that try fiber under fire. The current routine was lazily automatic, and was unconducive to growth or toughness. Only the available, accessible women approached D.J., from which, with Al's help, he made selections: weeding out some candidates and phasing out others who'd been permitted to start. D.J. resisted Al's strange force of logic.

"True, I find it easy to get women. But women find it easy to get *me*."

"Only some—only the lucky ones *now* but doubly unlucky to have their hearts more severely broken *later*. And it's all the more tough on the ones who temporarily succeed with you, for they thereby acquire a hope of marrying you—which you cruelly dash, leaving them strewn among the wreckage of crumbled dreams and shattered faith in Love itself."

"I'm not in this for charity. They'll recover. All right, I'm a heel. So?"

"So you're difficult for women. The odds are stacked in your favor. Be fair-minded, and equal out the odds, instead of retaining so obvious an advantage that you relinquish Fair Play itself."

"How do I redress these odds and advantages, and stop playing Fate's Favorite? How do I, in effect, handicap myself?"

"Since you're difficult for women, why not make women difficult for *you*? Obviously, you can't make the available, accessible ones difficult for you—they're pushovers, automatically. So I'll help you go for ones who, progressively more and more, are less and less accessible and available."

"But why should I go to the trouble? Why take such pains? What's the virtue of it? Puritan guilt? I like my simple life, which you bitterly envy but would have me exchange for one of complicated undertakings."

"I want you, masterfully, to assert yourself and take on 'tough nuts to crack,' instead of being the prey and game of women who crave you."

"I should go after women who don't want me?"

"Who *initially* don't want you. Take on the formidable task of breaking their will, breaking them down, overcoming their extreme reluctance. Be a gambler, pit yourself in truly competitive contests, for higher stakes and sturdy renown."

"Am I performing before an audience? Am I being recorded for history? Do my life and affairs go public? Am I no longer a private, pleasure-seeking man?"

"You haven't been pleasure-*seeking*—just pleasure-*accepting*. Now, go enterprising."

"What are you asking?"

"Be a big-game hunter, taking on graver risks, willing to brave failure or ordeal, in trials against increasingly formidable opponents."

"Are you recommending self-flagellation, with women as the whips?"

"Go for trophies of worth and hardihood. Undergo trials of severity."

"As?"

"Overcome progressively and melt down the various breeds of stubborn resistance: the wife whose love for her husband is a paragon of fidelity; the lesbian for whom men are a repugnant fungus of allergy; nuns with a sacred vow of chastity; saints of asceticism whose ideals have forsworn carnality; the pathological species of rigidly principled prudery; women guarded by mobster husbands of murder-inclined jealousy; women who, as candidates for high political office, must impeccably protect their career-dependent reputations from the scandal and infamy of a public disgrace."

"You're not asking much."

"I'm defying you. Where's your manly valor? I shame you now to fall back on softness!"

"Are you the guardian of my character?"

"You *have no* character. I'd *create* one, for you!"

4

By degrees, Donald J. Gervasi allowed Al Lehman to gain sway, to influence and remold him, acceding to a gradual takeover. Why did D.J. let this happen?

"Arduous ardor is harder—be a martyr," Al mellifluously insisted, prevailing, gaining supremacy, by D.J.'s permission. What was Al's hold over his "victim"?

Complying, D.J. took on mountingly strenuous odds and played more dangerous games, stepping up the failure risk in the frenzy of romantic strife.

From assured probability of conquests, he graduated up the scale of improbability till ready even to tackle the impossible. He tested the range of his capabilities by vast and foolish degree. He perpetuated the Don Juan myth, extended its lineage and dynasty as the sole contemporary representation at the crest and crown upholding a legendary succession with honor.

Contesting the stiffening wills of women, he endured, finally, heroic defeat.

Then he plunged into defeat's new habit. Defeat alone could sustain him.

Al Lehman had brought him down. One deranged ex-victim of the former Don succumbed to Al, by marriage.

D.J. retired—not from the advertising firm, but from women altogether. He ended up a biologically premature or precocious convert to the non-religion of sexual abstinence. He's become neuter.

Al left the firm to relocate, with his wife, in a new city. D.J. remains on Eighty-Ninth Street, more or less idly inactive. Even his easy, plush job with the advertising firm is being phased out. His work output leaks away, as does his diminishing pay.

No communication endures between him and the out-of-town Al Lehman. The effects they had on each other remain as reminders, but fade from the ferocity of consciousness.

A FAMILY CONFUSION

PART ONE

1

I'm now at the other side of life from the side that I started out from. So I have a lot to write about. So much, that I could even write indefinitely and not even barely scratch the topmost surface of a bottomless depth.

So that this tale may have a confined length and the modest readability of a limit, I must rigorously select only those significant highlights that survive a ruthless weeding-out of the inessential dross. How uncomplimentary, however, to the latter! If it was good enough to be included in my life, why shouldn't my life's narration retain all that went on?

So much time couldn't be compressed in the typographical space set aside for these memoirs.

The mother I was born from, being my own private mother and unique to the occasion of my birth, I now dismiss her as a conspicuous irrelevancy to the later unfolding of my life.

My father, the masculine accessory to my coming about, also gets no further treatment here. The sperm he spent gave him me, whom he turned over to my mother's care as soon as the spent sperm could no longer be recalled. He supported my mother and me, and later my sister, until he stopped working. Eventually, he'll someday die. He's hardly alone, in such a lonely end. But before that, there were surprises.

However, that's getting far ahead of where I've been left off in an early stage of existence by the trembling old hand—mine—which pens forth the creaking annals of my narration across a distant lifetime of memory; spanning both ends of a mud-speckled rainbow, whose flying arc comes cruising down to earth.

Speaking of memory, what were my earliest ones? I was such an infant in those days, that the combination of innocence, naiveté, and ignorance, to which a massive inexperience may plentifully be added, provided no conceptual base for distilling and interpreting my dizzily isolated little vivacious circle of sensations, so nakedly unreinforced by maturity's high art of categorization.

Re-enter my parents. How can I leave them out? They figured too prominently. They remain.

I was in my pram, or perambulator, pushed by my marketing mother on the wide shopping thoroughfare on a keenly pinching winter day that smarted my rounded cheeks. The area must vaguely have been in the proximate vicinity (if I'm to overcome memory's blur and etch out the vivid concreteness of a particular) of the Old Brompton Road, or the Fulham Road, perhaps Gloucester Road, or even the Kings Road. Along indefinite lines, surely that was the setting.

Being wheeled by my mother, hearing the honks of passing cars and buses, or the rumble of lorries, I sank comfortably back, lulled by the drowsing drone of pedestrian and traffic crowd repetitive with monotonous flux. The cosmopolitan environment buzzed me into the melting border of a sleep, to blend me out along the reaches of oblivion. This was the part I played, in the larger passing scene.

Such languor alternates with plenty of snap. I was awake, too, at times.

Incidentally, my name is Mark. Hello.

General dimness surrounds events contemporary to the one so pictorially depicted in the above rousing rendition. Being helplessly small in those pre-formed days of infancy, my faculties were distinctly underdeveloped for the recording and registering of later re-enactments in bursting raids upon memory's files.

The slow and sure progress, called growth, was meanwhile all the time underway, only sporadically accompanied, to the thread of a patchy and uneven counterpoint, by that rambling occurrence, consciousness.

Subsequent experience affords retrospective evaluation of those at-the-time undefined periods.

The color of my mother's hair, her smells and figure and facial expressive features, her clothing and attitudes, were the compilation cumulatively of later recollections retroactively permeating that dear dark dawn in the career of bright awareness, connecting my primitive island glimpses with the larger land mass in bridging beachheads gradually up the shore to the broad continuity, multiply-sequence-linking, that builds a margin of surplus from which informed flashbacks are securely subsidized with continual grants of support.

Microscopically, I mirrored evolution itself. Yes, but who doesn't?

What a beauty my mother was! And this is objectivity talking.

She seemed less conventional than my father. But he had to earn our living. He gave. Though not with gratitude always, we took. My lovely mother, and the tiny me. We were a pair. We were souls together. My father was "someone else." We didn't count him, did we? We took. He gave. Poor man.

2

When I was able to walk, I toddled along, pudgy hand clutching my mother's hovering fingers, on strolls and rambles, punctuated by use of public transport. One occasion lingers with fastidious firmness in the inventive upper reaches of memory's highly artificed craft.

From South Kensington we took a morning saunter to Knightsbridge; at Hyde Park Corner we boarded a bus going up Park Lane, around Marble Arch, along Oxford Street, and up the Tottenham Court Road just past Great Russell Street. In those days, I was an only child. My mother was restrictedly free, saddled only with me, before the advent of my sister her daughter, who was to further curtail her liberty and weary down her movements with clamoring imperatives that levied the usual constrictions on a wife already shackled by the modest earning power of my hardworking father, supplemented by no private means from either senior partner of this family that had me already and would add another in time's reproductive course of an actively coupling pair using moderate birth control.

But back to earlier before.

So there we were, my mother and I, on the corner of Great Russell Street and Museum Street. By appointment, a man had met my mother there. From my mother's point of view, which I identified with, this man (a stranger to me, but already intimate with my mother) vastly exceeded my father in the crudely refined power and erotic flavoring of a thrilling romantic appeal. Less conventionally dressed than my father, he was a sturdy figure of middle height and bright orange hair, shockingly pure of color. He was dashing, bright, and bouncy, with a wild sort of incessant energy overflowing in demonic zeal but honed to courtesy and good nature. His face was startling, and frank. But now, he was angry.

"Why'd you bring him along?"

"We can't keep affording babysitters. Tom works hard, but his earning power remains low yet. His company is fiscally bone-tight at the moment."

"Look, Liz, I want to be private with you. The presence of this brat doesn't allow for too much of that."

"We'll take him to your studio and give him some things to play with. Once occupied, he won't complain. Then you and I can sneak into the other room and do a little playing ourselves."

"Isn't he understanding what you're saying?"

"Give him credit for being too young for that."

"But Liz, look how he's listening to us—he's attentive beyond years."

"Ignore him, Lester. Trust me, with him."

They took me to Lester's studio, three flights up a decrepit but lovely pre-Victorian dwelling, with peeling flakes from the cream-colored staircase walls. Called a studio, it was Lester's residence as well. He was an artist—of the authentic variety.

In his muscular arms, I was put down on a prepared spot on the floor already bright with a crayon assortment and a large drawing pad.

But I was no prisoner. Winking humorously (it drew a trusting laugh from me, as calculated with expert precision), my charming host/rival drew something with swift professional skill to guide me by example in what was to be my earliest art lesson. I was avid to imitate his sure-fire technique, and so applied myself immediately.

Praising me and setting another example with a flurry of enchanting strokes in a variety of defiant colors, my mother's close friend had suddenly established himself as my private tutor. He won me off my feet, and I fell for him as my mother had. He was authoritative—he would always get his way. My mother and I were twin captives, joyfully, to this man bursting with the vigor and prime of life's fullest abundance.

His captivating orange hair was only a symbol. A glow kept leaping out of him, at all times.

My mother motioned impatiently. I was making a feast of his first attention to me. She beckoned him with that unmistakable gesture, universally traditional with the subtlest reference of emphasis, replete with implicit sex deftly explicit in the broad hint of insinuation that indicated invitation overtly overtured to a hair's turn and just the right shade between the overtone and the undertone denoting "Come on!"

Lester showed me where the bathroom was, and left out a glass of milk and packet of biscuits, to ward off complaint while he took my mother into an adjoining room and clicked the door behind them.

They were private. So was I. Oh, my poor father! Hard at work! I must tell him. My mother was *doubly* unfaithful—to him and me. I'd report, that very night.

Meanwhile, I enjoyed drawing. I used plenty of different colors from the wide crayon selection. Art was so much fun, and Lester seemed to be such a great man (in my mother's as well as my own identifying eyes) that I'd emulate him and be an artist myself. That way, I could retain my mother's affection, since she seemed to go for the artist "type," judging by all the time she took next door in Lester's private room in whatever they were together doing. She preferred Lester because my father wasn't an artist. This was apparent by the process of induced logic. I'd join Lester, in the upper realm of her love. He'll be my master and model. When he dies, I'll succeed him, as my mother's lover. By then, I'll even excel him as a painter. My father then will have *me* to be jealous of—or envious, as well. I'll take Lester's place as my father's cuckolder. It serves my father right, for not having been an artist. What a vulgar, common philistine! I'll learn all I can from Lester. He's my and my mother's idol. Art, obviously, is love's key; therefore life's secret.

How young I was to learn all that! And how determined I was, to learn it well. To dethrone Lester, as art's and my mother's master. On those twin goals, my future hardened, in a set mold. Firm motivation grew. I took precocious aim, on a world of adult art and love, in full fury flown to glory's high promise and the marvel of sure attainment.

I had interrupted my drawing, thus to muse. The door clicked open. Lester came kindly forward, bent down, and surveyed my progress, in the kneeling posture. (My mother stood over us, in a calm height.)

"Amazing, for a beginner. What pure talent!"

"Why not, being my son?"

"Tell him not to tell his father about this afternoon."

"He knows that. Don't you, dear?"

I nodded wisely, thus joining the conspiracy in a mystic collusion, an initiate to a secret, exalted cult that wisely tapped magic from a mysterious fund, solemnly conferring elective exclusiveness on my tutor Lester, my little embryonic self, and our enchanted mistress.

3

Until I was old enough to go to school, I was taken most weekday afternoons (mostly by underground on the Picadilly Line from South Kensington station to Russell Square) to Lester's studio, where I felt thoroughly familiar and at home. There, I served my apprenticeship to the craft of drawing and painting, while Lester and my mother would retire to their special room to play the special game I wondered about. (I assumed it was a game, since, by not bringing in any money, it couldn't be considered "work." Besides, they were so eager to go about it, that only a game could confer that delight, work being solemnized under the awesome appellation of "duty.")

My mother had tried to get me registered in a state nursery school—we were too poor to afford a private one—but failed because she wasn't employed. My father made what money there was. My mother was charged with tending to me. But Lester got a substantial cut of her tending. To make it up to me, he presided over my art education, with free lessons. It was a rare opportunity since, by great fortune, I happened to have true aptitude for art, by the accident of endowment, probably innate.

I got to love the studio. I shared my mother's love for Lester. Lester got to love me beside loving my mother, who, in turn, loved both of us males in our different capacities. The studio associated itself with love, and art. It was my temple, my school, my altar, the home of my spirit. My father seemed a minor matter at nights and weekends in our "real" home, down South Kensington way. He receded in importance or influence toward my true development. The shadow of the Museum in Bloomsbury, up in Lester's studio, pointed toward my future in the sun.

"Lester, I have something grave to report."

"That sounds fatal. What is it?"

"That child [pointing at me] will have a sibling."

"Mine? Or Tom's?"

"It's Tom's."

"How sure are you?"

"Too terribly sure."

"You've betrayed me."

"Stay with me."

"I will."

I was self-impressed that they said this in front of me. I was trusted, as one of them. We were three together, a band. Our enemy was my father and my impending sister or brother. True to his noble stature, his heroic cast, Lester stood loyally by my bowed mother, and the deeply-stirred me. Ours was the primary family, we three together. This was my life's strongest bond. Its support was my making. Only its severance would create my breaking. May it hold fast: to defy convention, my unsuspicious hard-working father, and the creature in my mother's belly that darkened Lester's and my access to our wonderful shared mistress.

4

Still during my mother's pregnancy, an important event to Lester's career was in the making: a gallery exhibition of his best paintings, a one-man show prestigiously presented by a foremost art dealer. Lester so

97

loved me, that a thrilling invitation was sent especially to me, to attend the opening party: a printed card with my name written on it. My father saw it proudly glowing on the mantelpiece. Seated nearby, my mother heard him say, "An artist friend of yours?"

"Yes, and fond of Mark, too. He's even given Mark some free drawing lessons. Mark's progress has done him proud."

"The gallery is on Cork Street—not far from my Hill Street office. I'll pop in after work and join you two there."

"Don't overdo the drinking, Tom."

"I'll need to unwind. The office pressure ..."

"I'll keep watch over you. And I'll introduce some nice friends there in the crowd."

"The friends of your secret weekday life while I'm hidden at work?"

"You'll like them. They're a whole different circle."

"I've wondered about them. They must have a nice effect on you. You're generally happy by the time I come home at night."

"I *do* like them."

"Is the artist being honored a special friend?"

"Yes. Mark and I adore him."

"Married?"

"No."

"Then watch out, Liz. Don't fall for him."

"He's not my type, unfortunately."

"How's the kid inside you?"

"Vigorous. But I'll manage."

"*We'll* manage, Liz. I have good news."

"Promotion?"

"With a salary increase. Timely, no?"

How cleverly my mother concealed our private life! She was more than my father's match, as Lester was. She was perfectly mated, though unofficially, to Lester, but went through the formal motions with my father like an accomplished actress. She knew the role so well, she toyed with it. How beautifully taken in was that good man, my father. And that *was* his role: ever earnestly trusting. His cooperation was needed; unsuspectingly, was given.

I was so excited. I was invited, as a special friend of the celebrant, to a glamorous party. More than a friend, I was uniquely his disciple. I was in the grown-up world!

The invitation said from six to eight. My mother and I were there a minute before six: the first guests, privately escorted by the artist himself, with whom we'd spent the afternoon at the very studio where he'd produced the works on display tonight.

My father would probably arrive near seven, for he usually worked late at his well-located Mayfair firm that finally seemed to be heading on the solvent track.

Attired quite sportily in the regal pomp of purple complemented by a loud shade of canary tan which wildly offset his orange hair blotch, Lester gaily introduced my mother and me to the gallery dealer and his two quite formally dressed assistants, who were equally divided between the two major genders in the symmetry of their representation.

More than important, I felt uniquely privileged. It was my impressive entry to society itself. I was already a transcended child—and not even of school age yet!

An air of sophisticated glitter, abetted no doubt by a full bar and two bartenders dispensing a wide choice of favorite beverages to the crowd that so thirsted for art and each other, decadently wove throughout the fluttering minutes that pulsated into the brain of the evening.

Conversation took place all over the gallery rooms in small fluid groupings rapidly interchanging with the sprightly air of promiscuous mobility, a gay pageantry of shifting tableaux woven with dexterous confusion to quite a boisterous scheme but refined to elegant pairings on civilization's highly cultured key gone brittle or brutal with uncouth delicacy along the enlightened lines of that exquisite phenomenon, Art.

The intoxication from that evening has never worn off. There I am, there I remain, forever.

Lester's paintings sparkled and sold out, one by one, to the eager investment-buyers, fashionable collectors, and shrewd speculators. My mother was drunk, merry, and possessive of the well-lionized Lester. With my father's late arrival, she modified her behavior on the right note of decorum, observing the proprieties as a faithful wife and second-time pregnant mother unfailingly should. The switch was remarkable. She became, on the spot, the true wife my father immediately recognized as his by legal right, family obligation, and old love that never wavered.

My father was soon swallowed up in the crowd, after admonishing me not to act too baby-ish. The hero of the occasion claimed me.

"Meet Mark, my little prodigy," Lester frequently repeated for introduction. But I was barely groin-high to all the people there, as the least imposing personage in the rowdy throng tempered by polite constraints on the prevailing drunken temper of the crowd that knew how to behave itself, in the cautious courtesy of its collectivity.

My mother let me sip some champagne. It was a mistake. I disgraced her by vomiting. But my little act went unobtrusive, in the press of contacts and connections pursued for preference, advantage, exploitation, and opportunity by many people on-the-make there. This hothouse bedlam became a marketplace, of sorts, among the sophisticates. The wheeling-dealing, sometimes cynically direct-to-the-point, raised hopes for improved fortunes and careers, for finer prospects, for a furtive deal here or there, a tenuous invitation, qualified promise, or open flirtation. Romance and business were put on the tempting scale, while enticement salivated from the leery corners of intrigue.

I was too young to know all this. But I sensed it, thanks to the wise retrospect afforded by the aged hand penning forth a scene so buried by time's brilliant transparency across the dim generational recess.

Arrangements were being made and broken, in the glare of suggestion or by tentative ploy or by the guile of decoy. I grew weary. The pace passed me by, in multitudes of footsteps and tongues. I reached for sleep, but fainted.

My mother's fun, thus, was cut short. She cursed my lack of stamina. But Lester argued that she must remain, not take me home.

In his trusty arms, I was carried, a-slumber, to a soft sofa in the gallery office, and gently deposited there. It was a loving solution. My mother embraced her hero, over my slumbering sofa. The din pierced the closed door, to penetrate this quiet sanctum.

Out there, mingling, was my father. In all his trusting innocence. Unsuspecting, happy over his raise and promotion in a reviving business, so timely to the advent of his second child being carried with unfaithful grace by the beauteous bride he was amazed to have married. Privately, he celebrated, in a wandering daze.

Where was she? Where was Mark? She was supposed to introduce him to her friends in the art circles. Drunkenly, or semi-so, he searched through the jostling swarm. In love with his wife. High on her, on improved prospects, and on concentrated alcohol.

"Tom, you're overdrinking. I warned you, remember?"

"You're hardly setting a contrary example yourself, Liz. Have you seen Mark?"

"We put him to sleep in that snug little office there—behind that door. This was all too much for him, but he's comfortable under someone's coat on soft sofa. Tom, I'm finally able to introduce you to the artist himself. Lester, this is my dear husband."

"Welcome. Your kid's quite an artist."

"I'm glad you've discovered him. Without you, maybe years would go by without anyone noticing. Your encouragement gives him a bright head start. You suggest that he dedicate himself to art as his life's work, and put aside all other types of business career considerations, and not try any other profession, but stick to this one right from the start and we sacrifice and stake everything on presuming his natural aptitude for enough genius and provide the training at whatever cost that will pay off with the guarantee of top-notch success like your own gala party triumph this evening, Lester? Is that what's in store for Mark? Answer me."

Lester looked shocked and angry. He looked like he was feeling, which was shocked and angry. If he *felt* that, then he *was* shocked and angry: directly socially communicated, via *looking* shocked and angry. Thus being comes from feeling, internally—or *is* feeling—and appearing is the way of letting others know it.

By appearing, a subjective phenomenon adds a potential objective dimension, for another or others who witness the subjectively feeling-being person and see, hear, perceive, what he seems to be, feel, think in his private inners.

The person being observed may be aware of being observed, and modify what he sends out accordingly. In that case, his "seeming" is an impure one, to the extent that he tries to control and redirect the now theatrical display he's creating for the sake of making an effect, playing to an audience.

Lester's shock and anger were spontaneous. How he seemed, then, was directly associated with what he was actually going through, irrespective of the people to whom he was seeming.

Lester wasn't the only one reacting to Tom, though his reaction sharply differed from the others'.

Tom's question had been roundly listened to by a sizable chunk of the partiers. Other voices had subsided, with Tom's first being the dominant voice and then the only one, like a speech before a formal and attentive audience. But he'd not been aware of becoming the dead focus of a hushed crowd's spontaneous collective consensus of following, in amused scandal, his every word soon after he'd begun addressing his elaborate question to the conspicuous popular hero of the evening.

Liz was too caught up, herself, in her husband's meeting with her lover, to notice at first the general reaction the former's address had produced between the gallery's walls in the well-entertained crowd thirsting for the kill of a juicy scandal of sorts in the form of a public fool uttering inappropriate words in an out-of-place tone of solemn oafish gauche philistine banality that was like shark bait for snobs scenting a natural victim in their midst. Too involved to partake in the detached hush, Liz, attractively pregnant, turned on her spouse with loud scorching reply that kept the eager crowd well entertained by advancing the impromptu drama another stage, a further open public bonus like a delectable bone thrown to the private gallery's wolf-like guests.

"Oh Tom, I wish you hadn't asked him that! You're too methodical. Let the boy *enjoy* drawing and painting. He has so many years yet just to love his craft and develop his skills in a pure way without your commercial scheming for him and your materialistic middle-class goals of art-for-business's sake. Be grateful for what Lester has done, for what Mark is discovered to be. Don't exploit natural resources for the careful calculation of gain so early in advance. Your attitude is so bourgeois! I apologize for him, Lester. He hasn't properly entered into the spirit of tonight's brilliant occasion. He's trying to con you into free expert advice and plan his son's future in petty terms of security and finance and harnessing the golden joy of art into the ability to make it pay off on the cold tabulation of an earning power. It's shameful of you, Tom. Release Lester. He's here to be celebrated; this is his night! Go back to the party, Lester. We're already making a scene enough; look at all the guests that have been listening to us! Talk to the important critics, reviewers, curators, buyers, art-world people, who are here to rave about you. Leave me to my husband's humiliation. Mocking sneers, derisive scornful smiles, cynical worldly contempt, come from this brutal mass of faces. All for you, Tom! How pompously paternal you are, for our sleeping darling in the next room! How you twist art to profit's dull ring! How you drag down the level here! Reckoning our son's future for the market price of what a lifetime's development in art can most likely bring, by your base standards!"

"You're only flaming the blaze higher with your fanning tongue. You're drunk, and the temper of the crowd is against us. They're rubbing in our shame. I see what I said now. But it can't be undone. Let's wake Mark and get us out of here. This scene has become too dangerous."

6

Though plenty of people in the crowd honoring Lester had known of his and Liz's long-term affair, and though Tom had mingled with them before he had made his bungling spectacle that quickly reduced him to disgrace and led to his, Liz's, and my flight, no knowledge of his wife's infidelity seeped into his curiously dense head on that score.

That was just as well. My mother and I kept up pretenses. My father was chastened, and continually tried to repent and atone for his thoughtless lapse.

My mother had to stop her weekday visits to her lover's studio accompanied by me for my art lessons, when her pregnancy reached the boiling point and she had to go into labor confinement for what issued out as the naked form of my baby sister. My days as an only child had now closed forever.

In addition, I now entered grade school. I'd become a schoolboy. And already, I was a thorough young artist in the embryonic precocity of immense promise.

My school was in Lexham Gardens, near the West Cromwell Road airport bus terminal. School activities kept me too late to continue my visits to Lester's Bloomsbury studio, even when my mother sufficiently recovered from childbirth to resume the visits herself. So now, instead of taking me, she took my new baby sister, an even younger disciple for Lester to make an artist of.

Lester was now a widely recognized, actually famous artist. Fame, power, and money added to his orange-haired attractive masculine toughness and powerful natural energy, made him an amorous object of a great variety of women in the art and society worlds. He'd become a culture hero of sorts, and was continually invited to meals and parties of every description, where he was beset and hounded by the sirens of temptation in all the cosmetic allure of their fashionably attired and subtly proffered flesh.

He did succumb, now and then, to situational irresistible enticement, the occasioned snares of seductive mutual impulse when framed by an inevitable aura of opportunity's perfect setting. But he never lost his heart, which had conjugated with my mother's on the firmest depth of committed fidelity maintained by a sweetly tuned accord and sustained on a perpetual note of rare devotion, borrowed from heaven to amaze cynical worldlings in its staying power so pressure-resistant that no vogueish flux could wash it over whatever from fickle waves and the dashing foam and artful trends that invited the heart to stray for cunning gains in the wicked power plays so fraught with romantic temptation from the higher regions that promoted reputation to the well-veneered sheen of total status enjewelled in the prominent belt of exclusive snobbish common property.

Theirs was a withstanding pure love. It would survive even doom, and stood as eternity's proof.

Saddled with two children, and no longer technically young, my mother outdid rich, influential women and young beauties everywhere in receiving the outpourings of Lester's steadfastness.

However, the hound of publicity is quick on fame's scent. Lester wore fame's scented suit, and was pursued by gossip documentarians that swooped journalistically to ply their public trade in periodicals of open print on the market of shared information of passing common interest. Thus the case, as hot news item cooled off for too long, was reheated on a four-alarm stove to so scorching a degree of bright orange crackling smoke, that no longer could this private matter be kept apart by stern right of secrecy even from the last man upon earth to find out: my ever trusting, suspicion-free, innocently practical, ideally married father. Established in the sacred institution of marriage that bore children-fruit, my long-deceived father's love for my mother had assumed the divine ordinance and traditional benediction of secure social custom. Their wedding foundation was proof against all irregularity, and would firmly ripen in absolute assurance like the righteous investment certainty of a legitimate federal bond backed by the mighty sanctity of a stable government hoisted secure on the combined industrial shoulders of business enterprise and commercial prosperity fixed and locked in place by an economy that has finally found itself.

What was stable is now shaky. The firm is fragmented. My father's shattered. His world crumbles. He loses grip. Illusions dearly essential to him become what they are: illusions.

He's too frail to withstand the shock. He goes to pieces. His firm of business regretfully discharges him, not even granting a decent medical leave with the promise of resumption should he get better. This inhumane treatment soured his confidence further.

With two children and a wife he never knew before, how can he adjust? He lacks the means. Nothing to hold him together. He dissolves. He's mentally certified, to an asylum. His recovery increasingly takes on remote unlikelihood. My mother and I dutifully visit him, then give up.

His grief hallucinates. He's lost his mind and soul. He's society's permanent reject now. He's apart. The world's affairs are not his. His business is too private to viably be conducted on any principle of communication or commerce. Socially, he's dead.

Death of the organism? No, death of the cell within the communal organism. Losing connections to the outside.

Not only am I no longer an only child, I'm no longer my own father's son. On my last visit to his poor state hospital for psychotic disorder and related afflictions of the soul on Hammersmith High Street, a red-brick building gone grimly brown with age, my former father stared past recognizing me in the ward he shared with a few sullen others of his own faded gender. Nor could I see myself on his blank face.

My grief was genuine. My mother cared mainly for her newborn and Lester. School, and Lester's work and social commitments kept me away from *him*. And now, that father I had stared quite past me, as though not only paternally blind, but humanly blind to me as well. Did I exist?

I kept my apprenticeship link to Lester for his future praise by turning out much art in school. School was also the source of new friends and companions, my class fellows of my age. So I was acquiring new identities. Spiritually orphaned, cut off from love's dear dependency, I worked hard at art, studies, and friendships, to grow healing tissues against the rot of despair.

7

To the man I never appreciated, choosing other models instead. With whom now it's too late to make amends.

Dear father. My memory flinches, recalling you. How contrite you were for that gallery party outburst to the celebrated artist of that occasion! How little you knew what part he truly played, in your carefully conventional own private life!

How late you found out! That twisted in the hurt the crueler. All of society preceded you. How lightly they cared! How they gaily consumed it, as their normal fare.

By then it was common knowledge that the raging hero loved forever, though pursued by women everywhere, a woman who happened to be my mother. It was generally assumed that my baby sister she was pregnant with and then gave birth to was, in the course of things and the way of the world and in the light of affairs, the artist's child. The fact that it was yours, father, would have been misleading to the currents of the social temper which beguiled itself with strict notions of the poetically apt, the sentiment of consistency. Popular fancy decreed, by the very spirit of the decadent tenets of democracy in the mass sway of things (heterogeneous orthodoxy by consent of the elective), that Lester was legitimately—in the standard reversal of values—my little sister's official illegitimate father. Should they be disabused of that just premise, the globe would be stood on its head, the earth turn flat, and nothing sacred thereon be left standing.

In your normal course of reading daily, weekly, monthly print, dear father, you encountered your demise as a man. Lester's very fame stabbed you with the dagger of truth.

His renown grew; your manhood flopped. It was the end of you.

Not ill-intentioned, not for vicious malice to cut you down, people in your regular business and social circles made harmless references, casually, in passing, or careless allusions, in your presence, in light innocuous chat, to that famous man of art whose name was daily associated with his known beloved, your own darling wife, mother of me your son and of the little daughter you also sired. The fatal words were let slip by normal people in your path, local ventings of our broadspread culture's prevailing fund of common knowledge. Our vast collective information estate is the domain and pool of all who draw and expel breath in these the times and property of our contemporaneous mentalities all, who share our slice of earth, the tongue and content that ring us round and band us to a community for whose edification such gossip is secreted that turns true and fatal for you.

Farewell, father. You never knew me, nor will.

8

A matter of economics. No more income from my father. Instead, my father was a drain on the National Health System, "living" at federal expense at the Hammersmith High Street gloomy asylum, where his lost mind made no progress toward being found.

The company he kept in his ward—his pathetic inmates—further discouraged communication altogether. The psychiatry interns couldn't prevail against the drabness of the meager mental remnants they were supposed to patch, renovate, graft new hope to. Instead, the resident doctors were dragged down to the uniform abject level of colorless apathy of those very patients they couldn't cure. Professional staff soon could hardly be distinguished from the pitiful subjects they'd been hired to treat.

In that atmosphere, my father languished. He contributed no more to the upkeep of his family. The Government awarded my mother a weekly maintenance check, in her helpless semi-widowed status, burdened with me, her schoolboy son, and my infant, still-sucking sister who fastened on my mother's alternate breasts as a primitive source of free milk to cut down on the dairy department branch of our overall grocery bill in a reduced household gone austere for want of a steady bread-earner to be the mainstay and support of a financially depleted family. We were the needy recipients of Socialist charity and were lucky to be so timely in the history of our government's liberal policy that now made poverty a positive advantage by the blessing of the economic system on those whose working power didn't exist enough to be a *contributing* factor to the overall country on the skids, but who, instead, were left to suck on the national dugs to consume the sorry dregs of a once flourishing monetary balance that's now been drained to a dry gulch by the immense force of unemployables whose mouths open wide above the stomach's anxious clamor for assistance.

Ah, Money! Over you, men have worried and fought. Over Woman, too, have they worried and fought. Then, Money, are you Woman? No? Sorry, I mistook you then.

That's what comes from fooling around with abstractions. Anyway, back to the particular.

On a beautiful afternoon in May, after school some classmate friends and I adjourned to the cricket field and had a memorable match surrounded by green trees, white clouds, blue sky, and the lovely lyricism of our play.

They were true comrades, on that field. I had art, I had them. I still had my mother somewhat, shared with my kid sister and the Lester I regretted to be never seeing at all any more. He was always so busy! (Though not for my mother. For her, love gave him time. His bond with her was more consuming and immediate and actively daily; he put me aside, momentarily, to resume later on.) Meanwhile, to prove my worth, I was building up a portfolio of better and better drawings and paintings to show that I was his true heir and apprentice. The opportunity would come. He hadn't disowned or abandoned me. My pulse still vibrated from his influence. I lived in his image. I was taking form, my outside art and my inside me, upon the sturdy example of himself.

Perspiring from my cricket exertions, having exchanged loud fond shouts of joyful departure with my chums of the match, hoisting my schoolbook satchel on my proud batting shoulder, I trudged my way homeward to South Kensington, my physical weariness buoyed up by an ecstatic premonition that didn't dare examine itself too closely.

In smothered expectation, a blissful shock readied itself for me. All I had to do was keep alive, and it was mine.

Superstitiously, I gaily fussed not to think about it too much. I didn't want to spoil the event from happening by lavishing eager premature mentality over it. But how could I empty out a mind so full? The premonition utterly consumed me. I blurred its edges to the indistinct vision of a trance, to ward the danger off in too precise an envisioning, which could prevent the desired miracle from taking its concrete place on the dream-dispelling, all-fulfilling, quite uncompromising world's stage of experience actually occurring in a way unmistakably real.

As I neared the goal of my familiar kitchen, I'd supposed by this hour my mother should have returned from Lester's Bloomsbury studio and would have my dinner nearly prepared, with my baby sister whimpering in her crib, or wooed cherub-like on a mild cloud of sleep by the harp-strum of innocence.

These expected figures were there. But a rousing addition was seated in our modest flat. Dressed in paint-soiled loose casuals, curbing his boundless energy to a light, disciplined mirth, vibrating his orange hair, robust with a blazing smile, Lester stood up upon sighting me and scared me with feigned fierceness and a pose of playful wrath. I jumped back, startled. Jolted off my shoulder, my schoolbook satchel slipped and fell. I screamed, involuntarily.

I resisted, but Lester grabbed me in a swooping snatch, hug-lifted me so that my head topped his, and quite crunched me till I whoozed breathless, subdued in a dizzy faint of surrender. I was quite annihilated to my mock-captor, in earnest.

My supreme moment had occurred.

In my favorite dreams, I would have chosen such a greeting. Now that it had happened, my faith rapidly converted to a reconciliation of ideals with reality. If life could find the relish of such occasions, however increasing their rarity in the mundane trot toward death, shouldn't skepticism occasionally leave life to its own devices on a chance happy abundance of dreams unaccountably creating themselves into not merely the images, but the whole substance, of truth tangibly brought fiery palpable manifest revealed into the light of what I've just felt, or thought I felt, in a dream-punctured bubble on the breathing course of the air? My dream turned real. Till it turned so, it hadn't been a dream yet.

9

Serious business was afoot: a major change, affecting us all, in our aspects with one another.

"Tell him," my mother directed.

Lester seated me sober, composed my exuberance, kept his hand on my shoulder to leave our contact intact, and announced, "We'll all be together now, Mark. I've bought a little house off Westbourne Grove, on the Artesian Road. I've dropped the lease on my Bloomsbury studio, and tomorrow I move to the new house with a hired moving van—not just I, but all of us. It's *our* house, not mine."

My breath jerked out in a hush. He went on.

"One room will be my painting studio, another a bedroom for me and your mother, an adjoining one your little sister's room, and you'll have an upstairs room all to yourself, big enough to make your own painting studio out of, as well as a place for study and sleeping. I'm so well-off now, I can share my prosperity with your family. We'll be artists together, in the same house. I can give you advanced lessons and you can experiment with mature technique. I assume your approval on this?"

Unbelievably, he couldn't, however automatic, however inevitable, it all so logically seemed.

Conscience, on my father's behalf, made me perverse. I raised objections to a scheme that would mean happiness for Lester, my mother, and me. I turned quarrelsome. I would destroy our happiness! How can that be?!

I found myself resisting. Was *I* doing it?

"But what if my father gets better and he's released from the asylum? He's technically still my father and still my mama's official husband. We can't bar him. He's got to have a place to live and be rehabilitated from besides finding work somewhere. Won't that complicate things not just legally but morally?"

"Don't you think I've considered all that? Does being a great artist mean compromising my intellect?"

"Let's not get cute. What would happen to my father?"

"He'll come to the new Artesian Road house and live with us."

"That's a generous arrangement, Lester. But my father would be jealous of you. He'd want to take your place beside my mother in bed. He has a wedded right to do so."

"Why worry *now*? According to your mother, he seemed so far from recovery on her recent visit to the asylum, that he couldn't even tell who she was. And on *your* visit, the same non-recognition happened. It seems unlikely he'll be well for a terribly long time."

"But you and Moma, protecting your love for each other, might actively intervene to sabotage any progress my father might make; you'd wish him to remain where he is, in his co-operatively dulled-off state, conveniently oblivious to your takeover with my mother. Unconsciously, you two would do what you could to retard that poor man's slim chances for any cure; you'd keep him crazy, to be out of your way and leave your love to flourish in peace. Wouldn't you?"

"But his chances are too remote for your ethical scruples. We have a right to be happy."

My retort was ready at lip, but for my mother's interjection: "Mark! What are you accusing us of? We're not bad people!"

"Leave him to me, Liz. His doubts and misgivings show what a noble, loyal son he is. I approve of his objections. He has courage and self-sacrifice. He's a good boy."

"Then are we bad, Lester? Whose side, after all, are you on?"

"Liz, it's not a matter of taking sides. Let's discuss the whole broad moral spectrum, not with partisanship, not with selfish interests at heart, but to see where the general good can be done, weighing all our special cases to the particular scale, to render the right and just decision."

"How pompously magisterial of you! Is this to degenerate from a simple fait accompli act of moving tomorrow, to a parliamentary debate with issues, protocol, weights and measures, pros and cons, and the flaming heraldry of rhetoric?"

"Don't mock your son! He has earnest objections, which we must dignify by giving him a hearing. He's too bright to be belittled, and what he raises has serious implications for us all. Not rhetoric, but responsibility, attends the consequences of this joint decision. It could stand examination."

"But the arrangements are all made. We're moving tomorrow."

"I'm moving tomorrow. Mark wonders if you should too!"

"Let him wonder. We're moving!"

"Do consult him on this."

"He's my little schoolboy. He obeys. I'm not going to fall in debate with him!"

"I'm on your side, dear. But our move must be agreeable to him. We should be unanimous with no qualm of regret. We should act in concert, as a united body, a true family, without dissidence of remorse to rankle any one heart. I want Mark's free consent, openly declared; not his injured obedience to a mother's power decree and rule by force."

"Then you convince him. Here's another hot item: dinner is ready."

We took our places at the table. The discussion was too serious to do justice to the pleasure of eating. We didn't savor our bites, being mindful of solemn issues at stake. This wasted a perfectly good meal. How untimely, that we couldn't have solved it before eating—a problem that I had raised, and would fully defend.

"I'll play my father's advocate. He's too insane to be his own spokesman. Who's responsible for his insanity? You two!"

My mother flinched. Lester launched a counter-assault.

"Kid, you and your family are damn poor. You're subsisting off the welfare system in threadbare socialism, as wards of the state's charity. Your father brings nothing in. Far from contributing support, he drains the state in a catatonic stupor. Maybe your mother and I brought him to this sorry pass, as you shrewdly accuse, but we couldn't help loving each other. Love is no crime—not even out of wedlock!"

I nodded and munched. My mother felt relieved and justified. My baby sister slept peacefully in her crib nearby. We were resembling a family. Lester proceeded.

"Not every cuckolded victim of a mate's infidelity would have gone under, as your father did. It was our bad luck (or maybe selfishly *good* luck), but was it our *fault* that your father's neurotic instability or inflexible inability to adjust, his rigid failure to adapt, should so collapse and crumble his unfortified defenses as to reduce him to expose so extreme a personality fragility, so violent a personal frailty, so feebly unresilient a pathological defenselessness to unforeseen disasters outside that violate the narrow focus of his vulnerably systematic happiness conditions? No. Your mother and I are in love. We withheld it from your father, but everyone else knew it before him; it was dense of him to find out so late. And once he did, couldn't he have taken it like a man? It's a commonplace, in our current society. It's a prevalent symptom of our times of enormous flux, rapid change, relaxed standards, liberated choices, individual freedom. *Other* husbands, in such a predicament, with their carefully constructed domestic worlds harshly caving in, have to *accept* it—fair and simple. It's their tough luck. It's in the chance of the game."

I was impressed. Lester had won me over. I'd learned a lesson outside art from him. I ate silently.

My mother beamed. She looked lovingly on her savior. Her moral rightness was restored.

Her infant daughter moved slightly, but went on sleeping.

Rather than leaving things be, in my state of surrender or at least of relenting, Lester would press his advantage further. He'd won, but wanted to pile up the score, and to dazzle by triumph rather than stop at mere persuasion.

"Spiritually, I'm your mother's true husband. By the same spiritual token, I'm your true father, teacher, guide. Life really resides *beyond* technicalities."

I acceded. His point was driven in. Now, he'd polish off his victory, with neat conclusion.

I stopped eating, admiring his technique. How he could get his way; carry the day, with gentle grace, dash, panache, humor, manly assertion, courteous fairmindedness, good sportsmanship, and great vigor!

My hero! My mother's hero! My baby sister's future hero, once she gains the requisite awareness at time's organic leisure.

To contradict this mood, I passed pitying contemplation over my father, in his doomed ward in the grim Hammersmith High Street building. *Here*, we thrive. *There*, alone … I wept.

"Don't cry. It's all for the best. I have money and power, and good will too. I take responsibility and assume all obligations for your father's wife, his two children, and him himself.

"Where he is now, he gets bureaucratic, inadequate treatment, in an atmosphere that already defeats itself. At my expense—*inspired by your protest, Mark!*—I'm going to have your father removed from this state dungeon of a mental home that hammers nails into his final mental coffin, and put him into the best, most advanced—at whatever cost—psychiatric private hospital possible. The best therapist will attend him—one who specializes in your father's peculiar species of affliction. He'll be cured!"

"What then?" That question didn't come from me—my mother uttered it. Once she did, it became mine by vital extended right and by my different concern than my mother's. She wanted nothing to interfere with herself and Lester; my father mustn't come molesting and meddling, newly armed with restored wits and legal family rights.

My mother wanted the status quo to develop and be protected; nothing must come between her and Lester. But to me, my father *himself* mattered, whatever nuisance it might carve into the great new scheme of solidarity already underway in the lives of the four people in this kitchen/dining room in South Kensington, a room I'm about to bid farewell to, with joy and desertion.

The rent was once paid by my father, now by the state. Here, my father had a thousand meals, in domestic customariness. Even on those occasions when his wife/cook had just recently come back from a fine sexual feast to assume the ordinary routine of her role with a spouse who would have been surprised to be regarded in the light of begrudging redundancy dutifully concealed.

I'm deserting this flat—but not my father. I've done well, by him.

I haven't betrayed my father; I've increased his chances of recovery. I've defended his cause, in his helpless absence, in his dim captivity. Great care and expense will now go toward his recovery. His recovery now is an actual possibility, thanks to me. It freshly raises my mother's question anew: "What then?"—a question now shared with wrinkled care and moral concern by my new-father-in-the-spiritual-sense and by my own grave, precocious self.

The meal is over. My taste buds had been at work, mechanically, like little animals. But I hadn't noticed. The major discussion of my life had taken the occasion away.

Tomorrow is moving day. Life's to enter a "new phase." Temporarily, in my father's absence.

PART TWO

1

By the calendar, three years passed. We were living three years—and a day—in the new house. New for *us*; it was a fine example of Regency architecture remodeled for gracious living with modern conveniences, progressive features, the latest gadgets, a streamlined interior decorated lavishly on the lines of Lester's precise specifications and exquisite design taste as a practicing artist in his own magnificent right.

But *outside*—the decor offered to the street—the building was its stately old self, intact. Nothing seemed altered but the paint. And even the paint seemed authentic. The right touch, to preserve the period-piece precious antiquity of the pure original—which it was itself, but on the outside.

The whole building was ours. Three floors. Unaccustomed luxury, for me. But by now, accustomed. It had become, through sheer living, "home." However opulent compared with my old South Kensington situation of barely genteel poverty, the Artesian Road mansion, by being daily lived in, nightly slept in, was good old "home." Home is where the heart is. Bodily, we all gave heart to this good new home.

My sister Mary was nearly four now. Toward her, I was the protective older brother, thus relinquishing my own "baby" status.

Lester seemed *my* older brother; my mother seemed like an older sister. I was doing well, at grades in school, at friendships with classmates, at cricket and soccer (I had too light a body for rugby as yet, being a delicately formed child), and above all, at art. I was committed to art as my true vocation, my perfect calling in total dedication. It was my one choice for a career.

Thus, a future artist and a present successful one toiled away in that fruitful house. The house wasn't just ornament; work was getting done in there.

Lester is the presiding genius, the master of the household, the kindling spirit, the generous proprietor, our loving host.

His orange hair has faded to dull orange. But his fiery nature reigns with unabated energy. His presence exudes such force, the house is charged with industry, joy, happiness, success. A great "growing-up" atmosphere for me and little Mary. It's the blessing of fortune. We're unaccountably blessed.

His is our bounty, and his wealth increases. So well, so prestigiously, is his art gobbled up by private collections and ranking museums here and abroad, that soon the Tate Gallery is honoring this man who's not even gray yet with a giant "retrospective" exhibit, commemorated the evening before the opening with a gala party for distinguished members and high-powered art world guests as well as notables from all callings of society, including members of Parliament, cabinet ministers, aristocracy, entertainment figures from show business and theater, and other limelight-kissed celebrities who bask in current glamor's glow on the fickle stage doomed to continual flux in fashion's changing trends that remove the recent and install the latest in "fortune and men's eyes." All is passing, and some are passing fair, floating before us, gliding from wing to wing while the curtain is raised.

Soon, but not yet, at the Tate Gallery. Excitement hurls its dart, in advance. But back to the Artesian Road house, off Westbourne Grove, in Bayswater, surrounded by Kilburn, Notting Hill Gate, and other neighboring areas in the Western part of this famous city immortalized by Dickens among others, as Dublin was by its defector, Joyce.

My mother is the reigning queen here. She's nature's own noble beauty. Lester adores her no less for all his rising fame. He's renowned as the coveted eligible bachelor of society who's steadfastly loyal, passionately devoted with unswayed purity, to a married woman, my mother, in a modern living arrangement.

Which I had initially objected to! But gave in, persuaded by my mother's persistent lover in vivid rhetoric akin to his art.

He won me over. But I won, too!

That crucial arrangement, devised three years ago, which I eventually consented to after a memorable debate with Lester over the dinner table in South Kensington on the eve of the move so momentous to all our lives, has worked out wonderfully. It's proven to be the right move. Our all living together has literally turned out to be precisely the "move" that got us all moving so well in the right direction. The center of earth is here, on the Artesian Road. It's our center of gravity, our nest of well-being, our hall of luxury, and progress.

I'm growing up in a charmed circle of magic that takes root in the genius of Lester both in life and in art; he weaves them both, to a delicious brew.

My own genius, needing careful nurture, finds it cleanly *here*. In flourishing rapport, Lester and I are mutual boosters. Respecting my natural development, he doesn't force his own mold or style on me, that's won him such rewards. With wise tips, generous encouragement, but judicious detachment, he lets me explore my own uniqueness as a fellow equal. Justly celebrated for his own brilliant trademark, he imposes no method on me, but lets me have my own set of adventures toward my critical self-discovery as my own artist bearing tools. He stands aside. He looks on. Hands off, benevolently.

He doesn't need to take advantage of being my idol by bending me to his own image, junior-variety. I'm forging ahead and finding myself. His value is in providing the means, the atmosphere, the inspiration—the example I needn't follow in the particular as "in-the-school-of," being no one's disciple, but by general precept and good working principle.

The household hums with work. Upstairs is my own workroom, my sacred private temple where I serve youthful apprenticeship to maturity's ripe calling which I learn acutely to heed: that far-off music that vibrates in my growing bones in the quiet haste, the calm alertness, of time's distant tune that gradually comes clear, in my speeding head, my nimble fingers, my trained and scrupulous eyes, the sense of discipline earned by dint of industrious application to the right point of pressure, the educated choice, the bold emphasis.

Below me, in the master studio, Lester's at work. He goes from phase to phase, in a continual development.

My mother cooks for us all. She tends to little Mary. Love is this house's dominant element. Love lightens hard work. The house is lifted off the Artesian Road, to meet heaven that comes rushing down to endorse it, support it, protect it, a benediction bestowed but rarely on hidden mortals in ageless history.

2

This house swarms with love and work, swims in them, permeated to the gills by their twin glories.

To their dominant notes, however, a discordant, harsh, jangling note tosses its disruptive, jarring tone of dissonance, upsetting the sweet instrumental sounds entwined by chords of orchestral harmonics, all melodiously beating away in concert, to the rhythm of sphere vibrations assonantly celestial by strict upper ordinance in the echoing chambers of faraway paradise, where music mystically originates in bleating murmurs and high choral bliss.

The music descends to the Artesian Road house, by transmission divinely kept lyrically continuous.

The dissonant note, newly arrived there from another place, is an irritant, but is assimilated by the prevalent note of harmony that gently throbs in the household to the agreeable pulse of love and work.

We put up with this new note, and try to drown it out to the tune of our well-woven sympathetic chords. Our unity will prevail against its insurrective, bitter, disruptive nature in our midst. We're organized in league to withstand it.

That note is my father. He's cured, he's come to live with us, parasitically off Lester. He idly thrusts himself in our earthly paradise, which he intends to soil, quite deliberately, in the gross semblance of a leech that doesn't stop at marring the host bodies whose internal substance it methodically sets about to consume; compelled to ravage in the keen clean glee of vengeance; all coiled up in the grim grip of dire dear retribution edged to a high polish to do the fierce bidding of malice tightly wrought, clenched solid.

I feared evil's deliverance from its responsibility; evil exulting in transcendent license, irresponsible liberation from the very morality it seeks so righteously to rectify, so vindictively to balance, so exactingly to redeem, so crusadingly to defend.

I feared this strange father of mine: wrongdoing's savagely yelping victim, becoming wrongdoing's "unwitting" exponent and arch, all-permitted advocate.

Justified in abusing those who abused him in a brutal moral ascendancy at his opportune disposal now, my father would, I dreaded, readily dispense with those qualms, scruples, compunctions, constraints, delicate niceties, that he'd quite clung to when wronged. He'd abandon those civilizing considerations, cast them gleefully aside, now that he'd be the perpetrator of wrong himself. The tables are his to turn, at will. The injured party turning his injury into the right to injure, a right he revels in, with much abuse.

Morality is a superfluous luxury, by his current advantage. Evil had been dealt him. The tide changes; he's handed the role's long-awaited reversal: being evil's *giver*, on the *active* end, past passively receiving. This is a fresh change to be exulted in. This invitation is irresistible. He accepts.

Pronounced sane, certified as cured, by the foremost psychiatrists granted the liberty to practice at an expensive rate; nurturing suavely barbaric weapons; fortified in the rectitude of an iron-clad, unassailable armor of rationale; wearing, besides, the aggrieved air of one to whom irreparably unforgivable wrong has been irrevocably done despite being pronounced cured and certified sane by specialists at an exorbitant fee Lester gladly paid; professionally assuming the role of one grievously injured, permanently harmed, damaged devastatingly—in short, destroyed—my father thus excuses himself from seeking employment. By his own testimony, he's disabled from ever holding down a job again. Professionally, he's a cripple, an amputee, for all business purposes. The reparation exacted, Lester must support such a disqualified refugee from the gainful field of his pursuit, him who's debarred from any honest means or measure in the rough-and-tumble task of making a living.

Equipped with these arguments, my father ominously descends on the old Artesian Road house with the new interior, somewhere between Queensway and the Portobello Road, near the shop-lined, bus-routed, well-worn thoroughfare for pedestrian and traffic alike, Westbourne Grove, Bayswater's handsome link with that exotic district, Notting Hill Gate.

How he arrives: with a vengeance! Certified cured, pronounced as sane as a daisy!

But in so helpless a state! Quite pathetically dependent.

Those who damaged him, he's at the mercy of. He's owed charity, and begs for it, at the hands of those who brought him low, to whom he owes requital, in any sort of kind that falls to hand. By this propitiation, he bides sure chance, polishing his closed-up reply by passive furtive stage held back to cunning's awful prime, to be released in the tide's full glory, to the ripe heat of time. Dankly prepared. Darkly gloating, well in audacious advance of the right deed to cancel out such perpetually flowing wrong.

He comes panting for faith, in trust. We take him in. The door closes on him; he's within. The house has his presence, warms his spreading ooze that will hatch toward what virulent contagion, the laid eggs of vipers, or a moist mound of vermin-seed foully fertilized?

"Our" father is among us, in our self-enclosed, holy house. Will it purify him, or will he defile it? There his grains are sowed, kernels planted, bulbs to take root. To pollute us soon? To quell the music? To kill the art? To freeze love out? And the kiss of a numbing languor to dull the tumult of our work and blast the fruit of it to withered knots that sicken with decay what so lives in that rousing house that loves us to trade love for love and grow greater abundance?

3

I'm worried sick. What's the weird bird up to? Were it not for me, he might still be rotting away in the bureaucratically inept, backward stagnation of that grim old asylum that's a blotch (one of many) on Hammersmith High Street, along the route to Heathrow Airport and destinations therefrom.

Cured and certified sane by professional pronouncement, he's supposed to be well now. But is he?

His wife, daughter, and wife's lover are elsewhere in the big house, behind closed doors, out of the way. On their behalf, late one night, and on mine, I confront this queer old bird, to bluntly "have it out" with him, to still my quaking mind alarmed with apprehension due to this odd bird whose sperm had spilled me forth into this odd old world in the queer shape of life in the weird growth of this human setup. I'll quiz him and get to the nonsense bottom of his weird queer odd somehow inexplicable form of so-called behavior, which is so boldly shameless in his cringing reliance on his constantly cuckolding host as though crazily to demean himself by means of which to gain control, to derive power, from the sponging insolence of his subordination so excessively meek, so suspiciously humble, so sickly hangdog, so threatening and terrifying behind the self-mocking transparency that shows the loud demand clamoring through the quiet protest of futility and weakness.

He's stubborn about something. We're sitting around a table. The only other living thing nearby is a cat—some plants too—and insects somewhere, not so noticeable. I'll get my father to confess. He's an odd bird. He's weird, that one.

"Daddy, you're shameless."

"Of course. My wife is sleeping with my host in the house he's letting me camp in. There's shame, dishonor, in that."

"She loves him, and prefers him to you."

"There's shame in *that*, too, while I still love her. Which I do."

"Lester saved you, at vast expense, getting you cured. You were crazy, but poor. Had it not been for Lester, you would *still* be crazy—and poor."

"Despite him, I'm still poor."

"Then find work. You're cured enough for that."

"I *am* working. But not for pay."

"Then what for?"

"To install myself here and make a nuisance. And to break up this happy household. To restore me to my family. But first to be the avenger. To pay Lester back, and my wife."

"In what coin?"

"That's what I'm working at. I don't know yet."

"Will you be cruel?"

"Of course. Revenge might be sweet to the do-er, but not to those done."

"Spare Lester. I love him. Please."

"No, son. Love me, instead."

"But he's won my gratitude. He's helped me enormously, at the heart of what interests me in life. He's famous. The Tate Gallery will honor him soon. I love him."

"So does my wife. She'll be punished, too."

"You don't understand me. *He* does."

"I'm jealous. That adds to my hate. I'll ruin him."

"I'll warn him of your intention."

"I'll disclaim it."

"It's *me* he believes. We have beautiful harmony. He knows me."

"He *owes* me. He'll have to put me up, here—no matter what you tell him. He ruined me."

"But Moma loved him, of her own will. She went to *him*—he didn't only take *her*."

"*She* owes me, too. I'll stay."

He won that little bout. Late next night: We sat around the same table again, he and I, alone. I was baby-sitting for Mary, asleep in the next room. My mother and Lester were out to a dinner party. Here's that odd bird, my father. Dazed, fanatical, stubborn, mild, peaceful, meek. I must protect Lester, and my mother. Against their sworn enemy. Whose enmity I hope, by discourse and reason's light, in their defense, to halt, disarm, dissuade.

But how can I win an argument? This man still gives a crazy impression. If his hate continues, may I disarm it from violence. May I plead peace, and call out for restraint. Let his revenge be mental, not carried out.

"It's no crime for Lester to love and be loved by your wife. It is human passion, that's all."

"What about *mine*—for *her*?"

"Give it up. It's no use now."

"It's not a faucet I can turn off. It keeps on."

"Divert it, reroute it, along another channel, to another woman."

"There is no other woman. There's just my wife."

"Go out more. Mingle in society. Mix about. Attend parties. Meet people, including women. Keep open."

"I can't 'keep' open. I've *stopped* being open. I've closed down. My love goes on for her, my only woman. It'll choke to poison. For her and him, and me too. That's its only transformation: the 'for' of love, to hate's 'against'."

"You live in the past."

"But my past isn't passed, yet. It's quite current, I assure you."

"Be kind to them. It's selfish to persist. And it gains nothing."

"It will gain their defeat—in *some* way."

"But that's bad."

"Not for *me*."

How could I argue with him? Then the pair of his hate returned from their dinner party. He greeted them with conventional phrase. They returned the courtesy. All very polite.

I tried again the following night. The pair of his hate were in bed together. We sat around the same table as before.

How would I attack, this time? To what avail could words be? He was determined. He swept me lightly aside.

"Please, Daddy. Listen to reason."

"I have no reason to. Shut up."

I did. I must avert calamity. I warned Lester and my mother, in private. "Daddy wants to destroy you. Even *he* doesn't know how, yet."

The endangered pair worried. But my father, on the surface, behaved with obsequious, fawning deference, in an invariable manner that seemed to disguise no threat. After a few days, the endangered pair dismissed my warning, paid no further heed. They attributed it to my fevered love for them, my protectiveness that stood vigilant guard sniffing suspiciously at a father I had mixed feelings for.

"Don't disregard it. It's a real danger!"

"We can't expel him," Lester explained. "He's here, for better or worse. He'll get used to us, we to him. He'll accept the situation. We're making him comfortable. He'll warm to us. He'll change to gratitude."

"But he loves Moma!"

"To no avail. He knows it's in vain. They never talk anything hut polite phrases to each other now. Just conventional courtesy, never letting communication ruffle the smooth superficiality of their meaningless words. *I'm* like that with him too. Only *you're* different with him, Mark. He's trying to scare you. He couldn't be in earnest. He's too mild."

"How long will all this continue?"

"It's up to him, not to us. Liz and I feel quite safe."

"We do, Mark," said my mother. "Have you heard the bad news?"

"What?"

"The staff employees of the Tate Gallery have gone on strike. For the duration of that strike, Lester's retrospective exhibit and the gala party on the eve of the opening—the special night's preview—will have to be put off."

"When will the strike end?"

"Union negotiations and arbitration are going on now. Art will have to wait. No, not art, but publicity of it. Our hero's career summit. The highest tribute to his fame." My mother beamed on Lester. He beamed back. They were arm in arm. I warmed myself in the circle of their glow.

My father passed. He caught this cozy tableau, but kept an immobile face, and without breaking stride, but uttering a vacuous courteous trite phrase of an almost impersonal greeting conveying automatic respect and mechanically high regards, walked past with innocuous serenity, leaving the room as empty of himself as it had been before—and tidier, as though in passage he'd whisked the floor of any dust.

We stared at the nothing there was to stare at. Lester broke the silence.

"I for one am not worried. How about you, Liz?" He spoke with no bluster. He was calm.

His appeal to his loved one was rhetorical. Her reply confirmed, word for word, what he seemed to expect. Since living together, their minds seemed double instruments of one understanding, in three years' closer growth. What one anticipated, the other delivered, as though they lived a natural music to the twin pulse of thought and act. How could my father ignore that? In blindness, or in wrath, my father didn't accept the obvious. Or else, madness was in further evidence. A refined madness, post-psychiatric.

Lester had proclaimed himself unworried, and handed their shared opinion to my mother to pronounce on.

She agreed knowledgeably: "I know my own husband, which he still is in the nominal sense. He's much altered. His spirit's broke. But he won't lash out. You're wrong, Mark. I respect your judgment. But he's harmless. We needn't worry."

I still challenged her, with some vehemence. Again, her assurance: "Mark, please ignore him. He loves me yet, that's true. He's furiously jealous of you, Lester. But he shows no sign of making trouble. He may brood, fantasize. But his action is safe. Knowing him—though he's changed—I know that. Be easy."

"I can't. He told me himself he means trouble."

"He's still demented. He'll recover here. This is a good household."

"But his 'bad' will pollute it."

"It hasn't yet, and won't—the 'bad' is all internal. He keeps it well checked, with extreme caution, under compulsive lock and key. Besides that, our house is protected by magic. God rests security here."

With that, she and Lester exchanged smiles. They left an open space for my smile to join. But I stood unconvinced. My worry grew graver. They were so trusting! As my father had once been, till he found out.

Will *their* trusting also meet a shock? If so, to what disaster?

They refuse to worry. Then I'll increase mine. The worry they don't do, I'll do for them. Not quite the moral burden that Christ took on, in his wholesale redeeming. Still, a cross to bear. Our household's guardian.

That's my self-imposed function. Lacking allies, it's my own self-created emergency. I'll answer my own alarm. I'll *prevent* damage, rather than attempting to repair what's too late to repair. I'll avert. Before the fuse blows off.

I'll eliminate worry by working on its source: my father. I must change him. It's our only chance.

If I can't alert my dear endangered pair, I'll put them out of danger. I'll attend to it—as a doctor. A doctor of the soul. To ward off evil, by plucking it out, root and all, from the diseased one.

My method? Let him talk his evil out. It takes time. I'll take it.

I keep seeking my father out, most nights, after school and painting and my friends and sports and all, to encourage him to talk, in the hope that he'll talk out his hate and revenge like a patient undergoing psychoanalysis who comes to realize what he's up to and comes to his senses about it and is able to make a rational choice instead of being internally beset by dreadful unconscious demons, repressed convoluted phantoms suffocating in fixated fantasies that contemplate violent hate. My therapeutic sessions will show him face to face all his stuck obsessions, while he takes the treatment of talking it all out and reaching some reasonable sweet solution of a peaceful purging and a change-of-heart catharsis that lets him examine the matter in a new light. He'll talk himself sane, at last. His love for my mother might linger, and jealous resentment at Lester. But he'll come to terms with those unactable-on feelings. That will open him up, to face jobs and new people again, in the outside world where he can start life over, on a new footing; find useful work that suits his capacity and restores his long-lost self-respect; and even remarry. This is my role: therapist.

Here's one session's account, blow by blow. I wearily recount it. I reel, from sessions like that. Grueling reiterations, fencings that cover the same ground endlessly. I make myself as maniacal as he, so that we wear similar uniforms, pressed together in combat, matching witless wits without strictly defined rules in an interminable arena that loses sight of what was said and hopelessly keeps circling about trampling on progress treadmill-like. We're caught in coils mechanical. Words succeed words, in unremembered succession.

"Daddy, don't you have any shame?"

"Sure, a highly developed sense of it. Excruciating at times. Or I *did* have. But I discarded it. It's excess baggage, in the current setup."

"Lester had you cured at vast expense."

"You're talking about money. Yes, it cost a lot of money. He put me through the finest specialists, who charged an awful lot. But money isn't the only way Lester's paying. It's costing him, it'll go on costing him, to control my wife and family on his own terms. If that's what he wants, I'm charging high. The price is constant blackmail. I admit that. But I can get away charging him that; the market will bear it."

"Daddy, please ..."

"He's sleeping with my wife in the master bedroom. I think that's what they're doing at this precise moment. I heard a noise in there when I passed—an unmistakable acoustic impression from my own broad experience that was so lovingly confined to just that same woman."

"All that psychiatry cured you to be rehabilitated as a self-respecting man to make a comeback in your previous line of business; not with the same heartless firm that let you go without a medical leave while you were cracking up, but with a new company that could value you for your industry and experience. You were proving yourself in that field.

It's work you're suited for. Why deprive yourself of it?"

"It helps to punish Lester and my wife. My idleness is a protest. I want to sit around here all day and all night, as a reminder, a visible reproach. They've assimilated my presence as though I were an old grandmother they've willingly taken on in goodhearted compassion, in the decent gratitude of memory. But that's not what they feel to me. They put up with me by reluctant moral obligation and guilt, because I've foisted myself on them as an obnoxious reminder. I'm in their way always as a self-advertising martyr to the ruthlessness of their selfish love for each other at the expense of ruining my happiness, crushing my self-respect. I want to accusingly display what they've done to me, at all times. I can't act crazy, since so much cost went to cure me of that. But within the bounds of sanity I can poke at their conscience incessantly in little ways by playing the injured role—morally, grievously, permanently injured—and playing it to the hilt, relentlessly; damaging them by being damaged. I want to make a display of my ruined sense of worth. I can't make them cringe with remorse—after all, I'm being supported by Lester in high style, as are the wife and two children he's confiscated to his care and keep; but I can keep snipping at them, with little daily and nightly irritants that gnaw at their peace."

"It's failing. They've become hardened, inured, immune, indifferent, to your devious ways. Daddy, please regain some dignity and self-respect."

"My relinquishing them is my subtlest weapon, to work on their conscience."

"It's not working. Can't you see that they ignore you?"

"They make a show of it, but they can't ignore me in their guilty hearts. They'll dwell on me; I'll be their obsession."

"No, they're quite oblivious. I assure you. Give up, Daddy."

"You are on my side, Mark?"

"I'm on *everyone's* side. I see all points of view."

"Some son you are!"

"I'm his too. Yours I am technically; his, in the fuller sense."

"You're my only allegiance, my only bond of confidence. I can't talk with *them*."

"And you're not affecting them, either. Get a job, Daddy. Get a decent job up to your capacity. Move out of this house as its resident parasite, find a flat somewhere to rent, be self-sufficient, be self-supporting, self-respecting, accept my mother's demand for a divorce, make a fair settlement, find yourself a new woman, get romantically involved, marry her, start a whole new family."

"Did I sire a son to hear all that advice?"

"*You're* the child now, Daddy. You've made yourself that, to torment us all, as a way of protest, bitterness, accusation. You're acting pathetic and helpless deliberately, like a child. You're being willful, petulant, spoiled, dependent, demanding. How can I treat you like a man? You've waived that right, you've abdicated the role itself. It's true, Moma did deprive you of your husband role, stripped you of that conjugal right. But you can still be a father to me and Mary, and a man to stand up to Lester by refusing to leech off him, leaving his house and board like a man, and become independent, self-supporting. Then you'll deserve to be treated like my father. I'd respect you, and not give you degrading advice, as I've just done. My advice is to *take* my degrading advice. That will change everything around; it'll turn everything over. I'll have a new tone to you. I'll have no right, and no grounds, for offering degrading advice. For that to happen, *take* the degrading advice I've just given. Clear out. Let them alone. Don't haunt them. Go! Go!"

"Sonny, I stay right here. But thanks anyway for your good intentions. You're a good boy. You have a higher ranking in this household than I do. How fallen is your Daddy! I *like* this fallen state. It fits me fine. I'm degraded pleasurably. It's my chosen way of life. I retain the moral advantage, from being the low man here. I show the others up. I must continue it. I can't let go."

"But it's not working! They don't care!"

"Well, I'll win new humiliation, new disgrace, and blame them. Let them keep paying. This is the goal that upholds my life. To keep them paying. To turn out costly. To turn out *too* costly. Their ultimate price will be—their love itself. Is it too high a price to ask that they'll have to separate? Is love their highest sacrifice? That's the very fee I'll force. I come expensive, you see."

There was no answering that. I left him high, on his own words.

I treated him almost nightly. Lester and my mother knew this.

They indulged the both of us. It was "harmless." They went happily on, together.

＊ ＊ ＊ ＊ ＊

When my father donated the sperm toward—quite unintentionally—the making of the very me who later tried to purge this maker of malice for the partner who assisted in my making and the one she chose to supersede that maker in her displaced affections, did he then, or did I then, expect that some years later the me he helped make with his sperm would be trying almost nightly in an unlikely place to purge this maker of malice for the partner who assisted in my making and the one she chose to supersede that maker in her displaced affections? In all likelihood, even by a wide margin of impossible miracle, no.

Yet, it happened. Not now, but years ago. I record this memory with disbelief. Yet memory speaks. So loudly that words must be written to silence it. These words speak in memory's place. For their veracity, their amazement stands. "I'm my father's analyst. To save two lives. To keep peace. On the Artesian Road. In a modern house with a preserved old exterior." That was me. With my father. There we were, and that's *how* we were. *That* we so were, is inconceivable. Yet so we were. It was happening. Those evenings with him seemed normal, simply by occurring. Occurring makes an actuality of the unlikely. And actualities must *force* credulity. Reality makes strangeness common and wipes mystery away. Such reality took the strange mystery's place, in the world of experience that happens to people—such people as I was then, and my father then. I was ministering to him. My own maker!

It came to be. It was. It did exist. I was there. That was me, then.

PART THREE

1

I borrowed a tape recorder from a classmate and recorded a session with my father similar to, even longer than, the sample quoted dialogue above, leaving it unabridged in its oral verbatim of mechanical fidelity to the actual original caught in exact transcription.

On appointment with Lester and my mother, whom the recorded session quite directly alluded to and concerned, I played it back for them. Their skepticism soon changed its tune when faced with this evidence of what my father, on his own confession, in his very own tone of words quite recently uttered (ignorant of being preserved on tape but the more candid, wild, furious, free and unchecked, unmonitored, uncensored upon that necessary ignorance) to me in the strict confidence of therapy I violated in deceit to unlull the endangered loving pair from their supposition of trust and refusal to suspect threat and smell a rat, putting aside all my warnings and misgivings till I thought of this device of irrefutable evidence, a tape recorder that doesn't lie. They listen to it in horror. But I hadn't taken the precaution of making dead sure my father was out of the way from the time and place of this playback. Passing outside the room, he heard his own voice behind the closed door, then mine answering, then his, so he stood with straining ear against the door and didn't need to see to know that, within, Lester and my mother were the audience and that I had betrayed him, as his own confidings were used to warn his intended victims, whom he immediately decided to add me to, as being Marked for punishment along with the ones I had sought to protect.

"Thanks, Mark. We believe you now," admitted my mother after hearing her husband's and son's recorded conversation in a distinct fit of chills and shocks.

"I heard scuffling behind that door," Lester whispered, rising, dashing over, and flinging the door open, catching my father trying to back away inconspicuously in the corridor as one guilty in a bare-eared act, a flagrant culprit detecting himself in the act of being detected at the spot of the scene of his hearing what wasn't meant for his ears, though what he'd heard hadn't been meant for other ears either, privately having been made by himself for my consumption in the confidence of the informal therapy I'd devised and administered.

My mother and I stood behind Lester in the corridor outside the now open door to the room of the overheard recording. My father stood with his back to the opposite hall wall, stunned and caught, trapped. He confronted us openly, nakedly, unguarded. He'd dropped his guise of meek courteous civility, the impersonal obsequious deference or bland politeness, the ritual mask of resentment undeclared, defiant accusation seething in the brooding ferment of vindictive fury, all held amiably in check, now quite pouring lividly forth from his pretense-stripped face baring the barbaric fangs, evil taking bold courage in its own wicked gleam quite frankly displayed, sincere and frightening.

My mother suppressed a tiny scream, the outmoded female stereotype response of weakness under stress.

I gasped, as a young schoolboy does in the primitive presence of demons previously only imagined.

Full blast, the evil trained itself upon our strongest: Lester.

The well-known artist, still orange-topped but not to his youth's primary intensity of blinding dominant hue, braced himself, held his ground, found words equal to the occasion, hurled in sly strength, in blunt point of provoking mockery and a showdown of challenge.

"You were listening to yourself plotting by vague means but underlying sure malice to undo—with all your power in the trial of patience—the love between Liz and me and not only our love but us two as people too. Since only by destroying us as people can you come between us to separate us both from the love that shares duration with our bodies physically themselves, those fragile sticky membrane linings that barely keep mortality in or out in flimsy hours of blood remaining and numbered pumpings of our breath."

"Lester! So passionate?"

"Divorce her, you fraud!"

"How much do I get?"

"Don't even *try* to bribe! You have no further claim—legal or moral. I owe you no debt of guilt. Get out of my house! I don't care where you go! Get out, be a tramp, a vagrant bum, sink or swim, or fall on your feet again, but out! It's no concern of mine. This is my house."

"This is my wife." (Pointing at her with contemptuous possessiveness as to something owned more to the detriment than to the benefit of the owner who's learned to regret his possession and yet, despite all, still clings to that perverse thing owned.)

Lester lashes back, in the fighting ferocity of his might, to drive home the heart's lyrical point on the ground of an uncompromising nature, in plain, unalterable fact.

"Your wife in name only. A title that's long been hollowed empty of any significance it once had. Your claim to her is hopelessly dated, a nominal vestige of the past. Fair and square, I took her without coercion. Nature ripened us together. She 'grew' mine, like time falling due. In peace, it came about. The slow course of violent inevitability. An organic flow. A new spasm to the pulse. Like life, it 'took place,' in its simple mystery. A change you can only accept. Your disease prevented you till now. Being cured, belatedly accept this event."

"Not now, or ever." My father was unmoved. Lester's power to persuade, his magnetic charm over people's hearts with energy overflowing at the will to sway even the obstinate, met its total exception: my father.

Lester appealed to plain sense, to worldly odds at practical utility, posing a threat bearing ultimatum not lightly disregarded with impunity. With all reasonable patience, Lester dealt in simple terms that led to obvious conclusions which my father would be truly mad or foolishly idiotic to treat contrarily.

"Liz isn't yours, whether you give her up or not. She's not chattel. She dispenses her own destiny. Your consent is irrelevant, your protest carries no weight whatever. In free will, she left you to go to me. If you want to contest for the children, go to court. You've already been a trial; now bring it all to law trial. Psychiatric evidence will be telling against you, from the Hammersmith High Street asylum records to the documents of case history preserved at the private luxury homes of treatment I paid for so willingly. I suggest you leave and stop bothering us. Immediately is the best time. It's already whizzing by, so catch up with it."

"Trying to get rid of me, Lester? Do I detect a hint?"

"I'll oust you bodily. You've no right to be here except by my express permission which is now withdrawn. Pack your bags."

"You passionate lad! We have my wife in common, don't we? She donated her earlier prime to me, her recent years to you; with some crucial overlap (or underlap) when she had already begun with you yet conceived our child Mary from me. A tiding-over phase, I suppose."

"Yes, Tom, you're fertile, I'm barren. But you overstay your leave. Get packing."

"By her own choice, you've won my Liz off me. You're her clear preference. You've taken her over. Aboveboard. By her consent."

"Go, Tom. Must I wait? Or throw you out? Please take the step."

"And you're more Mark's father than I am! You're making quite an artist out of him."

"He's doing it himself. He's earned his own credit. These insinuations weary me. No more banter. Gather your effects together in your room, in that suitcase I gave you for a gift when you showed excellent improvement under the special intensive therapy I hired for you. Then leave. Simply go."

"Just like that? Devoid of ceremony, of further ado? Lester, you lack breeding, manners, tact. Does art give you the right to be unsociable? Does art attract oafs by its special permit for temperamental crudeness? Will this license tempt my Mark, as well?"

"Tom, speaking plainly, please go."

"Lester, no."

"Have I run short of words? Is another tactic necessary?'"

"Most likely."

"Go. We *all* ask you. Your children and wife too." (Mary had just joined them, to complete this cozy scene of an entire family, plus one.) "On behalf of all of us—but from myself mostly—go. Need I say more?"

"I'm unwilling, Lester. You'll have to use physical violence. Though you're slightly shorter than I as a technicality of height comparison put pedantically to the measure, you're much more powerful, with sheer robust energy ceaselessly generated by your bursting vitality whose radiance compels others—such as Liz and Mark, and Mary too now—to do your bidding, dance and shuffle to each tinkle of your everlasting tune. Not me, though. I serve notice of resistance. Of the passive kind. Go on, initiate."

They were eye to eye. Mary, Moma, and I backed up to give them room, as in a cowboy drama, to "have it out."

They stood there, neither yielding by stance or gaze of eye. For all his anger, Lester was loath to use force—only its threat. But threat alone wasn't going to work. My father invited more, in a brave show of test. Lester was up against it. He was vacant, at a loss.

They stood ground. Locked in stalemate, the impasse brought about by Lester's backing down from a fight he would have won with the masterful ease of his success in art and love. It would have been no contest. My father won; Lester backed down.

An adjournment was declared, a truce for the evening. We all went to bed, in our usual respective rooms.

2

For a few days, my father made himself scarce; kept out of the way, while managing to remain indoors all the time in rooms and floors not strictly barred to him, in that well-used, functional home where he stood out, even in invisibility, for the decisive and haunting quality of not belonging, having no business there, gracelessly redundant, an imposition uneasily under sufferance by all concerned.

School took up my time, preparing for end-of-term examinations. My latest phase of painting—a breakthrough toward mature technique unbelievably in advance of my chronological age—also engaged me, as did classmate friendships and my continuing cricket progress, with soccer put aside till the cricket season has its full spring innings out. Then the summer holiday break; and when the fall term begins, the soccer pitch once again will get pitmarks from darting runs and abrupt, twisting dent-diggings on the contested turf for that elusive ball.

Spring was warming to the full. My sister Mary was attending pre-kindergarten infant nursery school. Early indications indicated that she wouldn't be following my example in following Lester's example of becoming an example-setting artist. That's perfectly fine. Two serious artists are enough, in this household of four. Swollen temporarily by a fifth to fever-puff surplus of glandular inflammation; but the pus mound (not found plus) will be lanced out; and the unhealthily soaring temperature will, disencumbered of that infected sore-point, come merrily tumbling down to normal, freed of the invading disease tribe that momentarily puts an embarrassing impairment on our trim-set bustling procedure which will resume when our organic housewholeness slims sleekly down to its functional four, its structural flourishing brisk economically managing self, operating in full gear when purged of foul bloat.

Meanwhile the pestilence, lying low, putrefies us from hidden corners, keeping out of the way but secreting poisonous emanations.

Whiffs of the slimy malodorousness flagellate our stiff nostrils. But we keep busy, in the vile interim.

3

The Tate Gallery staff employees settled their working grievances with management and arbitration, so that a definite new date was set for the grand evening preview bash in distinguished celebration of Lester's retrospective exhibition, an extraordinary achievement for an artist still in the prime of his own lifetime, overcoming the handicap of not being dead enough—or at all—for posthumous honor to be heaped on him by fame's glorious crush on, predilection for, favoritism toward, the grandly, all-reaping dead.

Meanwhile, Lester lives. Thank God.

Ascending the Tate Gallery entrance steps, to the near-the-door top, one is rewarded with a view back down to a chunk of the running Thames, that long-sung wide river that splits the large city into the much-more-important north top and the much-less-important south bottom. Despite that topographical imperfection, the city politically is strongly based on a longstanding, upstanding stand of high-minded rock-bottom spaced-out political democratic equality protected by canons of the law and embedded in a soundly firm, nobly established, aristocratically upheld, loftily-mindedly liberal respect for the individual, whoever that is.

Lester's paintings were carried up those steps, into the grandeur of that temple of art. His career has already ascended ambition's topmost steps. And proudly, I might call him "father"!

So can my sister Mary—in fancy. How he overtops our mere technical "blood" father! He's our elected father, in the high freedom of our choices.

For our mother, too, he excels her husband as a far greater "husband." By her soul's sacred affinity, and by unofficial conjugation in the bed.

What a pre-public opening is the party coming up! By engraved, embossed privilege of invitation only, so exclusive that it excludes all but members of the press (television, periodicals, and other vehicles of publicity-tinted information), aristocracy, the art world elite, critics, reviewers, celebrities—in short, the culturally eminent, society's select, the creamy elegance atop civilization's layer cake, so delicious at the upper crust, so so-so at the lower crumbs that decline rapidly from mediocrity's substantial slice of the middle class pie that tapers down into the dry dung of dregs.

To honor Lester! In actual fact, to honor Lester's art. The artist of which, though, is the man Lester.

Is he apart from his own art? Not while alive, yet. Actively still turning out more creations. Works of art.

By a working artist. Who can tell the artist from his art?

Who's the most logical living representative of one's art, but the artist himself? All homage, then, to Lester—his works' maker, fleshed out in living form as the artist of his own art works. Who else has a greater right to call himself the artist of them? None but Lester, in his own self.

His biggest day since birth is about to be! (Actually, his biggest *night*, in point of fact.)

His birth, of course, was vital to his life. But who noticed it? Very few.

But the big night coming up—ah, what a public view! *So* public—so *very* public—that it's an exclusive evening. By invitation only. The public is left out—but interested in this event. It intends to attend the show, on general admission.

Whereas, at Lester's birth, not only didn't the public attend (the spectacle was sorely limited to his own parents and some doctors and nurses whose so-called interest was of the merely professional kind), but the public showed no interest whatever. An ill-promoted event. Universally neglected, overlooked, slighted by sincere indifference born of ignorance: a nation-wide popular prevalent unanimous ignorance, save for those concerned within the narrow circle of the scene.

Now Lester is making up for it. He's widened the circle. Fame comes pouring in.

4

The big night is even closer than before! That's due to time, of course.

Lester had to interrupt painting to help in the preparations. My mother helped him to help, sometimes even by staying out of the way. She knew when to do what and when not to do what not, as regards Lester whose private life sometimes had to give way to its public aspects and applications and at the same time not compromise his strict essential privacy as a practicing artist and a dedicated family man whose "children" weren't his by blood but whose woman was his by everything.

My father lurked in the shadows. No renewed confrontation, as yet. We're all so busy, one way or another, except my father with his self-enforced idleness as his living strategy now.

My father struck Sunday morning, the day before the big gala scheduled event for special preview guests the eve before Tuesday's opening to the public at large of the month-long show of works on loan from private collections or owned by other galleries or museums. Fame's prime, full, official flowering is already coming on ahead. My father's interception is also schemed—but in dank diseased privacy of envy foully gloating its revenge.

Which will reach Lester first? On Sunday morning—Christianity's specially allotted time put aside for church worship by ritually old reverence lately a lot less observed—here comes my father, slipping quietly out of hiding. His glaring presence can't help but be noticed. He's the "other." We're closer together, due to the intruder.

May's sunshine gains entry via the windows. Four at the breakfast table, in domestic symmetry disturbed by an odd fifth figure emerging in open stealth.

He addresses us all, but specifically Lester—his only non-relative of our chummy batch.

"I appeal to you, Lester."

"For what, Tom?"

Thus began what promised to be quite a conversation, building up for a long time, now spilling out into the bright splash of indoor Sunday daylight.

"Are you announcing your departure, Tom? It's high past time."

"That's not my theme."

"No? It's ours, however," Lester emphasized, with a sweeping arc in wide gesture to include my mother, Mary, and me—or, on the other hand, implicate us, to my condemning father.

"That tape recorder—playing my own voice back to me—it seemed to incriminate me."

"Only 'seemed'? It decidedly *did*."

"Your conclusion's too easy, Lester. I beg your skepticism. The evidence was tainted."

"It lied?"

"*I* did, for a hoax."

"On whom?"

"My artist-son, Mark. To scare the boy. As, of course, a practical joke."

"Why pick on *him*, to play a dirty trick? If, indeed, trick it was, or hoax or joke, which I doubt. We caught you in deadly earnest. Or *he* did—Mark."

"No—*I* caught *him*. I'll explain how, and why."

"Elaborate, but don't take too long. It's a busy day ahead. Getting rid of you will ease our task somewhat. Proceed."

"A little mischief—to scare Mark. In all innocence, that's all I did."

"How sadistic! Why?"

"He's so high-strung, nervously inclined, ready to spring alarm on the fright and fabrication of any invented pretext, of slight or no base in people or events themselves, that he was my ideal invited target for the trifling hoax of pretending I meant the harm he had a sure dread of and so I played along with it in seeming earnest of evil intent by confession in psychiatric interview, for he thought he concealed the tape recorder but I detected it and him setting it on to trap me making the threats you then heard but all in idle play. I swear. Spare me."

"No. Why should we? The jig's up. If you don't leave, we'll have you arrested—on the tape's evidence."

My father couldn't undamn himself. Lester was convinced of my dear Daddy's concocting an off-the-spot lie to weasel his way out of the tape recorder's heap of damning evidence—all linked in vocal array—exposing a hateful heart disposed to actful harm in dire dreadful admission, of even boastful bravado letting malice in green glittering gleam quite nakedly squirm forward darkly to prelude its own high projected deed cast so unmistakably in frank cunning and the bold insolence of its guile.

Dear daddy stubbornly refused to leave. Lester dismissed the "hoax" theory as itself being an alibi hoax of huge monstrous pretense. The theory, and what it tried to hide or evade responsibility for, required sharp punitive action. Delay would quite dilute the deed. Time falters on, toward noon.

"You meant every word," Lester concluded. "I'm phoning the psychiatric division of the detective department of the central police force to have you put away. You're the menace Mark said you were. Just as prevention in the health and medical fields is considered as important as cure treatment, so it is also in current criminology emphasis. Two criminal investigative psychological specialists will handle your case and have you put out of our harm's way and society's at large. We have your own confession on tape, enough to lock you up. You'll be officially certified as a dangerous lunatic and go into a State detention center. I won't assist by private means, but let you rot there in the rust and rubbish of a hopeless penal system full of grisly methodology laid on by psychiatric banal enlightenment."

That should do it. Bravo, Lester! Finally, after long delay's lasting ache of misplaced mercy.

My father to be locked away. How free we'll all be!

Lester went to the phone to dial and bring justice in. His enemy made a last interruption, to avert finality by pronouncing it as unfinal.

Defiant, my father promised, "I'll do as they say on good behavior. In time I'll be released. Directly, I'll kill you three, in violent separate crimes. So much the worse for you. Death! Imagine that! I'll play up to the authorities. I'll show them how eager I am to reform, to rehabilitate, to be self-supporting with a job and land on my feet. Society will owe me another chance to prove myself and make good. I'll use the chance to do completely away with not only my wife's lover the artist, not only my wife herself, not only my artist son, but even my innocent little daughter. Let that hang over your future. Let that weigh on your peace and nibble at the collective stronghold of your happiness. Being doomed will devastate you before your natural term is up. I'll outspeed nature's slow decay of you and, in the bargain, inflict your horror on nature herself. *She*'ll recover, though. But not you, in your cozy quartet. You'll spend four deaths for what you've cost me. Once paid, your debt is cancelled out. Then, we'll forget it."

Could anything be more explicit than that? My father as a murderer! To undo two he'd brought to life, a third who'd assisted his bringing the first two to life, and a fourth for taking away the third from him.

That would be quite a feat, if pulled off.

Four of us! Three others, and me myself. A feast minor enough at Death's gigantic open banquet gluttony. Minor, maybe, but dreadfully personal.

5

Were we *really* doomed!? No, God, don't let it. Tie up my father legally. Let his *threat* die out—and not its several targets, who all face happy lives in full remaining futures. Protect us. Let's not spoil tomorrow night's big party with Worry and Fear. Let violence cut them short, to eliminate my dear father along with years of worry, four people's overhanging dread.

Legally, how to kill my father? Or if not, then illegally but with no punishment.

I'm a criminal? Yes, but circumstantially. To win some peaceful ease, freedom from care, for four threatened people. Was ever "crime" more justified? Thus, my reasoning. In wild tremble.

Lester's strategic phone call to the right authorities was crowned with the fruit of result. Our Artesian Road house (bulging with drama and tumult within, vibrating with murderous plots afoot and anti-murder counter-measures such as my brooding murder-preventing murder of my own dear father whose spent sperm gave me my biological start on our huge chemical planet now cluttered and choked in the coils of its own technology) was the scene of entrance from the outside by two investigative officials from the insanity division of the Bureau of Criminal Psychology of the department of the justice of the police to protect society from various destructive misfit activities such as, in my father's case, murder of wife, wife's lover, and own two legitimate children. Such violence just isn't right. The very idea is itself a violation of people's rights: the right to keep on living by surviving a reprehensible intent, on my father's part, of murder—foul murder, depriving its victims not only of the right to live—an inalienable right—but also, and more fundamentally, of life itself, without which there are no rights whatever.

And where there are no rights, then wrongs may breed. Right? If not, how wronged we are!

"Welcome!" Lester greeted the two officials who were making a purely duty call. This warm reception inclined them favorably to their genial but troubled host.

My mother had cooked a big, big lunch. We all repaired to the kitchen to gobble it yummy up. The same kitchen where Lester, my mother, Mary, my father, and I had sat around for an interesting breakfast discussion brightened by Sunday light streaming in—beautiful pure May sunshine filtered transparently through our immaculate window panes.

Panes? They were *pleasures*, to let such sun in. Such a lot would we *lose*, oh, without our good old *win*-dow. Without? Yes, for what it admits within, from without.

The light of day's Sunday in May was brightening the whole city, not just that dining room/kitchen setup of that specific house on the Artesian Road where the drama takes place.

The two officials join us to partake in a good lunch, a big, wholesome Sunday lunch. How much more wonderfully better it is to be eating like this—consuming *life*-giving substance—than to *be* consumed by that revolting non-phenomenon, death, especially death caused by foul murder such as what my father contemplates to do in his heart's account-book that registers a measure of revenge to dole out payment for evil received on the balanced ledger page of two columns, ruled, objectively tabulating sums of delicate justice.

May sunshine on holy Sunday poured over the entire famed city of cultural renown in western civilization, a city prominent in the annals of history—especially of the history of the country within which the city takes its prominent place and vast historical renown.

That's the overall setting. To focus more microscopically on a slice or cross-section or slim segment, we return to the room where munching is done by two officials, my father, my mother, me, Mary, and that celebrated artist, Lester, hero of tomorrow night's gala party occasion that's already been receiving much advance publicity and a favorable press build-up.

Lester presided. Courteously addressing the two officials, who were his specially summoned guests under urgent direction to place my multiple-murder-inclined father under arrest for consignment to confinement in jail or in locked padded cell for "emotional disturbance," our courtly host lifted his wine glass to toast the health of those two aforestated officials who were grateful for a huge, wonderful meal while on a duty call in professional service under bureaucratic wage-hours that paid them in good salary despite austere State socialism and a depressed economy.

"Gentlemen," Lester requested, "please arrest Tom."

"Gladly. But why?" equivocated the two indecisive officials.

"Because *here*'s why," said Lester, producing his trump card with a smack of triumphant finality: that telltale tape recorder adjusted to a loud range of volume to unleash my father's voice overheard in confidential treatment consultation with me in a therapist role that encouraged my parent-patient to speak his evil thoughts out in full oracular spectacular absolute revelation of murder by foremost premeditation.

The two officials listened, with increasing interest, gradually widening their eyes open to hyphoid bulges capped by lifted brows on faces vivid in rapt attentiveness and acute auditory concentration.

Oh, how they listened! It was, of course, their business to. Quite in keeping with of course their professional status of police criminal hostility and insanity investigation to protect, of course, that oblivious creature, the public.

Finally, the tape record was over. Well?

The officials cleared their throats. All the others wondered what the official reaction would be, with intensified interest and straining of waiting ears quiveringly on the alert.

The two critical officials, in solemn issuance of pronouncement in their well-trained judgment-making capacity, rendered this decisive verdict: "That evidence damns and condemns the accused. It's sufficient to indict him. Evidently, he would have been quite a criminal had we let him be, in the loose anarchy of his liberty. He ought to be deprived of his freedom, for the sake and safety of others. This, of course, is to state what patently sounds obvious. Moreover, what actually is obvious, in no uncertain terms, and to such extreme degree and truly dire extent, that we promptly, now, with no further ado or beating round about the bush, place this would-be assassin—proven by the tape recorder—under official house arrest, while we finish this delicious lunch, prior to escorting our man, in handcuffed captivity as a primary suspect for four not-yet-committed murders, to the police station to be booked and given a cell behind bars to await trial by stern due process of solemn justice to protect the innocent public."

All except my father, bowed in guilt, applauded that verdict. We drank a toast to our cordial guests, these two officials who were truly discharging their offices and mission for which, summarily, Lester had summoned them in a telephone emergency of importance so utmost as to rank in priority almost with wars themselves on an international scale of flare-ups that rise to the boiling point of quite excruciating crisis.

"I protest!" feebly retorted my father. The two officials greedily went on eating, heedless of that pathetic protest weakly uttered by the suspect they were in charge of now, under their guard, not handcuffed yet at the eating table but soon to be when they escorted him to the police station.

Nimbly, however, my father bolted. He rose and ran, ran out of the house, escaped into the early Sunday afternoon of lovely May sunshine along the Artesian Road either to the Westbourne Grove end conveniently nearby, or to any side street bisecting the other end. He'd flown the coop, in a burst of flight: first to flee, then to be free. Damn it! Just when they had him!

"Well, there goes our man," mumbled the two officials with full mouths between bites. It would have been an insult to my mother's cooking marvels to rise, leave the table, give chase to a man they'd wisely convicted of planning the high crime of homicide on a four-unit scale to murder's awful tune.

Politely, the two officials remained to render exact justice to my mother's awfully good cooking. "Well, he got away, I guess," they said, between healthy bites and chunky chews and wolfing gulps on the ravishing food with famish they fell upon with devouring jaws.

"Delicious?" asked my mother, beaming with vanity in the sun-gleaming room of slowly dawdling May afternoon in what was formerly the central city commanding an overpowering empire to the extensive scope of far-flung oceans over the vast terrestrial globe.

* * * * *

Lester scolded the two officials for negligence. "How dare you let him get away! A culprit like that on the loose—why, he's a public menace!"

To which my loving mother added, or amended, or appended, "A menace to *us*, dear. He doesn't care about the rest of the public, but focuses his kind attentions on Mark, Mary, you, and me. Beyond us, his concerns totally diminish to the point of no homicide whatever."

"That's true, Liz," assented Lester to his dear devoted.

"That's true, Mommy," little Mary joined in.

"That's true, Moma," added I, partly completing our homely little chorus, which became fully completed by the two officials, still gulping down gigantic portions from their endless bowls, who echoed, "That's true, madam. That's true."

How united we all were! One big happy family, temporarily increased by the two officials, who refilled their plates with almost comical rapidity.

* * * * *

Mary, Lester, my mother, and I had all finished our meals. The same couldn't be said, however, about the two officials, who were dressed in inconspicuous business suits of unassuming, modest, self-deprecating gray, now spotted and flecked with drops and drippings from the drooling stoking of food in opening and closing mouths like coal being shoveled into a furnace before technology found more efficient methods, instruments, and material for converting fuel into household warmth.

The two officials, already stout to begin with, were, by leaps and prodigious bounds, ceaselessly adding to their ever-widening bulky girths in rotundity's expanding dimension on all fronts in bulging volume.

"Are you enjoying your food?" my mother needlessly—yet nevertheless sweetly, quite endearingly—asked the two feasting officials. Their assent, between mouthfuls, was grunted out in full joint unanimity by a simultaneous stroke of consensus. This affirmative response was proclaimed with great mutuality, between the two of them, as though they shared a voice in common to dissolve all differences whatever, a synchronization with perfect beat to the timing (to take a musical example in metaphoric emphasis).

"Help yourself to more!" cheerfully encouraged my mother, delighted that her home cooking met with such frank approval.

The food was being dispatched with enormous gusto by those hulking two brutes all dressed in nice suits of grey now streaked with dribbles of sauce and juice and all matter of droppings from the whizzing coursefuls of swiftly emptied plates and bowls graciously replenished by the generous hostess, who shouted gaily over the slurping, "Help yourself! There's more, if you'd like."

"May we?" the two officials eagerly but academically in mere rhetorical nourish asked, quite complying to the literal letter, with the gallant zest of tireless appetite, with my mother's kind command that displayed a flawless hospitality.

"Of course!" my mother found fit to answer. "We're not poor, you know."

* * * * *

"Go on eating," suggested Lester agreeably to the two officials who were serving in the unofficial capacity of guest. "But I have a clue."

"A clue? What to?" with bulging mouths responded the two officials who had fallen to their food with a vengeance that tickled my mother's proud esteem and did fabulous wonders for her entire confidence in her own culminating acquisition of skills eminently culinary.

"To where the fled Tom, that escaped convict, will most likely show up tomorrow night, I can guarantee."

"Really?! Where?" asked the two guests in their official capacity as enforcers of the law in apprehending criminals potential or otherwise who are fugitive from the law's lengthy arm of detective search. They managed those words despite the internal congestion of food compressed in mouths so overcrowded that there was room for no air to mingle with the chewed-upon food packed in there so solidly.

Later, a burp trickled out. From one, or both officials? Both probably. Followed, in rapid succession, by a resonantly resounding belch of brutal degree and high impelling ferocity with a pedigree pistol effect of terrific explosive expulsion of food-driven breath in the reverse act of swallowing to the loud impact of "bang!" What a blast!

"The Tate Gallery is where he'll be, so guard all entrances with your entire police staff at the party tomorrow night. Oh, I apologize—there's only one entrance, for all ticket-holders bearing as tickets the embossed, engraved cards of fancily inscribed invitation specially printed for the swank occasion."

"Does he *have* an invitation?" the two officials pressed, in hungry intervals between chewing.

"Definitely!" asserted Lester. "I saw him take one from a stack this morning and put it firmly in a pocket of the very trousers he wore when he escaped from your close guard. Officers, I just *know* he'll turn up for the Tate Gallery tomorrow night party in my distinguished honor."

"In *your* honor? Why? What did *you* do?"

"Do? Why, I painted all the paintings for the retrospective exhibit of my works that will be on preview display tomorrow night, to the tinkle of a gala party occasion crowded with more exclusive celebrities than most probably you've ever seen before in any one set of rooms, I vouchsafe. Is that correct?"

"It must be, if it's true."

"True? Sure, it's true. As true as true."

"And all for you?"

"Sure."

"Then *you* must be a celebrity, yourself."

"Obviously, dear officials. Obviously."

For the first time in hours, the officials momentarily interrupted their eating to whisk out autograph books from secret detective vest pockets for Lester to write his autograph in, which he obligingly did in a fair hand, putting a high flair of flourish in his majestically public script, showing an eager acquiescence to the eminence thrust on him by brilliant genius and fortunate circumstances.

The two officials were awed, thanking Lester profusely. They turned to their bowls and plates once more, only to discover that the consecutive-eating spell had been broken—they were too stuffed even to continue to the overlapping stage (the meal's final phase) of an inspired dessert my mother had prepared. "Don't be offended," they let out, "but we're full now. That's our signal (an internal one) to stop our eating altogether. Please don't construe this, madam, as an adverse reflection on your cooking, which we indeed found excellent—in fact, even excelling excellence itself—and that's no exaggeration, but a modest understatement of the case. Will you accept these words as the compliment they're intended for?"

My mother actually curtsied! So gallant was her guests' full-hearted or full-bellied gratitude, nothing but that old-fashioned gesture could convey how touched she was—indeed, overwhelmed—by the justice they did on the eating level and the verbal one to the splendor of her cooking.

7

The bright May Sunday now turned to later afternoon, by stealth of time itself, like the thief of our lives that time most assuredly is, in slow destructive process of gradation subtly imperceptible save by intervals of lapsed inattentiveness.

The two officials were suffering from acute indigestion, which had been brought about by many too many helpings at the lunch they'd been invited to stay to join in, when on an official business visit to our house, brought about by an urgent phone call placed by Lester earlier that morning to their big correction institute office that rendered a vast protective national service against wrongdoing of diverse kinds such as the crime my father was accused of planning according to the evidence of the tape recorder played to the two kindly visiting officials whose lunchtime verdict placed my father legitimately under official arrest, an act he soon disobeyed by turning fugitive from the law's lengthy arm that apprehends to constrain people from wrongdoing done or intended.

The two officials excused themselves to retire briefly to suitable quarters to vomit in private.

That delicate business satisfactorily transacted, they felt somewhat better about their internal corporate stomach affairs, which had been cleansed of the intolerable aftermath of a pleasurable prolonged bout of really solid eating.

Now, the two officials were making preparations to depart from the place of a meal even more memorable than it had been unexpected. Once again, my mother was commended—a formality discharged exuberantly—for the sustained quality of cooking as a substantial though "perishable" art form—art meant to be consumed by a participant, not merely admired in passivity by thin cerebral spectator taste at an un-directly-involved distance off the passing event itself, however enthusiastic the connoisseur is in "taking it all in."

Lester's art isn't "perishable"—it's collected. It'll be the magnet of a glitteringly gala cultural affair that in turn will serve—if Lester's tip-off to the two twin-like officers of penal bureaucratic officialdom turns out right tomorrow night—to be the magnet that draws the escaped fugitive, that outlaw-on-the-loose, my murder-meditating father, bearing myself, Mary, Lester, and my mother most ominously in mind as the superbly logical victims of the pains he'll take, the risks he'll bear, in providing our exits from life by means necessarily abruptly violent, employing surprise as a key medium.

I'd thought of committing a multiple-murder-preventing murder of my father myself, thus making me a murderer in a good cause. But that was before my father was placed under official arrest, thanks to the tape recorder, by those two titans of gastronomy, those excessive murderers of prepared food, who, however, in pursuing their favorite pastime, let my father slip away from their by-then greasy hands that slickly manipulated some fancy flashy silverware, those ever-handy utensils—knife, fork, spoon—which they wielded deftly like knitting needles threading their way through yarns and spools of some sumptuous material, to the immense pleasure of my mother, the provider.

Our guests are taking their leave. They've already taken—and left in the vomit bowl—lots of food which, by the nature of food, is perishable stuff anyway. They put it away, tucked it away, in vast intestinal vessels, but then vomited so much of it away, but by then the damage had been done anyway and the nourishment taken on and conveyed to inner cells bursting at the beams and at the seams with the vital nutriment organically replenishing the whole system with health-affording vitamins, minerals, proteins, and other chemical agents positive to human physical nature in separate specimens of evolved biological structure native to the growth of our kind over vast tracts of pre-historical, historical, and mostly hysterical man-made time that measures our lack of progress on the incessant inching forward of process, mutation, change, flux, and alteration in small or large.

The above is amply illustrated in the twin persons of those two officials, who have warmly been our Sunday guests.

We escort them to the door, which opens on the declining afternoon along the entire length of the Artesian Road, off Westbourne Grove in the district of Bayswater near Notting Hill Gate but remote from such other areas of lengthening sunny shadows as Hampstead, Highgate, Belsize Park, Kentish Town, Tufnel Park, Chalk Farm, Camden Town, Swiss Cottage, St. John's Wood, Baker Street, Oxford Circus, Marble Arch, Edgeware Road, Little Venice, Kilburn, Picadilly, Leicester Square, Charing Cross, Covent Garden, Tottenham Court Road, Russell Square (scene of Lester's studio where I was taken by my mother as an infant and where I had my first art lessons opening out to a career in art as promising in the future—provided my father doesn't deprive me of that future—as Lester's is confirmed in the present), Hyde Park Corner, Knightsbridge, Sloane Square, Victoria, Pimlico (scene of tomorrow night's well-guarded entrance at the top of the Tate Gallery steps), South Kensington (where my father had actually been my father and my mother's husband in what seems like a few lifetimes ago, such changes having been wrought in our radically wrenched lives from before, changes stabilized happily, productively, lovingly, but now threatened by radical wholesale overthrow in a murder-motivated man's high lethal act of vengeance fatally fated for four victims chosen logically by his wounded sentiment and mortally offended pride, in logic's awfully lucid clarity that glitters by an insane beam of frenzy to decisive conviction confidently asserted by deranged delusion that strikes the will with such disease that only firm action can rigidly spring from the locked obsession of narrow viewpoint), Gloucester Road, Earls Court, High Street Kensington, Olympia, Hammersmith (where my father had been kept in a '"mental" dungeon for free on Government care), Barnes, Wandsworth, Clapham Common, Brixton, Herne Hill, Dulwich, Greenwich, Blackheath, and places even further away, such as for example Leytonstone, Bristol, Brighton, Sheffield, Bath, Tunbridge Wells, Leeds, or even, to stretch a point further, beyond the Channel itself, across oceans, straits, and seas, in radiant outer directions from our global orb's spherical circumference's direct center spot, which at this precise moment in universal time happened to be our front door, opened from inside our own house itself, whose residents face peril from without, thanks to two unalert officials undistracted from intensive eating bouts recently ended in regurgitation and weariness.

There, on the doorway area, Mary, my mother and I clustered behind our guiding light, that orange-capped tower of wisdom, ingenuity, resourcefulness, the ability to get us out of a scrape: Lester, our leader.

Respectfully but firmly, he gave carefully cautionary instructions to, while seeing off in parting, those two officials who had served in prodigious, awesome capacities as informal luncheon guests just on an impromptu, circumstantially (but substantially) "pot-luck" basis in last-minute invitation, an occasion to which they rose as eaters but from which they fell in the role of officers entrusted with an acknowledged dangerous man's captivity in passage to sentence and detention once the formalities of prosecution result in psychiatric and criminal confinement to make life safe and living secure for Mary, my mother, Lester, and me, the re-endangered, uneasy, upset quartet.

Those two officials reverentially listened to a discovered celebrity whose autograph they now prized—treasured even—in detective inside vest pockets, secret compartments within the clothes they wore on the outside, now bespeckled not only with flecks of juice and sauce but from subsequent vomit drops as a retching aftermath to eating of course excessively beyond even the vanishing point of too much, at the very minimum.

Their departure was on the note of stomach contentment, a healthy glow of visceral stability. They were as pleased as they could possibly be in the place where glandular taste buds were signally bewitched by a rare splendor in unique culinary annals.

Their heads, though, were somewhat clogged. Lester, however, penetrated all barriers of denseness either situational or innate, by putting this message strongly:

"Get a lot of plainclothesmen dressed up in the guise of fashionable guests to be on hand to mill around as a well-sprinkled security force armed with hidden guns alert at a moment's notice on the spot at any time to shoot Tom, whose description I'll provide you with, and identifying photographs to reproduce and distribute to the guards on duty disguised into incognito anonymity. These crackshots must shoot Tom down if unable immediately to handcuff him. If this isn't done, these would be, alas, the consequences:

"Myself, guest of honor and celebrant of the occasion, killed, therefore unable to receive that overwhelming honor rarely accorded to an artist in his own youthful lifetime;

"My lovely Liz, to whom your taste buds will be in debt forever, put out of life by an assassin who, not coincidentally, happens to be her as-yet-undivorced husband;

"Talented Mark" (indicating me with an intimate compassionate nod underscored by a wink of sympathy and understanding), "a future outstandingly recognized artist who one night will receive a similar honor to mine tomorrow, but not, however, if Tom, his father, undetected by your protective crew of accredited precisionists, manages to kill the poor unfortunate boy: which prevent, please, by every means possible known to police vigilance and your emergency task squad of crack, military-type personnel;

"And sweet little Mary, adorable angel of innocence, cut down even before she precociously grows to bride's unbridled estate of post-virginity license and loosened obsolete maidenhead of sinful knowledge of the apple of experience's eye? Avert such tragedy. Alert yourselves to her father, who wishes to wilt her prime and blast her embryonically gorgeously opening bud into withered retardation on the frost of her arrested biological right, blighted before ripe, to cheat time of beauty and sex."

The two officials listened at the doorway to a man whom they admired for being famous and whose impassioned plea they took in flattery's vanity's spirit of insipid hero-worship by trends of cultural hierarchy that degrades all by presuming at all to grade.

"Your appeal," they replied in quivering tremulousness all aquake and shaky, "shall surely, in all respects, be met." This flat declaration was unequivocal. Yet uncertainty offsets the implication of a guarantee.

Parting now completed, if not exceeded, all the remaining formalities that courtesy drearily tried to invent, reiterate, reaffirm, and redundantly cover itself with, as though afraid of missing some magic act of prescribed code in the appropriate shape of banal wording or superfluous gesture that effects the precise relief desired from dread's dreadful self-continuum in the vague floating dread mixed of anguish, malaise, despair, and that arch foe of joy, pessimism, in jittery morbid irritable anxiety that barely gives respite or abates somewhat in brief restitution to mercifully relent and relax the uneasy, all-alerting grip in tense alternating currents of pressure's irregular torment.

Both officials, together, were about to leave. Goodbyes, then, were the order of the declining day.

"Goodbye, you officials," Lester bade them.

"Goodbye, officials both," my mother added, "and thanks for pretending that my food was adequate."

Before they could rise to her assurance, I piped up myself: "Goodbye, you officials. Four lives are in your four hands. Symmetrically balance them, if you please, with expert professional protection of the caliber of even your high-ranking, much-awarded, duly noted, lofty capabilities. Be decorated heroes in our salvation, please, by timely rescue from those irreversibly devouring jaws of Death, ever-famished but in our cases too premature."

"I'll really appreciate you if you save us from an early demise," my little sister Mary joined in, to complete our full chorus in the linking linear sequence of solidarity doomed but devoted to grim survival's hope in the crisis of crucial desperation determined through the might and main of combined sheer will to prevail ultimately and triumph with lives flourishingly intact and left literally to breathe sighs of our several relief from eight inflated nostrils.

"We'll do our best," those two parting officials openly asserted on taking their dual leave. "Our best ought to be enough. Tom will be out-numbered by opponents he won't recognize but who'll be able to spot *him*—and *stop* him. The odds are terrifically against him. By a profes-sional estimate, Tom really doesn't stand a chance. He's a wanted, hunted man. We'll zero in on him. We'll cut him off, isolate him, catch him, nab him, or shoot him. Your lives are as good as safe. You four will live. Here's wishing you good lives! Including emphatically tomorrow night's portions, in glory and glamor safely protected from a tragically dra-matic culmination by a thorough, discreetly unapparent police guard scattered through the crowd but prepared to spot, nab, shoot, arrest—if he shows up—the man you stand in fear of.

"We neglected to guard him tight, and he's at large. We'll well atone for that slip-up—if our prey shows up—at the big party. We'll redeem our reputations, if given even the slightest chance. Our files bulge with a portfolio of his case history, his medical transcripts, dossier reports of vital documents from the Hammersmith High Street state hospital at national expense and from those fancy private homes at *your* gener-ous expense. And we're taking the telltale tape record with us, as well as photos and other descriptive material. We'll compile it all together, to track him down, detect him anywhere, to prosecute and convict, to sentence him to a life term in prison in escape-proof jail, where he can't interfere with your four futures all unfolding in full freedom and safety unmolested far from the tight cell that holds Tom."

With those words, the two officials terminate the lengthy official eventful Sunday visit. I'll have to be dead to forget it, or so senile as to be virtually dead. Which isn't too far off, as I pen this.

What memorable officials they are! Memory feeds on them. *They*'d feed on *anything.*

Their bulky figures vanish in dusk's distance. They're crossing West-bourne Grove, then they're out of view. They're quite a pair with food.

But will they prevent my father from killing us? They'd left us gracious parting words, those two officials, promising deliverance from danger from the man they'd had in their grip but let slip away. The odds, the chances, were all on our safety, they'd said. Still, fear's tinkle wouldn't leave me. I was obviously already a worrying type.

My father could be cunning and unpredictable. He might outsmart the network laid out to trap him by anticipating it and trying an unexpected tactic to evade the airtight foolproof coverage with some surprise move. He had enough money on him to buy a knife or gun or bomb. No one knows where he is, which is to his advantage. He can make a sudden strike, from nowhere, choosing his own time to dart in thrust when security lets down or defense is lulled relaxed from tense alert.

He could even come back here, to the Artesian Road house. Why aren't police posted by our entrance now? He might not wait to go to the Tate Gallery. He might strike before tomorrow night. Right here!

I conveyed these apprehensions to Lester, while my mother took Mary out to a visit. He was worried along similar lines from an independent train of brooding. We linked up our feelings, in united gloom.

"I'm unconfident in those two officials. They're bunglers," Lester pointed out, to which I joined my grave doubts that those two officials could really get anything right. Evening found us allied in misgivings, brittle with vulnerable mortality.

Could we count on being alive when tomorrow night ends? We were glad my mother and Mary were spared these forbidding contemplations. Despair found us an easy prey. My father lurked somewhere. Hidden in a starlit night. Bearing us in mind. Trying to rearrange such futures as Mary, my mother, Lester, and I could, might, would have, simply by stopping such futures short of all the living that adventurously remains in possibility's outflung realm. We *want* our lives extended. We're in a morbid state, not for love of morbidity, but for love and desire that life should continue. We dearly prize the exquisite thrill of living. What we'd prolong, my father would curtail. We're a family unit. Please stay out, Daddy. Don't break us up. Don't fling our scattered souls to the dust and waste and void barren of thought, pulse, blood, and breath. Don't annihilate us. Leave us here, to dread and hate you. We hate to dread, and dread to hate, but would bear those feelings rather than that you should deprive us of all feelings together.

Die yourself. That's better than troubling us. Please be caught and die, be killed, instead of us. We're four together, all separately valuable. Let us be. Lose to the police in backfired violence. Surrender your life, however unwillingly. What peace it would mean, for your survivors!

PART FOUR

1

We never got that peace, the peace coming from the certified death of our definite endangerer.

Now *lots* of time passes, instead of just only a little. I refer to *years*, not the mere panic of minutes.

Whether it was the deliberate form his revenge took, or not, what finally happened defied all our expectations. My father was never heard from again, ever. No word of him, no clue; and by now, considering after all how old I, the writer of these memoirs, have come to be, my father would certainly have been discarded by natural age, anyone's ancient doom and final hazard of patient fate.

Whether he lived to the full course of an old aging lifetime, or died somewhere along that obstacle-strewn, notoriously treacherous path that forces precarious lives on us sojourners in our variously episodic passage, just isn't known. Starvation or some other poverty peril might have shoved him to the wayside, or misadventure by insane distractedness or numb indifference to survival's cozy joy. These are problematicals, hypothetical conjecture given no seal of proof by any official report.

Anything could have happened or not. All we know is what happened to *us*—the uneasy "survivors" who never knew when or if we were surviving that poor man whose sperm led to this book I'm writing in old age by giving me a new age from the start.

A belated goodbye, Daddy. Thanks for life. But then I came to curse you.

I had reason to. But you had reason to cause me to. But you weren't reasonable. Anyway, I'm old. Even at great longevity, you would have to be chronologically dead by now. Whether you meant to or not, your disappearance and never turning up kept away our peace. That was clever. You took effect, all right. How cruel and diabolical. You were disturbing.

You whom I love, hate, and remember—I'll stop addressing you in the direct "you" person, and resume my narrative with you becoming my father in the third person. You, whose sperm has led me all this way, by giving me a shape, a chance, a name, a being: that's me. However old I've become, I'm still your son. Your dutiful son. Mark.

2

The central character in these memoirs seems to be less Lester and more my father. Those two major men in my mother's life.

My father's family became Lester's family. My father was exiled. He became alien.

But he put up a stink about it. Not passively but poisonously did he react, when his family bodily became another's and not his.

We, whose lives he threatened, lived under a cloud of apprehensive anxiety, worry, dread, for ever so long.

At first, we felt *acute* danger; that Sunday night a few hours after he'd escaped, was very uncomfortable. The next day led up to the gala party at the Tate Gallery, the most publicized social event of the whole year. A huge armed guard was at the entrance and inside. The place was swarming with detectives.

"Nothing" happened. As those two food-loving officials had brought forward as a possibility after letting my father escape their clumsy clutches, the elaborately prepared-for man never did actually show up. He *might* have, in disguise, but what a clever disguise it would have had to be to pass undetected the vigilance of the top spotters of the entire anti-crime brigade, themselves disguised as mingling guests in the distinguished exclusive bash.

3

I fulfilled my promise. I even eclipsed Lester in fame, when my *own* time came for being a recognized artist in a newer phase of art's fashion-reputationed history of changing trends and passing stylistic vogue-eries, each wooing immortality in its own peculiar and compelling mode.

Mary grew up to be a non-artist. However, she married an art critic, by whom she has non-artist children.

Lester's fame endured, despite my own rise. Gradually, white replaced his orange hair.

We remained good friends. The grief of my life was when he died.

The love between him and my mother lasted forever. They couldn't marry, because my mother was still officially married to my continually absent (whereabouts unknown, a wanted man by the police but ever in vain) father. Lester and my mother were made for each other in heaven.

If the divorce business can get cleared up there, that's where they must be married now. (This is, of course, mere theological speculation. It's founded on no evidence of truth, nor is heaven, for that matter—not that heaven is matter, at all. It does, however, matter.)

My mother died soon after Lester, in the Artesian Road house.

Mary, her husband and children lived in Putney. The Artesian Road house? I'm writing this there. Studio and residence it's ever been for me; I never left it once there.

I married, but my wife is dead. I had a girlfriend before she died, who moved in with me here in the Artesian Road house once my wife was dead.

I mourn my wife. We had no children. I mourn my mother and Lester. My girlfriend constantly keeps me company, though she's old too.

When I finish this by pen, she, a good typist, will type it, proofread it, and off it goes to the publisher (who commissioned these memoirs) for copyediting and then to the printer.

When the book comes out, my father will be too dead to read it, even if other circumstances could permit him to read it.

This is for strangers, this book: people outside our family, whether they be artists or non-artists.

Of course, Mary will read it. She's so old by now.

Hang on, Mary, a little longer. I'll give you an advance galley proof copy, uncorrected—just in case.

I'm reaching the last end of my life. I still paint, but feebly.

This is Mark. I've made my mark in life. I've made these marks on paper here. I was marked by my father, with three others. My face is all marked, with time, with all the worrying I did, by more problems than solutions.

Reader, goodbye. To *you*, not to *all* readers. To *you*—the one whose reading of this comes to a full stop just about here.

It's over with. Now attend to other matters. Enough of this.

Soon, enough of *me*. Goodbye.

GUILT IN SEARCH OF GOD

Eric Felldunger was just as usual as anyone, except when he was being unusually so. This was true even now, at a time when his receding birth was over twenty years distant and falling back at the same steady rate. His later development had been assigned, for further results, to the capable future, which would consume what was not yet. Thus his life was quickly falling into its lack of place, so bound was it in the temporal dimension. Space, to move in, seemed rather out of place, in the record of his progress. Being average, he earned his living as a manufacturer's salesman who traveled to retail stores—stationers; for his line was in greeting cards, giving him an affable disposition as a necessary trait in trade. He suspected books as being too literary, beyond the call of the normal intellect. So in college he majored in marketing, and was regarded as a potential extrovert. Some day, he'd organize sales routes in the office; now, he was getting needed field experience, and was enjoying life.

His parents were doing all right in another part of the country, so his responsibility was only to himself. Pressure was put on him by the boss to think of getting married; it would steady down his wild oats, and apply a serious coating to his youth. So Eric tried out different girls, with a miscellaneous series of results. Into these adventures he thrust an organ somewhat other than his heart. Besides, his work took him all over, and made it hard to settle down. Being a healthy non-prude, he had above his share of a man's right to a good load of fun. Life was behaving friendly to his senses, and kindly looked out to his well being. Eric had purely no grounds for complaint, since happiness was his chief mark of pleasure, in whose formation all general circumstances were prompt to cooperate. And his bank account wore a healthy tone of fat, to uphold this level in the finest future standard. As fortune's pampered pet, Eric had a fair outlook, and flung a rosy radiance, charged to account, on the suns not yet dawned.

His credit was drawn from that endless source of man's vitality: confidence. He was an assured man.

But yet—something was wrong. He wondered what it was, and discovered it to be himself. What he did was wrong, and he was wrong for what he did. This state of affairs didn't help to make him a contented man; he developed symptoms of guilt, and was plagued by the stirrings of a tormented conscience, in whose throes he was a creature in unrest. Why? If he could catch the cause, he'd crush the captive harm, and free his soul that was twitching from the stings of scruples. Shouldn't he seek outside advice, and be guided from his present plight, or be directed to the road of self-improvement? His quest was self-evident, and would begin.

Maybe he had a deficiency of religion? Should he go to a church and improve his faith? Or was the problem more basic?

What had he to repent? Was it immoral to handle girls the way he did? He always reduced their state of dress, then covered the main pit of their modesty by inserting a portion of himself in it—much to his delight, and subsequent sleepiness. Was this act evilly sinful, and perhaps wrong?

In one of the cities where he sold greeting cards, he made the acquaintance of a definitive physiologist adept at analyzing man's structural ingredients. In his spare, non-scientifically-devoted time, the physiologist, to improve himself spiritually, was secretly registered at a theological seminary, where he studied earnestly for the ministry, hoping to earn himself a collar. Eric admired this man's dual caliber, and so acquired his confidence, telling him of his core's doubt. "Can you show me," Eric asked, "how things are organized inside—functionally, of course. My conflicts are a mystery, so I have several layers of pain. Dissect them, will you?"

The physiologist broke into thought, wherein he contemplated the matter. He doodled out a few pertinent diagrams, humming most creatively. Eric waited, in a hush of steep suspense. The words he wanted would be woven in a golden web of magic.

The physiologist pucked his brow, then let a frown play lightly along the slanting shades of his face, while his brain strained to deliver the right group of facts that would ease Eric's curiosity and brush away his bruised gloom of tension. Yet the language mustn't be too technical. The description should be clad in terms that accord with Eric's simple business sense. It should be neatly presented, with the minimum ambiguity. That would effect the maximum communication, and clinch Eric's enlightenment. At the end of this substantial meal, a theological pudding may be thrown in, to round out a world view, with man at the center:

"The body manufactures sex, and is the basic raw material. Later, the intellect constructs a cozy retrospect. Pride and conscience also preside at this top-level assemblage, while the gland submits its latest blueprint. The joint decision that pleases the corporation is to undergo further action, either immediately or else very soon after. Then comes a general adjournment, a momentary halt in the mind-molested life of the body's sex-hungry quest. Nearby, in an overhanging cloud, God and the devil shoot their well-matched game of dice, from cupped fists that gamble in the great tyranny of indifference."

"That's an ingenious process," Eric remarked, "but it's fatalistic why God can't concern Himself more actively, with less moral apathy, in man's deplorable beastliness. Why must behavior include so much body? Isn't mentality sufficient?"

"You're naive," answered the physiologist, whose cynical future was to be a clergyman. Eric was indignant, and walked out. (They were in the physiologist's house. It was the season of mild weather. The hour was late.) "I'll explore further," Eric decided, continuing his quest.

Next day he sold greeting cards in another city. The local girl friend was bleeding out an abortion (not from Eric's causation), so when evening fell he felt the need for diversion and, attracted by the sight of a Ferris wheel and the sound from a merry-go-round, he repaired to a gaudy, bright-colored amusement park, in which his delighted senses took a very young pleasure, belying his mature occupation.

He soon spied, in the swarm of dense crowds, a human-operated weighing machine (based on gravity) which advertised to tell the customer's fortune on a principle of specific individual generality. Eric approached the operator, and asked if the machine could weigh in with advice (or warning) on what happens when love isn't repressed, but is grossly practiced. The operator, who was enormously fat, and wore a collegiate sweater, grunted out an assent. Eric got up on the machine, and the lever was cranked, with a crunching moan of noise. A hooting crowd gathered, to boo Eric. Out popped a card, recording Eric's weight (under two hundred pounds) and, under it, these printed, ominous words against man's nature:

"Ah, love is sweet, grand, and romantic, and is an appropriate toy with which the heart plays breakfully often to its own self-destruction. Girls always present kissable lips, as a device of utility upon which passion may first playfully practice, in prelude to the business at hand which concludes below, to the accompaniment of a world of guilt that earns its livelihood feeding on the bitter dregs of such conduct, leaving scars in the slit and broken soul that heal in reverse toward the innocence of a glaring immortality, the cruel religion of time that tampers with us, wounds joy, and bites us with ugliness. This tempers our nature, and fouls our scheme of love."

"Was this only for me?" Eric asked the operator, after reading the message. "Yeah, it's purely by chance," he was assured. But he worried. Wasn't the card's language above the usual patron of an amusement park? And how gravely did those prophetic words pertain to Eric's peculiar dilemma! How had the machine guessed it? Eric's dilettantism in love exposed him to the danger that girls might break down the accumulated morality of his soul, through physical pressure. The peril of losing out on salvation sorely grieved him. Troubled by his probable destiny, Eric retired to his hotel, where sleep eluded his pursuit and panic greeted him instead.

He thought of business, but soon his image was a cloud of God, from Whose staggering distance Eric was directly scolded. Then lust flashed out signals, to compound the infamy, the deep distress. He dressed, and went to a house of ill fame. How puny was the relief!

"The world doesn't smell right," sniffed out Eric, seeing dawn invade his hotel window with bland coloring of pink hues and some purple passages. "Its ugliness contaminates my breath, exploiting the craving of my lungs for the inhaling of any air available, as life's rhythm so often demands. Is evil in our very atmosphere itself? That's a frightening speculation. I need more information, to clarify the subject. Let me rise, and sell greeting cards. Then I'll look up some consultant on the odor problem, who'll blow my nose for me and clean out the passages. Then I'll view life from a more rosy perfume, and ignore the gaseous stink that pervades our senses. Ah, my pillow is comfy. I'll shortly live a small sleep..."

When he awoke, Eric was anxious. As a salesman, he was super, and sold out all the greeting cards, procuring orders for more. Even his samples were in demand; stock was depleted, so his cards were fiercely wanted. He phoned the head office, and received an earful of congratulations. A promotion, even while on the road, seemed due any day, by special messenger. If life could be measured by business alone, his success was heavenly, and won a royal road to God's front throne. However, other standards seemed to prevail. Sinning was the talent he had been granted in generous doses by the powers that be. No wonder his smell buds seemed to quake and ache, sniffing. He had inhaled the world's worst germ.

The nose specialist greeted him courteously, but then shoved a mirror rod far up to the adenoids. Eric passed a sneeze out, through his forward ear, and managed to adjust the remains of his tongue. "Is it me or the world, Doc?" he asked. Professionally, he was told:

"Deep breathing is our mysterious ailment, and the discharged air overloads the world with foul purity. Vegetables can hardly grow, from porous land where whiffs of dead breath blow gently from buried cemeteries. There is no bone, no matter how deeply rotted, that does not boast of at least a corrupted bladder of lungs. Even from pinched nostrils, outflowing breath pours local disease upon a world already vastly stenched. Chiseled teeth, blue and uneven, open gaping gaps, and the filthy breath of wine scares virginity away and makes holes appear in the sacred cathedral of the woman, whose apse is apt to lapse. Overhead, worms chew the moth-eaten sun, and urine drizzles from the sky's ugly manhole."

"But to avoid this hell, should I stop breathing, Doc?" "Suit yourself," said that expert on the respiratory tract, tweezing Eric's nose, while writing out an exorbitant bill. "Must I pay through this?" Eric asked, touching his own nose with a chattering forefinger. "I doubt a dollar would go through," the physician replied, estimating the girth of the canal. It was a shrewd financial guess.

Eric's commercial traveling gave him a new city to be in, but his mind was the same. Grim thoughts obsessed him. Was the world, or even his body, made with man in mind? Or was man made without care for the things that would assail him? Eric met a Professor of Pessimism, whose course was popular in the local university. But at the end of the term the professor had reduced classes, due to a wave of unexpected suicide that had not been recommended by the text. And those students would have passed, not failed, had they prolonged their lives so as not to miss the final test. The professor, of course, was puzzled.

He was a staunch academician, a scholarly adept. He walked on a compilation of increasing footnotes. He taught in the evening session. Eric audited the class, then asked the professor out for tea. Beer was preferred, so they found a quiet bar. "Professor, is life good or bad?" Eric asked. A predictably wise smile answered him.

"Can you describe," Eric persisted, "what things are like. I mean, how do things stand. For benefiting people, I mean; are we fit to be here where the living is; and do conditions subscribe to what's conducive for our well being? Are our circumstances fortunate, or the reverse? What's in us, that's against or for the best way to feel? Does a propitious star hang over our life, or have we oddly fallen out with every ideal we crave? Give it to me straight; you're a scholar, so you studied all this. And how you think is by what exists, I'm sure. And don't sugar-coat the pill; be nothing but objective, in your pessimism."

The professor looked sad, and crinkled his wrinkled skin. In kindness to Eric, he said gently:

"The world isn't quite right for people. The mind is lost in hazy arithmetic. The body, self-torturing and self-pleasing, sniffs its back with its front, while the helpless person is caught tight in the middle, clutching at his soul. Above, the sky mixes its poison. Below, the ground stands poised to drink in our dark and sick bodies."

"What a revolting concept!" Eric noted; the professor shrugged, so as to say, "Did I create that? No, I merely record. What's true, is true, whether we will so or not. Sorry, if it displeases you."

Each tugged slowly on the first beer. There was silence, where conversation should have been. Leaving the bar, they parted, on terms of deep mutual distrust. The unspoken hatred gave Eric a shivering case of horrors; his skin prickled, and his soul recoiled, like a snake frozen by human perversity. Had Eric political power to remold, or rectify throughout, this cosmic superstructure? This act of grand nobility and heroic endeavor was locked futilely within his breast; no, conditions would remain; only Eric must change.

He kept at girls, like the rake he was, city after city. The pleasure must go on below, though the mind above was free to sacrificially suffer and give up its peace. Rarely did the two clash; or rather, always.

Could the professor be proven erroneous, as to his view? Now in a new city, Eric met a novelist of realism; over whiskey at a party, they exchanged some details of erotic hardship, for both were connoisseurs in the science of women. The novelist brandished his latest book, a "hot item." "Can I read an excerpt?" Eric asked. "Which one?" said the man of letters. "To tell me what's actually taking place, unknown to most, in this sordid specimen of a universe," Eric specified. "That's a tall order," said the briefly-famed author. He thumbed through the pages, saying, "I never read this since I wrote it." "You should, it's interesting," recommended an admirer, who had overheard them. For his pains, this fan was thanked and had an autograph forced on him. It was studied minutely, as part of an extensive forgery plot. Thus worketh the criminal mind.

"Here, try this episode," the novelist suggested, and Eric read, in his throbbing greed for insight, two paragraphs—one of commentary, and one describing a dry spark in the annals of human contact—with the novelist dangling over his shoulder to follow each word in the suspended animation of criticism, occasionally blocking Eric's view, jostling the guest reader in their contest to absorb the shoddy matter presented:

"Faraway clouds hide in their caverns. Weather, behind the scenes, prepares tomorrow's forecast. Evil, having been transacted in broad daylight, divides itself into money, with profits for the few and mere wages for the many, and locks up the office, the factory, the schoolroom. Next on the agenda? Cheap love.

"It takes many mouths to consummate one kiss. Hands, released from their gloves, feel for the coarse texture of their true mate, but find it dangling, however gently, from a stranger's arm. Apologies merely rub more dirt into a friendly wound. At a certain hour, permission seems almost free. A well-scrubbed emotion, for no reason at all, yields to a slum impulse, overturning the neat lamp. They step on their brief fire, and quickly the ashes insure privacy. But a third guest, the odor thereof, has stolen between them. Something was scarcely burnt."

"Why have you chosen shabby content?" Eric asked. This offended the novelist, who replied that reality does very well, as a mirrored subject to tempt style. Eric thought the contrary: art should edify, and should aim at preserving morals. "A watchdog of decency," Eric said, defining art metaphorically. Sophisticated laughter greeted this prudent remark, and mirth hounded Eric to the door, the cruel hilarity of a twentieth century party. "I reject the reality you depict," Eric supplied, as a parting note. The novelist didn't heed this, his back was turned; he was bent on conquering a pretty flirt who fawned before him. "He converts mud to art," Eric said, walking out. He passed by a necking couple, closely knit in a kiss. "Why doesn't guilt stop them?" he asked of the Almighty, in a fit of profound pity and no less deep concern. Being shocked at others, he found, somewhat relieved the plight of his own conscience, so that he forgot his sins.

"Nature is the root of all immorality," he decided. He continued to fornicate, and to sell greeting cards; at each, he was an easy master, and success was a trifle, merely a casual pushover. What he wanted was a fight.

But not against his body. That would destroy pleasure.

So he was a theory tyrant, believing in virtue on principle. A self-righteous arrogance, an offensive overbearing morality, soon insulted his biggest greeting card buyers, and alienated a chunk of the market. Saleswise, he went downhill. "Don't antagonize us," said the stationery store keepers. But Eric Felldunger was a haunted man, and bitten by eager devils. Little that he was belonged to himself; his acts were "possessed," and not his own.

Love is suspect; in Eric's book, it's the arch culprit.

He examines his disgust, and finds it bitter. He travels, but sells few greeting cards. He looks seedy. His boss has sent him a warning telegram; but Eric is distracted, and makes no headway. Defeat and failure, those brutal vultures, circle overhead.

His sales record descends, rapidly. A rival firm gets a better greeting; *his* cards remain in his valise, and the unbought boxes are piled in the trunk compartment at the back of a weather-soiled car, which he drives, in careless abandon, to the wrong city. Along the lonely highway, the word "guilt" assaults him, with its murderous intent.

Stacks of greeting cards, far out of season, clutter his car. His suit is unpressed. He violates a traffic ordinance, and is hauled in. He neglects to shave, and his sales schedule is months behind. Even the women he "has" in each city turn him down for a date. He lacks that former dash and sharpness, that "line," that sold himself into their embrace. Now, he's a pathetic sap, and long gone.

He lost the list of his dealers, and memory is unreliable. Forgetful, he spills oil on most of his card stock. He doesn't brush his teeth, and keeps appointments by accident, but ruins the deal by slovenly ways, incomprehensible mutterings, and foul breath; when asked for estimates, he bungles. "He's deteriorated," say his old customers, whose custom goes elsewhere, to better equipped competitors. Eric is all but fired, except that the office can't reach him. Where is he, stranded on a delirious side road of his lone self, ranting prophetically. The single refrain, "guilt," buzzes continually about his head. His replacement, whom the firm has assigned, is seeking him frantically, to notify him of his dismissal; he drives hurriedly; the office fears that Eric has spoiled their major accounts, and ruined good will, on his ruinous campaign. Eric's sanity is proclaimed void, and his reason nullified. He had been a man of outstanding promise.

Eric enters a familiar city, puts up at a hotel, finds a telegram; it breaks the news. "I'm a has-been," Eric is aware. He phones his local girl friend, but she says, "Stop annoying me. We're quits, you hear?"

Eric broods, and loses weight. He's not balanced, inside. Either his conscience is too big for his guilt and needs more crimes, or else his guilt is too big in proportion to his conscience, and jam-packs it. The spatial relationship between the vessel and what it contains should provide a workmanlike harmony, on a scale of sure functioning. So Eric needs to consult a psychic anatomist, with new and used models. A spare conscience might be wise to buy, as an annex in case of a surplus of guilt. Or ready-made guilt, already prefabricated, could be stored away, in case the conscience feels empty. Eric was endowed with a good mechanical sense. A solid mental structure, kept constantly under repair, is a worldly asset for a man to keep his head above the storm-tormented riot of the emotional ocean. Reason was Eric's fortress; let the waves lash and the hurricanes roar; it would weather even God's wrath, and be unpierced by the divine thunderbolt. Eric believed in his constitution, as a strong ally. It had much adversity to face, and would muster all its impeccable fortitude, under the sternest duress. It was crack-proof, and endured the mightiest blasts.

Ruggedly impervious to misfortunes without, Eric is in a messy hell within. That's his softest weak spot, all mushy. One poke in that flabby area, and he's in pieces. How unsettling, this crumbling stability in wholesome Eric Felldunger, who started out in a brave suit of happy armor, and now is reduced to ragged bones that sway in any wind. To reverse the trend and restore the origin, Eric must see a specialist quickly. But under what category does this disorder fall? Then maybe a *general* expert could define it for him.

"Doctor of Internal Evil" was the title on the placard outside. The aluminum shingle reflected the sun, to catch Eric's wandering eye. "May I have treatment?" he asked the nurse at the desk. "Appointment, sir?"

"No, I'm new." "Wait your turn." "But no one else is waiting." "It's for an appearance of prestige, to pretend so. And when you do see the doctor, he'll first diagnose you. He's very proficient, and has a time-worn system. You'll be cured almost before payment. Then a bill will be sent, or we'll have to sue. Symptoms, sir? I'll notate them, to give the doctor advance billing. To be waylaid, or startled, by an unprecedented case, demoralizes his esteemed confidence. He's not a steady man, I'm afraid."

"Is he a quack?" Eric asked. "No, nor a fraud, neither," the nurse assured. "He'll mangle your disease, even if you have to die. He's a thorough man, and almost went to medical school, were it not for failing the entrance exams. Sir, you're in good hands. May I help you with your prayers?"

Eric felt befuddled. Then the doctor appeared, with a dignified moustache and an assertive belly. His white eyebrows were arched diabolically. He inspired horror, if not confidence. "Do you respect me?" he asked. "Yes, your honor," said Eric, duped and won over by the professional's easy manner. "Shall we examine you?" the physician stated, with rhetorical polish. "If it pleases your majesty," Eric replied, tilting on his crumbling knees. "Posture!" the doctor warned, and Eric immediately rightened himself. "My authority is omniscient," the doctor mildly declared, almost carelessly. Eric was proud to have to agree, as he stood in signal dread. "I'm Doctor Deity," said his master, "but I like you, so call me by my nickname: God." Eric was obliged: "Your Sacred Holiness, bless me, your servant," Eric intoned, with devout and all-suffering humility. "You have the correct attitude," added the doctor.

"You're my first patient. I've just set up practice, so tell me: what's your complaint?" "My guilt is gigantic in size," Eric estimated, "like an elephant too high for a zoo. My awkward conscience must work overtime, to keep building higher bars. The cage continually grows smaller."

"That's rough," sympathized the doctor. "But should I classify your problem medical or religious? On this point, my unclarity perhaps betrays my inexperience. In fact, I hardly feel adequate for the task. I'm having an affair with my nurse. Isn't that immoral?" "Perhaps you need a priest's counsel," Eric recommended. The doctor protested, "How unscientific!"and Eric blanched. "Pardon, I'm not up on the latest progress," Eric explained. They entered a strangely complete empathy, and fast became friends, sworn to lifelong devotion. Then, a bond of hostility released them from that companionable freedom, and they were angry antagonists.

The nurse entered, with a glass of water for the doctor. "Technically, it's good for the health," said the doctor, simply. Eric nodded. He loved to be made, confidentially, the intimate to such inside dope. He advised remedies for ailments the doctor never dreamed of; but the latter was kissing his nurse in sibilant frenzy, wearing out her lips with passionate vitality. She screamed, and ran from the office with her skirts flying. The doctor admired her stubby legs.

"On with me," Eric strongly hinted, annoyed at being disregarded. "Oh yes, you," the doctor replied, and fixed him with a glare. "For you, I give a lecture. Listen to this, attentively. It's a case I studied as an intern; I wrote a doctorate thesis, on my analysis. But I wasn't officially a matriculated student, so they discharged me for disrupting classroom procedure. How I wept! Till this day, my revenge was inactive; on you, it's practiced."

"I'll die?" Eric asked, alarmed at this eventuality. "No, just sit back; it's not therapy, nor catharsis, just a term paper. I must have my audience, and you're it."

"But does it apply to my grievance?" asked Eric, with his fastidious precision. "Certainly. I wrote it, prophetically, in anticipation of the symptoms you demonstrate!" "May I hear?" Eric requested, with a little boy's obedience. "Certainly, my child," said the Doctor of Internal Evil, glancing at his script in a trembling display of nervousness. To cure it, he gave Eric anesthesia, to put his listener asleep. Then, no longer hesitant, secure in conquering all criticism, he read loudly (for Eric was gasping in choked snores) this important medical statement, in a voice proudly bursting with insight into the moral nuances of recent psychological breakthroughs, featuring the enlightened absence of innocence:

"The conscience is a container for guilt. I knew someone, whose tiny guilt seemed practically lost in the enormous spaces of his conscience. But someone else had but a small conscience, whose walls were jammed and trembling with the packed mass of guilt inside. For proportion's sake, they traded corresponding parts, and thus bulged with the same empty unbalance, but in reverse. Evil remained operative, and sin's stubborn sense of remorse poured out the suffering of atonement. Thus change retained its internal changelessness, and the nature of self-accused immorality was shaped the same, in the sad human guise. The torture-machine inherent as the soul's private punishment prolonged torment in the usual emotions, which specialized in bliss's rarity. Happiness functioned in a miserable discontentedness, and was severely short-changed as an ideal. The advancement of imperfection developed unimpeded, in the worldly perfection of its progress. Who's to stop it?"

At the uttering of "it?" Eric violently awoke. "I'm cured, purged, Doc," he declared. "Subliminally, it worked," boasted the physician of human badness. "What's your rate?" Eric asked, suddenly suspicious. "For you, a bargain," said the business scoundrel. They haggled, and wound up cheated. From Eric was minused the dollars that added plus to his therapist's enriched wallet and, on that transaction, they closed the deal, parting terms in coolness akin to impersonal animosity. "Did you cheat me?" Eric asked. "Not one bit," said the charlatan, directing his patient to the door, from which point Eric received a fitting departure, being flung down and kicked, knocked to the pavement, a discourteous gesture socially unceremonious. "I deserved it," Eric said, gloating in hurt glee, thankful for each bony ache. "How splendid simple pain can be!" exulted Eric, whose wounds rang about him in a swelling chorus, a festival of bruises, a merry displeasure in the physical realm of sensation. The contrasting purity of soul was worth this excruciating humiliation of the senses; it provided Eric with the loftiest release in the chronicled pre-death moments of his explosive spirit. God, being in the neighborhood, greeted him with casual equality. "How exalted my rank!" Eric spoke, on behalf of an ambitious soul. Heaven would be a fine outfit to join. It did flourishing business, despite periodical turnovers of personnel; it was a going concern, and Eric, with his sales experience, could prove an invaluable asset. He'd get to know the territory, and win undying promotion. And maybe, some day, he'd be God's heir, and run the whole works from a well-placed central office. "Felldunger's executive stature is undoubted," the praise would ring, among corporation stockholders, whose dividends would multiply. "But having attained to such a height, wouldn't I slow up with complacency?" Eric worried. Then his progress would slide backward, until the familiar thud of the pavement would echo on his favored backside, releasing evil pains and other diabolical stings. Pleasure, that primary virtue, should become his permanent possession, the chief prize of his power. Then the problem is to conserve it. Its loss is no mean thing, but gives rise to so embittered a complaint that paradise is defined by the extent of a pleasure regained. It pleased Eric to forego pain. On this negative goal he focused his metaphysical fury, in painstaking dedication. On the keyboard of his moral nerves played dexterous fingers; strains of cosmic dissonance converted Eric to religious inclinations and other high-minded states of a supernatural, mystic order. God had replaced guilt, as the most consuming echo.

Next month, Eric was still on the road. There was no reason to be. He had been fired.

The firm had sent a new salesman to replace him, and repair good will along the broken route of Eric's commercial delinquency. Eric evaded him, leaving no forwarding address at the better hotels; for now he put up in low-quality shacks, where inferior lice bred and cheap wine lingered in the stale breath of the uncouth boarders. Prematurely, Eric flirted with poverty, despite his providential bank account, the savings of his sunny successes. He apprenticed himself to a saint's ordeal, as a resolute journeyman, working his way through his favorite alma martyr. Gradually, he'd graduate. Then, God will have an up-and-coming rival for the lucrative religious market, jeopardizing His monopoly. Free enterprise, which had spawned Eric, was now used on another plane. Eric was a candidate for an angel's wide-flung wings, as horizons beckoned with luring repose of infinity. Their values as real estate, not yet assessed by landed opportunists, represented a solid investment in invisible mansions of the future. Eric would buy and build, from his resourceful capital. Since when was ownership a spiritual handicap? Eric was greedy for intangible gain.

Meanwhile, the site of his body's days remained world-bound. Yearly came four seasons, succeeded by the next year. Slices of time were cut from eternity's endless loaf, that had risen in the yeast, and was yet to set. Eric ate himself middle-aged, as the well-bread embodiment of time's abstract tendencies. His new occupation could only be called "former salesman;" even its bonus was unremunerative. Prosperity, as a worldly accomplishment, took place more and more in the past, and was fast becoming the least active principle of Now. Thus, Eric submitted to Change.

However, he still lusted; fewer women succumbed, but those who did had to last longer, and were used more often. They were never pretty, but Eric had sworn off aesthetics in his simplified economy of a life radically reduced to its non-essentials. Spasms of guilt afflicted him, after each debauchery.

He stayed longer in each town, loafing and drifting. Short of God, he was aimless, and found oddments of leftover gratifications to console his impulsive abandonment to the wild vagary of whim. Instinct warred with conscience, and guilt intervened. He denied himself no outlet, then glibly phrased a prayer. He tricked conscience by sinning with its back turned, then protested innocence. He learned to get away with what he committed, and escape consequences. If not accused, he keeps his impunity intact. In one of his missions of iniquity, he chanced upon a fellow hypocrite, who needed no introduction to say, "I was once a social worker. But I terminated the career, and became a reprobate, as more suitable to the natural bent of my character. As an outcast, I can afford to be objective, and see where misjustice carries. It's more fun to find fault without conceding to the compulsion to reform. With no solemn purpose or sacred mission, I'm free to indulge my propensity, here in the shady habitats of man in the seamy underside of the world, to laugh at how some guys shake off a rap, while others are pinched. Like once I did a little daring piece of wrong, I admit, but trumped up the evidence, to revenge a grudge, on a guy who was wrongfully accused but lacked the wit to convince the law how it was I and not himself who deserved retribution. And that wasn't all. With my typical pair of guts, feeling sorry that the bum was so lonely, I legally offended the jail and the whole crime system by daring, sinner as I was, to pay the ironic courtesy of a visit; though the ones not locked up are the most hardened and successful criminals, and the fall guys jailed as scapegoats for the rest of us, like Christ on a cross, were probably too innocent or nerveless to make a slick getaway unpenalized, with all the loot. So justice is like the survival of the fittest, and little by little the innocently clumsy fall into the ways of extinction, while the cruel and brutal survive with smart distinction, honors, and a crooked set of sons and scheming daughters, that sneak in and out of the law like a tricky pack of sharp crooks that earn the role and rank of society's most upstanding substantial citizens, imprisoned comfortably outside our arbitrary jails, breathing the contaminated air of freedom and subduing, at all levels, the non-official off-the-record remorse that trickles up from a crushed conscience. Yeah, I know I didn't get away with being rich, but I'm out here, while he's in the pen, that unlucky sucker. Don't you think that's inequity, for him to pay, without conscience, for what I'm unpunished for except by my own guilt? I tell you, because you're a stranger who won't stay around long, and if you talk I'll kill you. My crime is concealed. The penal code is unjust. There's no fair apportionment; but he'll get the best afterworld assignation, and I the worst, maybe, to even the ledger and balance account. Now look, there's a pal of mine—see?—he's a judge. Come here; let's talk to him. He frequents these haunts because he's a regular guy—though he's worse than most. But respected? You bet. Open to graft or bribe any day.

"Hey Judge, come here. Talk to this guy, will you? He was born tomorrow, and don't know nothin', as the saying goes. He needs to be set straight, as well as a shave and haircut. Ain't it true, Judge, that rewards and punishments aren't allotted properly? How do you dispense a verdict, and deal out a sentence? Do you allocate, depending on merits and deserts, fair play to all comers, with impartial heavy-handedness? Or are your callous ethical standards cynically arbitrary? Inform him. He won't tell. He's one of us, a bum. Your court decisions are famous. Yet you're kindhearted, with your orderly dispensation of the law. We all love you, Boss. What you got to say?"

Winkingly, the judge said, between furious puffs on a smoking manly cigar, these judicial words of honorable confession, punctuated with polite regret and philosophical renunciation of humanist ideals and other goody-goody dreams kindly impractical in intention (He was a big man, and gross, smugly pompous, self-assured, and girt with ill-begotten money, puffed up; he reeked corruption, and was its principle exponent.):

"My heart is in the right place, but at the wrong time. So when I'm kind, it's always to someone who's just done something not to deserve it. To correct the disorder, I deal out cruel punishment to a victim who merits nothing but kindness; and everlasting harmony reigns without interruption in a world uncomplicated by poetic or prosaic justice, however evident the case may be. No one asks for perfection, but must imperfection be the rule, the steady and daily rule? How un-ideal. Something is out of order. Is it correctable? No, possibly? Foo. Space, time, good, and bad ought to join within unity and organization. A little more justice, hey?"

His impromptu audience laughed, or they would have been shot down. Prosperous vulgarity personified, the judge was. His henchmen had bulges in their suits, lethal iron. Eric was scared, and meekly mild. "I want him to like me," was the first thought that survival dictated, and a wise one.

"He's not fit for his profession," he thought privately; but no one had seen the thought, so he survived. It was a close call.

The main thing is to escape accusation from the outside, and indictment. Do what you will, as long as you don't get caught.

But what of self-apprehension, self-condemnation, self-conviction? —that internalized exposure of guilt, the superego: how culpable one is, in its eyes! It severely makes one inform on one's self: an internal spy system. (Eric had fled to another town; his safety was grateful.)

He looked within. Nothing there, wrong place. So he looked outside, and found a fellow willing to talk. It was in a crummy bar. The guy was nervous. He kept looking at Eric, with some imagined resentment. "What's wrong?" asked Eric, somewhat defensively. "Me," the answer was.

"Why?" said Eric, cool. "My conscience has a million people," said the fellow, who was thin and not very big, "looking in. They inform on me. Or comment. Or respond, in some form. I'm a marked object of non-indifference. Each thought I think is examined by outsiders. And whatever I do, my conscience either applauds or boos. I can hear it, too." "You an athletic performer?" Eric interrupted. "No privacy," he was told; "a big stadium watching my every move, analyzing it. And on Sundays, a double header." "Then why don't you go on strike?" baited Eric. "Too much, as it is, I'm striking out," said the fool, who was peeved. They drank, and shook hands, taking leave. "Am I as crazy as he?" Eric pondered. There, in front of him, was an abandoned blonde. He kissed her. Soon, they were sitting on the same stool. They were observed by drinkers. So they retired, for privacy.

Into the world's condemning eye. From mankind's collective guilt, what could one man, and a woman, hide? Conscience was a public document. The retribution is universal. Redemption occurs on an open stage. Self-testimony is heard by the jury of the living population, and the sin of one is visited on the entire race. Eric released the blonde, and didn't dare to walk the street; he'd be seen, and his secret would be shown by critical daylight into a glaring popular view, the scandalous topic blaring on all tongues, exposed by foreign dialects and an unsympathetic press. Wrong-doing was obvious; no one was fooled. Eric hid tight, and kept to shadows. He poured himself a scarce rationing of breath, so as to be less heard. Outside was a clamor; hunting dogs were inducted, and pressed to the scent; the threat was boldly coming closer.

Eric fled. He entered a mental institution, as a visitor: they wouldn't suspect his purpose. "Who you visiting?" asked the guard, while polishing his bayonet with soft rubber foam as a glistening instrument of delight. "A paranoid," said Eric, swiftly getting out of that one by a flash brilliancy of thinking. "There are several," said the guard, in a voice halfway divided between malice and humor. "I want to interview the most confirmed, notorious, far-gone, incurable, and actively dangerous," dared Eric, with audacity that paid little heed to safety. "Can you present a credential?" the guard required, jotting down a note in a memorandum pad, and so discharging the duty of his post. "My courage," answered Eric, bristling. "A handsome attribute," the guard commented, stepping aside. Eric passed, but he felt a rip in his sleeve. It was the bayonet's tip, having inadvertently been caught there. "Pardon," said the guard, whose sadism was on display with rather jocular relish. Eric was scratched, before the bayonet could be dislodged. A few drops of dark blood presented him with a panic; either he must faint, or whistle. He chose to be indignant. "Unhand me, sir," he said; "I happen to be a citizen, and my taxes pay your salary. Therefore, I employ you. Guide me to a talkative paranoid, whose confession I'm eager to hear. Then retire, instantly!"

This was done. The corridors were white, smelling of electric shock. Crazy eyes peered through the bars. Screams poured forth from all floors, and other symptoms of mental nightmare. It was exactly at the thrust of visiting hour. Eric was admitted to a big room: its walls and floor were padded, and the ceiling too high to endanger its occupant. There, in the center was a man frothing. He wore the standard pajamas, and looked suspiciously at Eric, as much as to ask, "What you want?" The guard left them together, as cozy companions. Of furniture the room was devoid, or of any other article, however practical or decorative its utility or design. The door was locked from the outside, but sounds of listening indicated that nothing said would be unheard from without. "You're a paranoid?" Eric asked, cautiously. "Paranoid is an adjective; *paranoiac* is the noun," the uniformed captive revealed, with mild ferocity and other alarming manifestations peculiar to a member of the occult cult of insanity. "Oh," Eric said, subdued, as though his knuckles had been rapped and his abuse of English chastised with castigation. "But you're neurotic?" Eric inquired, and was relieved to hear, "That's correct." They were getting on famously, with singular rapport. This worried Eric: was he in the same class with a wild madman, imprisoned by an official institution? What an irrational supposition. "Are you a stranger to logic?" Eric asked the wild, overheated beast in front of him. "By no means," was the gentle reply, masking the deliberate insult. "Not the least offense was intended," stressed Eric, with reasonable force. They sat on the floor, for there was no chair. They resembled sailors, sitting cross-legged. It was bad for the heart.

Eric ventured to say, "Strokes of conscience from within are externalized, and consequences of retribution are feared from the outside. It's a dread that disturbs peace. But we're safe in an asylum, so don't be worried. I'm harmless, and too cowardly to strike you. What's your mental affliction? How are you disturbed? You're here because of upset emotions. I understand you, for I don't feel so fit in this category, myself. Be friends with me. You sound like an intelligent man; along the way, something went wrong. A misfortune has deluded you. Please tell me what ails you: it won't be held against you, or used to your malicious destruction. I'll be fair, and merely listen. Now tell me how you see people, and what you think they think of you. Do they mean harm? Have they joined in a plot to do you in? What's your opinion, seeing how central you are to this subject?"

"It won't be printed?" said the inmate. "Unless you first die," implored Eric, injecting the personal note. "A likely event," said the sad man who reasoned in subordinated conjunction with his aberration, his distorted hyper-fear of being blotted out by phantoms of his own conjuring. Then he whispered a vile oath, bit his lips, and pronounced this verdict on himself:

"I shrewdly try to angle out this world, and chart its bumps. Hidden assailants, behind unseen weapons for my versatile and complete persecution, wait for ripely times to do me in and molest my artificial patchwork peacequilt, disturb the woven threads and unstitch the pattern. I'm watchful with only two eyes, and wage vigilant blindness with my remaining impediments of vision, assuring my sight of remarkable insufficiency and so dooming my defense. Others wish to attack me, that's clear; my guard is openly down, and I present an easily focused target centrally convenient to any conspirational enemy for whom my downfall would give him vigorous access to joy. I may be soon spotted, and done with, away and for all. A pity I survive, to apprehend such immediate doom, and die in retaliatory advance, murdered by expectation. I live by temporary junction, and the roads of my removal come perilously near, closing to foretell the deep imminence of my disaster. People are so cruel, I know; friends betray me, and plot and plan the rotation of my fall, as I alternate between a tragic fate and a dire destiny, and they clamp a unity of destruction down on me, to oppress my downtrodden ways and dog me under, devoid of a fair or fighting chance to uphold the guilty innocence of which, illegally, they throng to accuse me. I maintain what they do, so we concur: then let them get me, rub me out, and eradicate this detested conscience. I'll help them, as the first to honor the attack against my maltreated skin to which is attached the soul complete in villainous blame, waiting to receive its penalty and accept, from all concerned, the immense gift of my punishment."

"Can you relate your former history, to show cause how you came to be this way?" Eric bargained; the paranoiac's revelation had been incomplete, and not explanatory enough. The door clicked, and the guard came in, preceded by his trusty bayonet, sparkling in the dismal air. (The room was windowless, and got light from air holes, invisible to the eye, at the corners of the ceiling. This was considered sanitary, as well as morale-uplifting; it represented progressive aid to those determined to be mad. Scientifically, it was supposed to help the victim concentrate on his indigestion. The flaw in this theory was the lack of food on which digestion could malfunction. Thus, life was cheerful, indoors.) "Hello," said the friendly guard, "did you have a nice chat?" His smile was generous and radiant, like the sun of nostalgia's heyday. "Yes, of course," Eric said, as well as the patient. "Would you like to change places?" the guard asked, glinting mischievously an eye-twinkle of arch brutality, like a cat preying on a dead bird. "You hate me!" accused the paranoiac, backing up. He raged, and for his conduct took pains to receive a jab from the bayonet. Sedately disciplined, he saw with fascination a drop of blood emerging from the wound, like a red-clad king striding out of his palace. The guard chuckled, and took great delight in the fine points of his job. The salary might be low, but some compensations abounded, on staking one's initiative. Said Eric to him, "Please conduct me out. " "Out where?" the guard bickered. "Of here," Eric insisted, and was escorted by the tip of the bayonet, so that he had to dash to keep ahead of the guard, who wielded his weapon with deft sureness and a light, rather spry, hand. "Goodbye," said Eric to the prisoner. The latter, in return, suggested that Eric remove himself to far hell, where the climate was ideal. "He's not treated well," decided Eric, to dismiss the case. "Pay me," said the guard, as they neared the street exit. "With this," said Eric, slapping him, and being pricked by that persistent bayonet as a rather sharp retort. He ran, and made good his escape. The hour was fading dusk. Nearby stood a park. Like a fallen drunkard, Eric stretched out on the grass. It seasoned to be late spring; there Eric, the former greeting card salesman, reflected about everything he could think of; how busily blank his mind was!

The tree over him had big leaves. We'll, that's the tree's business. Why should *he* worry?

"That paranoiac tried his case in his own court, and was self-convicted; yet he protested the legality of the verdict, and demanded to be sentenced to less guilt. But by behaving as though persecuted, he confirms, by increasing, his own admission of guilt. So he breeds more of the ill, by acting on the basis of the ill. It's a killing cycle, and I only hope that his therapy is advanced, and radical. Thank God I'm not he," wound up Eric, rejoicing. Then he reviewed himself, and fared little better. "I'm my own crime," he concluded, after examining his known soul and testing random samples from its unknown deposits, deep down. "I hate to be me," he said, looking about. Observing wanderers, he envied no one. "I wish I didn't have to *work* so hard to pile up all this guilt; it's a stiff role, that of a bad conscience, and the responsibility to replenish it is arduous and exhaustive. Can't someone perform my evil *for* me, and carry it out with better grace? To be a sinner, in the professional manner, is quite a job; couldn't I hire someone to do all the dirty work for me, while I get the discredit, and retain my evil reputation? I'm too lazy to be always sinning, though heaven knows how many bad acts my guilt needs to absorb per hour, as strength-producing nourishment to keep its vigorous constitution robust. Where can I find a real master who, with discretion, can do what I get blamed for? Then I can still "be" evil, have my conscience working overtime, and yet take a rest! What a scheme, to relieve me of hand-soiling, soul-defiling labor, while adding to my store of guilt! It's an idler's paradise, the devil's commissioned sinecure, free-loading on hell without being actually evil myself. Whom can I delegate? I'll consult the classified pages of the telephone directory, and see if his services aren't listed. Ah, what work I'll be spared, what desperate deeds I can clean my hands of, to await the result! I'll capitalize on sin's profit, while leading a virtuous life! This reverses all known creeds of hypocrisy. I'll revolutionize vice!"

Eric looked under "Crime Committer" and found only one listing. "As a monopolist, he might charge high," he meditated; his bank book could only quote a low figure now; his savings had been all but depleted. But Eric still owned a car—though it looked like a monstrosity—and wore what was once known as a suit, shirt, and tie. His shoes scantly negotiated between feet and ground, so hole-ridden was that ancient leather. Eric often slept in his car, and "bathed" in public lavatories. The values of his society were not exemplified in *him*, poor soul. But how God-closer he was, having traversed the worn path of guilt!

Next morning, owing to a misty misconduct of the skies, a hazy unclarity curtained the weather. Most prominently veiled was that chief source of sunniness, the sun. Under such conditions, which it termed "adverse," it damn well refused to shine, for no matter what. The clouds snickered, and huddled to confer. Their plot was ominous and thick. The outcome was rain, more rain, and still more rain. Down below, Eric became wet. "It's raining," he observed, getting the message.

The day couldn't exactly be called bright. Eric phoned the Crime Committer, and was told that no appointment was necessary: he only had to "show up," and the deal was clinched. "For how much?" Eric asked, but was hung up on. "Obviously, he has customers aplenty, or he would have been more polite," Eric observed, calculating his monetary distress. He drove up to the office, and took the chance. "Will he charge me for an *estimate?*" Eric worried. How bad to be hard up. It made one pause, and things seem inconvenient. Necessity, however, was adamant, regardless of expense. The secretary showed him in, where the waiting room was crowded with standees as well as sitters. "Perhaps his rates are popular," Eric hoped. He looked through a magazine, listlessly leafing its pages with vacant perusal. Hours, interminably, glided by. "Your turn," alerted the secretary, who led Eric to this unusual servicer of psychic needs. The individual was plainly dressed, and bore himself nondescriptly. Except for what he was, notice would hardly pertain to him. "You look poor," he told Eric. "That's me, all over," said the impecunious patient, smirking wistfully, with a reticent shudder. "My services come high," he was told, with direct bluntness. "Then, in detail, could you describe what can be done for me, in what your labor consists, and with what predictable outcome? I must, of course, deliberate, so to receive your prospectus in advance would help me to decide. Have you a printed pamphlet, stating your proposition, and for free?" "Gladly," offered Eric's would-be moral agent who'd intervene, as a broker, between a guilt-laden soul and the acts themselves that must freshly earn the devil's decisive approbation. The one-page prospectus, printed with white type on the red paper, was handed to Eric, whose eyes dilated with trembling and whose conscience suspended its uneven breath as, hesitantly, in the bold blush of timidity, he read these strangest words of practical religious intervention, and ethical passivity, he had ever encountered in his lifetime of literate theology:

THE PRIVATE SOUL'S NEW IMMUNITY

"I commit other people's crimes for them, and do the acts that they are blamed for in the guilt of sin. Then, my opposite, Christ, redeems them of the hole I put them in, and absolves them (while they stand passively acted on, first by me and then by Him) of the perpetual responsibility, the shame and moral wrong, in which I represented them. Thus caught in the middle between me, their evil-doer by proxy, and Christ, Who atones for that evil in His greatly publicized suffering, the people are deficient in the do-it-yourself rage that is *said* to plague this most self-reliant age. But really, everything is done symbolically for them; so what can it matter what they actually *do*?—having delegated their power.

"Their conscience is a mental appendix, in the obsolete progress of evolution, and must be surgically rooted out. Those amoral creatures!"

"But aren't you hurting your objective, in satirizing humanity?" Eric finely pointed out, looking up from the paper. "People love to be debunked," was the answer; "their neighbors are incriminated, with exposed folly, just as they are. I tell people what they want to know. Their image is low, of themselves. So they need intermediaries, for they're unable, in the sense of being incapable. I collaborate with Christ, and people stay at home, nursing their receipt. Why not? Would you call my service an exploitation? Don't be silly. Humanity is feeble. It was weaned too long; their salvation is at long-distance, by installment: I call it "Grace on the Absentee Plan," and have processed it minutely. So, is it worth while for you to pay? Or does your poverty forbid it?"

"Your method presupposes, or postulates, a belief in Christ," remarked Eric, monetarily scrupulous in the affirmation of a gravely devout orthodoxy, to conceal his reluctance to pay. "Your scorn of evolution, in the final paragraph, insults me personally; I consider conscience a boon to man's progress. You give no examples of your service, but only vague promises. And how did you contact Christ, to agree on that double-deal treatment of man's moral cycle? Why would He conspire with the likes of you?"

The window was a picture of inclement weather. "Go home, and do it yourself," and the agent dismissed Eric. "That's what comes from being broke," said Eric, in a self-aside, as he gamed the rain and reached his car. He roared off. "When Sunday comes, I'll see about Christ," he pondered, planning June salvation, for the good of a world-tired soul. Sky-water formed rolling puddles on the dents atop his car. He rode to another town.

It was where his mother and father lived. They were as many years older than he as before, despite his own "coming of age." "Where you been?" they asked.

"Away," he said, entering the door. The car was parked in the garden. A few stagnant pools of water collected on top. The rain had dried out, and come to a stop.

"You look unprosperous," said Mr. Felldunger, eyeing his son. His wife, seeing that this was true, fell to weeping, intermingling tears with prayers to ease her maternal negligence. Had she given birth to a failure? What a waste of dutiful pain! No other son or daughter had she formed into creation. Eric was all they had. He was their heir. "Dying soon?" he asked.

"Not yet," they retaliated, pleased at their ancient health. "You'll go first," they even insinuated, getting nasty. "No," Eric said, in a voice that feigned youth. His parents cackled, naughtily. "Can I borrow a loan from you?" he asked. "No," he was informed. "May I sit down, and eat dinner?" "No, please leave," said his doting parents. "Are you retired?" he asked his father. "More legitimately than you are," was the reply. Being unwanted, Eric left. He loved his parents no longer.

He rode through the night, to another town. On the way, he stole gas from attendants, without paying. It was his illegal way of fighting poverty.

Then he remembered he had forgotten something. He returned to parents. "What, you again!" they gasped. (They'd expected another twenty-five-year interval between visits from so chronically absent a former son.) "Yeah," Eric said, trying to gain admission. They barred him, at the threshold; the door was open an inch, and they peeped out. Hearing their voices was all Eric could see of them. Those invisible parents, irresponsible for a wayward son. "Couldn't I have more love?" he asked. "Yes, but not from us," he was told. "You treat me cold," he observed. "As deserved," the reply went.

"What did you come back for?" demanded the father. "Don't be so stern," warned Eric, forgetting that an irreparable bond existed between them, of blood kinship and primal descendancy. "I'll call the cops," threatened the father. "No. Could you instead give me advice?" Eric implored, from a genuine genuflection of the knee. "Arise, knave," commanded his father, imperious and haughty, like a God disdainful of his inferiors. Eric did as bidden, and was told, "Never seek advice. Wherever you go, in all your travels as an itinerant wanderer of the modern automobile, take no opinions, accept no influence, have no heed to others. That will safeguard your independence, and will stress more reliance on your own self-sufficiency, a man trading on the experience he himself collects, ordained by an internal will. Take my advice, and you'll be better off. Now go."

"But Pop, please help me. I'm so lonely." "Here's a dollar. Don't spend it, and it will always be yours." (The bill was slipped under the door, as a safety precaution.) Eric stooped, and picked it up. "It's money, thank God!" he said, pleased to have made a profit. He turned to give lyrical utterance to his gratitude, but the door was shut with tight lock, sealed to an intruding panhandler whose shameful sense of honor was well omitted. "Well, I got something out of them," said Eric, fingering the hundred-cents piece. It was a lovely denomination of paper; too bad the number printed on it was such a low one. "So far as money went, quantity was basic," Eric calculated, shrewdly regaining his business sense. "I used to be a salesman," he remembered, "for greeting cards," he added, to round out that autobiographical precision. His occupation was never forgotten. He, now seeking Christ, had won a flirtatious bout with Success, only to be punched out in the second round. He drove a long way, and stopped somewhere on Sunday. He bathed in a park fountain, and found a suitable church. It wasn't open yet, so he waited, until morning should be bloated into proper piety and the minister arrive; he'd join the congregation, be preached a sermon to, and be God-delivered. What a fate, and how heavenly was his destination's fond ambition! But he was sleepy from driving so long. He had stopped along the road, to nap. His clothes were actually foul. His pew neighbors might turn up their nose, then. But June wore gorgeous raiment, a plentiful adornment to nature. How that tree spread out! He sat on the steps to the church. From the distance, he could see his car. It received a parking ticket, which meant a summons, from a passing policeman. It begged to be ignored, but he'd have to travel far; the law's arm stretched long, troubling Eric in his mind. It woke up his conscience, which yawned and went to work. How it would plague him, and unsettle his peace! Alas! But the sun was ablaze, and the sexton, a weak, lame-footed old man, unlatched the church. Eric was hungry. The soul was free to feed, but the body cost plenty. Wasn't that disproportionate?

He remembered his father's advice, not to beg advice. He followed it, since no adviser was handy, the church deserted, the sexton attending his offices. It was clean and pleasant, this Sunday morning.

The stained glass window allowed the sun. It gave one a holy feeling.

An ordinary man entered the church, spoiling Eric's blissful solitude. The man was walking toward him.

"Are you so religious as to observe Sunday?" asked the man. "But Sunday is invisible, it can't be observed," stated Eric, seeing nothing but sights. "Once I was waiting for Sunday, but when it arrived I was in another town," regretted the stranger, who appeared anything if not ordinary. "Sorry you missed it," Eric commiserated, bored by this whole conversation. He suppressed a yawn by cramming ten fingers in his mouth, but they belonged to the stranger's two hands, who yelled, "Ouch!" "Did I bite you?" Eric asked. "Yes," said the man, showing bleedy tips. Eric spat out the fingernails, to have done with it. It had been, as aggression goes, a very satisfactory attack. "Hasn't the churchly sanctity been violated?" said the stranger, whose hands hurt. "Why did you come so early?" Eric asked. "To take a bath, and envision, receive a visitation from, the Lord." "Who, God?" asked Eric. "Who else?" shrugged that name-dropping stranger who liked to walk with the great. "He speak to you?" Eric wondered, pinched by jealousy. "Yeah, He scolded me," the man had to confess. "Is that so?" Eric mentioned, now somewhat curious. "Tell more," he welcomed, as they stood near a holy image: the plaster cast, bust and all, of a saint-idol, who, in the old days, had been martyred. In front, a candle burned.

Nearby, stood an altar. It sure was holy, inside the church.

Eric questioned him more closely. "When was it?" he asked, assuming it had been in the past. "I was being kind of bad, see, and it was tormenting me. I mean, I got a conscience, like everyone else. Why exclude me from the guilt department? Anyway, I was sin-haunted, and sought redemption."

"Through Christ?" Eric asked, anxious to learn the technique. "I went a step higher, to His Pop," the stranger boasted, sanctimoniously; "or rather, the Old Man came to *me*. I was so flattered, I'd nearly faint." "But wasn't His wrath evident?" Eric asked. "Sure. He was irritable, that's why," the guy said. The tone was apologetic; he sincerely wished to be good. Only his own nature prevented him.

"And it happened on Sunday?" Eric prompted, fishing for the full story. The stranger guessed this, and asked, "Want to hear more?" "Why not?" asked Eric, matter-of-fact. He subdued the show of too tense an interest, to extract a more relaxed confession from this visionary who claimed to have been spoken to by God. By now, worshipers began to arrive. So for privacy, the two "friends" stepped outside on the glittering lawn. In the process, they disturbed a bird; the little citizen of the air, offended by their bad manners, made a swooping dive, after rising, and let loose. But Eric and the other fellow were too absorbed to notice. Their hair had a patch of a foreign color.

Oblivious to being splattered, they stood in the sun's steady path, fully illuminated. "Go on with it," Eric advised. "But why confess to *you*?" said the stranger, shifting to suspicion. "Because you gave me a hint. Now I want more," said Eric, with clenched fist. His attitude was decidedly pugnacious.

"Very well, then," meekly objected the other. Eric was taller of the two. The Sunday bells rang. More churchgoers arrived, stepping up the path, while Eric waited. The stranger sighed. "Cut out the pause," shouted Eric, "and tell me what God told you. Damn it, I want to attend service. So get along. Deliver!"

Frightened by this bluster, cowed to submission, the man narrated this crucial episode in the life of his personal morality, when God saw fit to intervene. His voice, quaking with scared hesitation as Eric glowered over, described this deep inner sequence:

"My soul was in a mess, and first I tried salvation. It didn't work. When Sunday arrived, which is God's weekly birthday, I took a bath in an empty church, and came out all black, and feeling bad. That was no good. Perhaps a crime was on my conscience, and was haunting my guilt to pieces. My soul was rapidly deteriorating, and things were getting worse. My agony was so complete, I managed a little laugh, for evil effect. I must get on.

"At once, a vision occurred. God said, 'Sinner, get the hell out of here. You're spoiling the world. Your offense is odorous, mangling the sensitivity of your neighbor's nostril. I advise you to quit.' Then the vision stopped. Well, God was direct. Without an ambassador, He Himself stooped to deliver His message. Yet His words wounded. They hit home, and, even were I to obey them, death would sorely result. What a hideous malformation of things. I nearly went nuts. In fact, I did. Which of course promoted my insanity, and led to craziness. I hate being a product. Yet that's what I was.

"On Monday, the day after Sunday, somehow the world resumed, and I didn't feel bad. Some kind of empty vigor was restored, at just my speed. I sort of got into step, and saw the day through. Good going."

"Is that so?" said Eric, in pointed commentary. What an interesting Sunday tale. "And what's the moral?" he asked.

"Consult the sermon; it should start soon," said the stranger , whose wrist was self-examined for a watch. It was time. Suddenly, this strange man, in a startling transformation, dipped down the neck of his shirt with a sure finger and pulled up a collar: he was a clergyman! "Now for my regular sermon," he said, heading for the pulpit. How embarrassed Eric proved to be! He had wronged a rector, or minister, with flagrant insult! How tedious his misconceptions, how flurried and inexact his conduct! The service began. Should Eric attend it?

He had administered injury to the preacher, in ignorant abuse. But was he expected to penetrate identity, spy an unworn frock, guess divinity? He wasn't that talented, theologically, and knew no magic formula.

He fled, not wishing to hear. He started up the car, and roared to another town.

His hunger was acute. So he robbed the charity box in a humble church, unnoticed because the congregation was wailing some mighty hymns in such a way that one would have thought God was deaf. The mice scampered away.

Sunday wasn't over yet. Eric ate himself blue in the stomach in a restaurant that specialized in food. An abdominal bulge was the result.

Then he sat in a high park, waiting for sunset. It was due any second now.

A flourish of clouds preceded it. The florid procession featured the sun. It sank, transforming the earth.

He thought about God. Wouldn't he ever meet Him?

Perhaps not without an introduction. But his contacts were few, he knew no influential people, now that he was down and out and cast from the world's favor.

Though there were plenty of benches, a stranger preferred to share his, and abruptly sat down. "Were you just thinking of God?" he asked.

"You must have amazing powers!" gasped Eric, "and very keen insight. Could you explain your station in life, and to what I owe the honor of meeting you? You're not dressed well. Are you as poor as you look?"

"All of that," admitted the stranger; "can you buy me a meal? Then I'll tell you of my friend: God."

"Can you introduce us?" Eric asked, relenting to a social-climbing impulse. "No, He's out of town, on business," regretted the stranger, who was honest for a bum. "But if you treat me to a restaurant, I'll describe, from personal acquaintance, some facts about the Almighty, and reveal the lowdown. How does that sound? A bargain?"

Eric consented, and let the man order six courses in a seedy diner. Stolen money would cover it.

Cheered by the fare, the tramp said, "I'm an intimate buddy of His; we carouse together, as boon companions. He's my all-around pal. A great guy, if you want to know. And he's not conceited, and he don't put on no airs, but He's just like us. He's out of town on a business trip, but He's really everywhere. There's not a place you can name where He ain't been. He really gets around, that Guy!"

"You speak so familiarly," Eric remarked; "have you no respect? Surely you place Him above you?"

The vagabond, tattered and ill-kempt, couldn't deny this. But he was a great believer in, and voter for, democracy, a state of affairs that gave the lowest equal equality with the highest. This principle raised him to his present perch.

They sat over coffee. Their booth adjoined a night-darkened window. They fell to being silent.

Eric asked, "Has your friendship with God made you religious?" "No, God leaves His professionalism behind, when He consorts with me," the hobo declared, entertaining generous sentiments. He peered out the black window, seemed to detect something, and then, in the style of an orator, inspired by a vulgar excess of ultraworldly joy, feeling the fellowship of all things in common, suffused with a deep sense of his Friend's immense vastness, he declaimed in great round syllables on the most eminent Being known to the wondering unknown on the mystical outside of the mundane scope of man's God-mingled mind:

"God isn't concerned with religion alone, no sir. God cares about people too, even such as you and me, though we aren't lawyers, presidents, or archbishops. God, you see, is democratic, and was one of Lincoln's most influential supporters. Let's praise Him; it doesn't matter how. He loves atheists, too; also Negroes, chickens, and cows. God, in other words, is universal. But He's sometimes homey, too: He visits farms and superintends the crops; He visits factories and improves the efficiency; He visits the honeymoon bed and invents new strokes. God, you see, is everywhere. There He is now. Catch Him!"

"Where?" and Eric looked outside the window. It was too black to see.

"Right in your heart, there's where He is," directed the feasted stranger, absorbing his digestion. Inverting his vision, Eric made no such discovery. He felt cheated.

He scolded the tramp for having equated Negro humans with chickens and cows of any persuasion; an apology was forwarded, soothing his nerves.

He should have faith, and believe! That would cure his ills of doubt.

His dinner-guest bum, disdaintily, was extracting rot with a toothpick from stumps in his mouth. To avoid puking, Eric searched the air, with skeptical hopelessness, for a passing view of God in flight. His sight returned, empty.

If God had abandoned him, he'd reject God. This cold dose of reason would rescue his fallen pride.

With his inner temple destroyed, all outward things were barren. Decadence was in constant display; rampant corruption scored a field day, razed harmonies exhibited their crumbling ruins. Belief was clownish, and absurd. Nothing holy was sacred anymore; or else, the least and mere of anything was holy or sacred, by exalted inflation of God's general decline. Values had surrendered their absolute, and were now pathetically relative.

In disgust, he said goodbye to God's undistinguished friend and repaired to his car. It was hard to start up, due to internal disorder; then, the lump of garbage whizzed away, bearing Eric, its disconsolate driver, morbidly in need of a shave. He drove beyond the night, and landed in Monday, July's time elsewhere.

Pulling up, he parked the heap, and skipped traffic. He ignored the summons ticket, having torn it up; what had he violated, since laws were not the rule, and rules had no law, in his private immorality? The absence of God had disappointed him; his was a bitter quest for strife, a menace to peace. Trouble brooded, in stifled agitation. He'd be capable of an action humanity would regret; privately, he'd gloat to create misery and distribute some of his excess hell among undeserving customers for having dared to live, or even coexist, in his own lifetime's exquisite misery. What foul revenge should he perfect, what feat of enduring malice? He was in the market district, scaring shoppers because of a brutal bearing. Office workers charged out for lunch; seeing Eric, their appetites flopped down, like a fish tired of struggling; he radiated a poisonous banality, a kind of cosmic venom. Instinctively, all avoided him, as though his presence were something incomparably vile, fell, deadly. Murder was not one of his impossibilities, during his present state. Palpably, God owned no substance; nor was He a ghost within. The outward void, and his vacuum inside, negated Eric doubly. Whose counsel would save him, what solace would administer balm? Evil fed on itself, chewing him Godless. He meandered to the slum district, and spied a soapbox orator, who was a reformed priest now given to lay preaching on secular matters in which the deflated figure of God was pathetically stripped of omniscience and shorn of effective intervention. The lecturer was a huge grizzly man, hardened by the world, with an obviously disappointed soul. Somewhat of an egotist, he was dressed like a laborer, and appealed to simple folk. His audience included students and other intellectuals, for the speech was riddled with paradoxical forms of irony and an exalted profession of cynicism, in grandiloquent language surpassing human understanding. The crowd was gathered around the soapbox, and Eric took a close position, listening as though these words would determine his life's fitful plight and allay his ambiguous remorse. The speaker called attention to himself, with boisterous assurance, and assertive pugnacity. He said that nothing could be certain. Ideals were debunked, and death warned about. God was scorned, roundly, for enduring beyond His time in a debased state, hanging around pitifully, seeking a power forever lost. Faith is a subject for believers, but God Himself lacks it. Man continues to ply his own nature, in discouraged idealism. The picture is bleak. The hulky orator, in a colorful summer sweater, a handy man with his fists and conceited in the mind, hands out these words over the rapt heads that surround his pulverizing skepticism that batters brutally the Infant of hope and light, in sneering condescension. His harangue exhibits those sharp upper teeth, as these sentiments, so world-weary in their triumph of disillusioned regret, crash softly on the collective comprehensions of the crowd moved to the thrill of such forbidding godlessness, voiced by a renegade man of God whose disinherited heaven spurns comfort and clutches the negative underside, in despairing rapture, of an ignorant warmth whose sacred protective covering has worn off, shoving fact into life's opened eye, the nihilistic gospel of bare experience disenchanted of dreams that so fluttered where now the images stand distressed and barren:

"I only pretend to be affected, but I'm honest by nature. All my insincerities add up to the truth, through multiple subtractions. And the truth is part of a great lie, a fabulous inconsistency. In a similar way, life is one side of an enormous death, an inferior dimension of it. Death itself belongs to something inconceivable, a sunrise supremely overwhelming the imagination. Beyond that, surely, awaits another surprise, like a bear behind a mountain bush. Ah, we can stretch on. So let me wisely conceal my smile, and the fawning world be servile to that superior adding machine, my brain. Pardon me, humanity only faintly disagrees with me. If I puke, I drown my human meal in an excess of tribal glee, the zeal of my race. Read my facial expression, if you will; isn't everything summed up there? Or if not, just read it in. I articulate, as a vehicle, all known pressures, the truth-lies that churn to the emotional upset of our digestion, since our favorite world fouls the nest of dreams with dung that breaks the egg before the song of the rainbow bird can be composed and hatch.

"Too bad, isn't it? Don't blame my fault, I only came along when it's too late. I tell you, don't believe too much; cherish a few ideals, suck them against the milkfast of your breast, and when they grow up, and bear the fruits of reality's toil, kiss the humble, sun-worn earth, and praise, up high, Old Man God. He made us all, including the imperfections that might unmake Him. We'll bite His hand, by whose crafty art the ugly beauties of our existence were carved and undone; and the fast air we breathe, conscious in degrees of our pains and pleasures, spills back into the wasteful vacuum, and our souls drift free.

"'So what?' you might ask. 'Your attitude is intolerable,' I answer, and slap all your faces, with the decisive effeminacy of a gnarled aristocrat whose blood, by blue degrees, decays in a backwash of corruption into an ocean of degeneracy, the black tide of democracy's onward progression. Let's breed, and preserve ourselves. Always, we must survive. Remember that. Pass it on to your children, those inferior creatures of our selfish love for reproductive pleasure. Born on a panting bed, shaken out of a laboring mattress, an infant inherits the hate of love, and its crippled health strives toward the flower of maturity. Oh, drink the pure air. It's pure, you damn bastards, pure. Drenched with the uncanny sun, our golden days halo us. What a mockery. We are the professionals of sin, to protect our amateur rating as Sunday practitioners of the deceitful arts of deliberate virtue, ringing from the clock of a towerful bell. With every breath, we catch disease. We stink, and rot. To perfume, we laugh. Our flesh is a riot, our mind a hole where cynical pus collects in disgust, ruining immortality forever. God stands by, and watches, with helpless passivity. Worshiped, He explains, 'Myself, personally, I'm an agnostic. I believe, you see, but yet, I don't. Faith, that's the thing. I ask you to have it, to cover up for My own doubt. You have to understand Me. To understand is to forgive. Have an open mind. Mine, it's closed.' Then God bows, and we all boo Him. A few devils yell, 'Encore.' But the curtain is closed. And God, or His impersonator, has died, in real life. Only religion remains, and a few devouts. To sort of sing the praises of His memory. Songs, lifted up. They fall back down. Because gravity is the law. The world has new rules, but we're sentimental. The past ruins us, for we sob with nostalgia, and ignore present opportunities. We're loyal to a regime now out of power, and are crushed, annihilated, disgraced, by our modern oppressors, whose forces and tactics exploit our short foreconscious and the long slope of buttocks that incline to the sweet life of our birth, when candelabra halos lighted nimbus brilliance like the sad angels on a Christmas tree, lit up by agonizing electricity. Wake up. We face a new dream."

The speech was over, and hands clapped. Then came the question period. Eric, in need of a shave and not otherwise well groomed either, in his unwholesome appearance, doubted the true death of God, and voiced this reservation. The speaker threatened Eric for dissenting, and begged him to accept the contents of the address as an article of faith, a goodwill grant to the authentic dogmatism of the author of so wide-flung a lecture. "But you advised us to despair, to dispose of outmoded ideals, and cease to believe. According to you, God is absolute—I mean obsolete. How were you so sacrilegiously ever ordained a priest, as a title you've blasphemed and a role you disgraced, now that you rail in abomination against the conservation of archaic purity, which the busy world has, layer under layer, crushed and all but extinguished, man being only but a man? Answer, you bum."

Eric had said this, a defiant tirade, while meanwhile the soapbox of the speaker caved in, giving vent to a sprain in the region of the leg, whose owner howled a roar of healthy pain. The crowd dispersed, leaving Eric to administer balm and improvise a splint. His efforts were ineffectual and the victim died—but not till nearly half a century later. That showed how delayed his reflexes were.

Eric was out of gas, with no money. And his belly tank needed food fuel, if his own locomotive was to gain the incentive to keep on going. The town had an employment agency, to which he applied. The way he looked, the prospect was limited to manual labor, on a tedious basis, where he would acquire physical fatigue. He was hired, on the spot.

The indignity, for an ex-sales representative of an actual greeting card firm, to be reduced as a sorry figure in degrading employment! He dug a ditch, under a whipping supervisor, who lazily lashed him all the while. The July sweat oozed out. Eric was a bearded hireling, a wage slave of fiery degree. But what he earned, he saved, save what was stuffed into his empty guts. In two weeks, all but dead, he purchased gasoline, and drove far off, into an adjoining area of that large national region. He slept, fitfully, on the road—or alongside, to assure decent safety. Mingled in his dry dreams were visions of God's wonderful glory, as a traditional Western myth. Driving by fields of immense agriculture, he tried to picture how God was, at present. These times must be awfully hard for Him. Yet survival was part of being immortal, so God was in some state or other, a mystery that would yield to the sturdy pressure of research. Now Eric was a scholar, to investigate piety's personal center. He pulled up at a library, around which had grown so vast a city that enough people resided there to justify the upkeep of a "house of books." Eric headed immediately for the theological section, ignoring fiction and other compilations of creative endeavor. What was the latest on God? A recent book, and not a daily newspaper, might supply this exalted information. It would make good reading.

The Celestial Being was obscured by devotional literature and gospel tripe, thwarting Eric's objective. He consulted the librarian: an old maid who wore glasses. Her dress trailed to her knees, which were knocked. Her ankles were dense with hair, and her shoes very spinsterish. She wore a brooch, on top, and unpainted lipstick. Her nose, in itself, was overlong, like a sign indicator that pointed to a prominent direction. She was thin beyond belief, which ought to indicate how thin she was. This gave space more space.

That caricature of a female personage, keeper of an orderly collection of tomes and volumes as a public service to bookworms, was seated at her walnut desk, carved from a tree in her native land, a habitat from which her location had not been removed, so steadfast had her whereabouts remained in conformity to the past. "Yes?" she motioned, for Eric was standing in front of her strict line of attention. Her voice squeaked, like a door being slowly opened, despite stagnant hinges, in a house haunted by hereditary ghosts that were joyless and given to perpetuating horror with livid vocation. Eric paused, frightened. He looked a sight. He felt, momentarily, agelessly old, or else precipitantly young, so carelessly was time lodged in the transience of that temporal situation. The breathing moment was soon dispelled.

Eric fumbled with his voice, which had taken the occasion to break in hoarseness. A window displayed summer shadows.

"Well, Ma'am," began Eric, in a dilatory fashion, without evident conviction. A slow hour unwound itself, unruffled by that tremendous dialogue.

At the corners of the room, dust curled, or seeped, on venerable pages of interminable volumes. Somewhere, a faded dictionary began to sneeze.

Eric interrupted the swift conversation to apply his homespun handkerchief to the stricken lexicon, and wiped its wordy nose. Several verbs came off, not to mention a rather technical noun. Eric folded the learned handkerchief, so vocabulary-soiled, and thrust it into his abridged pocket, for later reference. Knowledge was an acquisition casually come by, in the lax formalities of day-by-day chance. Eric had slackened his discipline, drifting toward wisdom with no special diligence. He'd get there, by a course so slow it seemed motionless. Movement, at a microscopic inch, was sure, compared to a mile's speed in the moving telescope. At any rate, Eric soon came about to state his problem, while the listening librarian deafly pretended to hear. The words were consumed by the air, and made no dent on comprehension. The entire message was uncommunicated, at its precise tone of delivery. This cut wastage to its irreducible maximum.

Eric had not made himself clear. Before he tried again, the assistant librarian intercepted his troubled words, advising the scholar to explore a big-town library, where the likelihood of books was greater.

Eric thanked him, with much effusion of courtesy. Then he bowed to the librarian herself, whose flat rate of dignity took on haughty airs with the brazen pouting of a flaunted coquette. She winked, and expired.

Eric headed toward the big city. The library there would be so capacious that God would be trapped in residence, catalogued in a cell of print. While driving, Eric remembered how the librarian had minced. It was hot weather. His beard was breeding insects. And on his mind, topping the whole deal, was the tenacious idea of God. Never was thought more cosmic.

He went to the central branch, after reaching the exciting city from the vicinity of that populous metropolis. He was referred to the Theology Department, and took the elevator up high. It was self-operated, and he felt serenely independent.

An eccentric character officiated at the desk, nominally a clerk, but also a receptionist, God's literary agent and public relations representative, altogether a very responsible post. But the job was poorly paid, and ecclesiastical poverty burdened its narrow-shouldered occupant. "I'd like the lowdown," Eric began, "on the incumbent God's ancestral delineage, the derivation of His authority, and how He usurped His way to power. This commercial coup, so hushed-up as a post-historical scandal in high places, should depict the present title-holder as a fraud Who purchased Lordship and rules in outstanding vulgarity as a heavenly parvenu. Please refer me to the source, so that I can confirm this information with salient detail forbidden to the common reader. On what sacred shelf of enclosed biography can be disclosed this disgraceful exposure? I won't betray this secret to the world that's being victimized by that power maniac in Whose reign this century transpires. Don't tremble. If the book is protected under lock and key, trust my discretion; my intention is pure: to attain knowledge, not for exploitation, but for the pleasure of my old age, when the bitter acid of irony shall yet preserve my years. Don't deny my curious curiosity, nor deprive my emphatic wisdom of facts so delectable that all chronicles pale and falter that omit reference to an outlawed and condemned truth that I alone seek. My pursuit depends on you. Please yield."

"Sir, the information you want is decidedly a secret affair. The author memorized his passage, and all printed copies were deleted, branded detrimental to public morals, and burned at a celebrated bonfire. But we've bottled the smoke, for you to sniff. And we've preserved the author. Consult him, at so tenuous a risk that I'll ring him in (for he's on call) and arrange a sound-proof booth for the interview. This is all but fair. Information *must* be disseminated, despite the official ban. The procedure is illegal, but libraries are self-ordained. We retain the privilege to confer wisdom on whoever applies. Then accept my gift of knowledge. I'm authorized, on behalf of learning, to permit you the right to your own blasphemy. The rest is conscience, but beware of God, in His vindictive mood. He's capable of the most extreme spite. Enter that door, be seated, and wait. When the author arrives, request of him what you wish. He's demented, but that shouldn't invalidate his story. On the contrary, insanity possesses uncanny insight, intuition on a divine scale. Follow instructions, and you'll avail yourself of this auditory service, which the library provides free of charge. As atonement, for burning the book."

After cordially thanking his benefactor, Eric repaired to the room indicated. It proved to be dark; strain as he might, Eric couldn't see the author, who had also arrived and was seated facing him. In blackness, they traded white words, out of print.

The booth was overrun with smoke. A jar had been opened.

"That's from the fire in which burned my book," the author elaborated. Eric listened, from a cracked chair.

"I anticipate your story," Eric ventured, "and in fact briefed the librarian with an outline that displayed what I have the right to expect. I trust your memory is not rusty from abuse. Then ingratiate me with a fine rendition of this tale. It forms the occult splendor of a myth."

The author was intrigued. "The saga has been so guarded, residing only in my own person, how'd *you* get an inkling to it?" he inquired, highly mystified. Eric admitted, "I'm psychic. Besides, the truth deserves me, so I've discipled myself out to it. God has been in my bones for years."

"That's well said," confided this bookless author who'd committed the burned-out words to his solitary head, where his memory had its lodging and stored up the story. "Should I pitch right in, with no prelude or even an approximate introduction? If you'd like, discussion can wait upon my termination," offered the discharger of so impending a shocker that the world's ignorant public was protected from so unpleasant a contradiction to their assumptions. "Thank you, all at once; spill it," commanded the former salesman of greeting cards. The author rehearsed his voice, for sound effect. He hummed a few notes, in off key. The suspension gripped Eric. He stretched his hearing until both ears were implicated in one united attention to this crime, which a crazy man would relate. It began innocently enough:

"The beefy man with the delicate interior, having sipped from both mammalian breasts of his favorite neighborhood tavern, has lost what the taste of logic feels like, and is busily stumbling after his equilibrium. The equilibrium, like a swift dog, is allergic to his fumbling grasp. He catches realms of fantasy, superb vistas of womandom, deep stretches of magnificent views, sheer photographs lovely and inspiring. Transformed into an artist, he lusts for a model. Compressing himself into an oversized kiss, he attaches his rape upon the face of a huge woman, who drops her stinking glass of beer, and calls upon her husband, a professional midget, to save her honor. The drunkard nearly kills the poor little guy.

"The victor won her spoils, and gave her a walloping love when he dragged her into his sizzling apartment. Their exhaustion made a heap of dead tissue. The air, poorly ventilated, kept echoing their recent odors. They piled up in a mumble of snores, and dragged a confusion of limbs upon a rambling shuffle in sleep, ugly and thick with the peace of morbid passion. Then the midget and a parcel of police, having traced down the uncouth bum's dirty apartment, tore through the ill-hinged door with war whoops, and descended upon the pair caught in adultery. Bringing up the rear, with bulbs brilliantly flashing, came a battalion of photographers, eager for the truth of pictorial proof, to keep a world standing honest in its mudbath of scandal.

"The guy was sued for his shirt and his undershirt, the whore tank of a wife was overthrown with insulting divorce, and the midget quit his circus job and got a position as a martyr with a religious outfit, and came neat to work each day sporting a brilliant halo, the idolatry of widows both far and near. The religious business perked up, and the handsome midget worked himself up through the hierarchy of angels, and finally, just as the profit motive threatened to expose his success as basely materialistic, he bought out God Himself, and set up shop with a handsome office right in heaven, overlooking our taller New York buildings, with a view that took in the prosperous horizons of our busy little world. During His regime, the business cycles stopped being so depressing or inflationary, and the ranks of the unemployed, because of capital punishment, became less each day. Warfare was abolished, and in its stead a militaristic peace was established, which depopulated the working population because of its purely disciplinary routine of exploding advanced hydrogen bombs. This had a crippling effect on juvenile delinquency, which correspondingly reduced the police force, and lowered the pension burden on the long-suffering taxpayer. The crime rate steadily decreased, and the earth, finally, was reduced to two people: Mr. Adams and Miss Even. Theirs was a natural law wedding, as unglamorous as possible, attended only by a snake. For wedding feast, they ate an apple. It went to their head, and taxed their immoral temptations to the limit of resistance. They went to bed, took off their fig leafs, and re-evolutionized the world. Species after species flowed from their fertile loins. Finally, birth control was introduced, sponsored by Mr. Malthus, which tended to take reproduction from love and substitute mere pleasure. Out of this Freud evolved the pleasure principle, which set loose a new wave of licentiousness that wiped out all preexisting morality. Lawyers, judges, and juries, overworked, set a new fatigue endurance record, and a deep reaction made religion exquisitely fashionable. Churches sprung up everywhere, and debutantes affected nun-like behavior. At a society ball the hostess masqueraded as a Mother Superior, and was attended by her illegitimate children superior. The new God, weeping with delight at His progress, almost slipped from His silver windowsill in His beaming heavenly mansion, so smothered with mirth was He when viewing the merry proceedings that philosophers wisely call folly from their secluded distance."

In the black booth, the author had stopped. Eric couldn't see him, but saw a floating picture, overhead, in depth, to illustrate the proceedings narrated. It was an image, projected either by Eric or the author. Blackness displaced it, and visual silence filled the void.

"Was that an extract, or the total story?" Eric broke out; what he'd heard had been a confirmation of his own divination; as though a modern legend, packed and ready, had been capsuled in as a birth legacy, along with the purely physical genes. "It's what you make it out to be," said the creator of that fable, or its scientific discoverer, with ambiguity suitable to the unscrupulous occasion. Eric requested a review, to undistinguish some clarities as a general tendency to blur. He liked being weirdly unsettled.

"Can you blunt the sharpness?" he hinted, broadly missing the point. Both of them, frail creatures, were well in the dark.

The air seemed haunted. Each sat in a ring of space, linked in vagueness. Momentarily, the world lost its orbit.

But found it, the next instant. Happily, humanity held on, in firm recapture of its teeming collective life. Cycles revolved, day and night alternated, all was as it was. And would ever be.

Eric thought of the story, and summed up: "The key figure," he recalled, in the dark enclosed booth, "was that dwarf. He got beaten up, by that big lump who infidelitized his wife. Then the little guy bought out the Deity, after climbing up the totem pole ladder to mankind's ruling myth. Attaining his ambition, he thinned out the population considerably, to work on a new turnover. The numbers were reduced, ultimately, to our two sparse ancestors, who then began a new race. That led us to our present crime, through routes of devious decadence. Broadly linking history, evolution, and theology with one sweeping family myth, my dear bard, you've given us humanity's lost-and-found tribe in the ritual of its highest up and lowest down, its liquidation and restoration, presided over by the one smallest God ever to unleash a terrible retribution for his own painful loss of pride over another man stealing his wife. That was in his human guise, before ascension. His revenge was awful, personal, and complete. He had swallowed the humiliarity of the inferioration of his masculine usurped role; and he redeemed his size, for now none's taller than he. But we're speaking of our Father, are we not?"

The author admired Eric's summary, and they two, in the blackness of a tiny booth where no light was shed on them to see with or be seen by, shared in a secret legend, known only by them both or either, of the King's illicit background, Heaven's degrading past, the unstable Power that reigns above. They sighed. How had they known it?

Through clairvoyance. Each, through his vehicular mysticism, had had the revelation passed through him. But their knowledge was doomed never to become popular. They were the sages to the Unknown.

Their communion was over. Eric was told to leave the booth. The author remained.

Eric thanked the official librarian, but not without registering a protest: "Why'd you tell me the author was mad? I found him eminently lucid." The librarian smiled, like some mysterious idol preserved from the time of multiple deities, and said, cryptically, "It was you, sir." "But I heard *him* recite it," Eric corrected. "But you never saw him," insisted the librarian. "That doesn't make him me," Eric maintained; "the room was entirely black, from his arrival, through the narration, and till I was told to leave. He's there now, himself." "No, he's where *you* are, in you," insisted the smiling librarian. "Infernal mystic!" Eric called him, and stalked out. "I'm through with stories," Eric impatiently cried; " now I want to come face to face with my God. Or else, acquire a new version. Who is He, that Wonder One, Whom in guilt I sought, and in redemption shall secure?" He stayed in the big city, earning a job as a messenger, despite his prophetic beard. His car was in the scrap heap. It had broken down, and been stranded, then hauled away, from where Eric parked it. Now, he was on his human feet. He lived in a flop house, true to his professed humility. But at least he ate regularly, no small feat. Life was hastening him to death. And still, he had seen no God.

But been told plenty about Him. Belief postulated Existence; Eric wanted to see for himself.

With the car no more, it was redundant, he felt, to have collected so many unpaid parking tickets, speed detections, license-revoking ordinances, and other traffic passports of driver delinquency. By having spread his whereabouts in so many towns, he had divided apprehension from directional pursuit. So he wrapped the court orders in a bundle, and drowned them in the river that fed the city. Thus, he was liberated from justice, and free with undetected anonymity; his name was one of many names, and all names spelled one.

He was fed up with enigmatic libraries; he would seek God in the woods.

Outdoors was more appropriate, since nature was rumored to be at God's source, His primitive root. Taking up this cue, he joined the Hiking Club, and took weekend trips, tied to a knapsack that fit on the upper part of his back. It restored his health. With kicking vigor, his health knocked him cold. It was too vital for him.

Luck was with him. A doddering member, in full fledge, of the same hiking club, turned out to be a rebellious nature lover who organized a cult of Natural Piety, of which he was the supreme president. He was a retired professor who had been a historian and won some kind of reputation. Now, he tended to rival God.

So he studied up on his Rival, to be informed about the nature of his Competition. It was going to be a Sunday sermon in the forest, with this amazing preacher grappling with the Almighty. A path would be cleared, in the brisk season between autumn and winter. The Hiking Club members were cordially invited. Some reporters would accompany them, to scoop some religious headlines. Beavers and birds were also invited, and whole squads of insects. It would be well attended, and the speech would be lengthy. The great event gave rise to moving expectations. Eric was fully prepared to learn.

What a wonder it was to be! The speaker was reputed to be a self-lover, who'd conduct group therapy on how God was even more human (therefore less godly) than the flattered listeners. The outcome would be confidence in self: a necessary lesson, and beneficial to one's well being. It would instruct, as a practical guide.

The egocentricity of the preacher would counteract God's awesome power, so that the struggle would be even.

But would God get a chance to answer? If so, the revelation would be welcome.

The great day arrived; the hikers plunged through the forest, roughing it, and gathered at a clearing, where, nearby, a brook rippled (or was it a stream?). Sunday had dawned, with brilliant effect. Eric puffed, being out of breath. He nibbled on a sandwich, for needed nourishment. The moment would be enormous.

Logs were rolled together, for a platform, which the speaker mounted. Quite a vigorous old man, and vain as any youth.

A hundred people constituted his audience, the majority being hiking fellows. What arrogance, that the sermonizer would try to equal the Lord! Was he worthy even of contention? This was disputed. Then a hush grew in the woods.

The speaker steadied himself on the logs. Ominously, they rolled, so some vine creepers and twigs were used to tie them together, by the sergeants-at-arms. Sun decorated the meeting, and rippling shadows overhead. The early December weather was dry, sparkling, and mild, and visibility could be seen for miles. The view afforded distant mountains. It was a God-inspiring scene.

The old man stood tall, surrounded by people and trees; his platform of logs shook no more, but held him steady. Huge pines bristled overhead, roaring at the clouds. The shine of the sun poured out vivid patches of gold and blue, relieved by white and earth brown. Sense perception quivered, eager to consume the words that were well awaited.

To downgrade his Opponent, the speaker would resort to petty gossip, as a scandalmonger, mudraking the love life of the Lord. He'd defy his Enemy, with scathing boldness, despite his frail mortality. He was too liberal to be traditionally overwhelmed by the fame of his Adversary. Yet he'd beg God to protect man's (and his) survival, and to help purge man of dependence on so capricious a Master. Would God cooperate? Or would the message be in vain?

At least God's emissary was present, the diplomatic corps of His clergical spokesmen, representing each denomination. Then, they'd send a report back to Him.

But would they interpret the speech uniformly? Creeds differed, to begin with. No one reference framed the scattered multitude of ideas. No Law was singular. Chaos ruled concepts, doubts and beliefs formed a formless disorder. The one word was lacking.

Under such handicap, the Natural Pietary cultist would labor, fighting misunderstanding with mere words, like a boy throwing wooden airplane models at a well-disciplined, fully equipped, desperately armed, rigorously led, modern army. So the speaker would "appeal" to his deadly Enemy, after assassinating His character and defaming Him: requesting equality, but plotting to supplant Him. Would the deception work? But the crowd was getting unruly. No more stalling. They were in readiness. It was sermon time.

By way of introduction to his long-awaited chronicle, the speaker prefaced a remark that all pronouns pertaining to the Subject would be assumed to be uncapitalized, since God already had so many advantages He shouldn't be given another. As it was, He was favored to win; the speaker would give Him no quarter.

Then, the title: either *The Sometime Adventures of God*, or *An Aside to God*. Or both. That cleared up the formal business. Eric acutely listened, packed close to others on whom the words would descend. A bird twittered, and was told to shut up. A mighty hush swept the forest.

Eric hoped that God would appear Himself, in defense. Words of Him were substitutes. It was tedious to hear *about* Him; why not the real article, Himself?

Man presumed to know, or defy. That's natural. Eric wanted to invoke the Real Thing; and actually catch a Glimpse.

The speaker would evoke the image. But would it be true?

So many competitive listeners crowded Eric, he found himself lost. But his ears struggled to hear:

"Today, like all the many yesterdays, God is in the habit of being a man. He comes, and goes, just like a real one. He's, when the occasion strikes him, religious, thus deifying himself.

"One day, atomic devastation struck. God fled to the mountains. There he lived like a hermit, fasting for want of anything better to eat. It interfered with his digestion, leaving him almost as emaciated as his Son, who had become a man and had been severely tried. God lacked nutrition, and his body, borrowed for the occasion, began to complain. He elevated his thoughts, and approached divinity that way, through a sort of mystic martyrdom. But summer came, to chase the atom away. Civilization prospered, and God chose commerce, to try his hand at an occupation. It profited him not, and he had to beg, borrow, or steal. As a punished public enemy, he spent time in jail. There guilt deflamed his evil, and he walked out a good man. To praise, he prayed. Himself, he got the message. Saved, and full of grace, he walked away. Rescued by a forward sky, he drifted on high. Now, his manhood forever unassailable, he lives confined in heaven, married to a lusty earthly wench. She penhecks him, and he, for his part, advises her to escape to hell. Being materialistic, she refuses to move. God looks down, and sees evolution. But his wife is a fright. Lately almost pathologically divine, he lives once removed from his skin, and pampers the soul part of him. This thrifty guarantee of a future, gaining immortality, both consoles and atones, and with a set heart he braces himself to endure. He looks clean shaven, to avoid being confused with unsavory types. Of medium high height, and fair in the disposition of his skin, his behavior is more youthful than his age, and can be strikingly modern at times. Morality interests him, and he pursues that science to an extreme. For hobby, he's taken up expert gardening, but the seasons weave their tyranny, molesting his brightest plans. He fell in love, recently, with one of the sweet young things that tempt the genius of the earth to have their birth and growth fairly promoted. Out of vengeance, his wife is seeking divorce. Being childless, the couple has no recourse. Now, God is a widower. His lecheries are harmless, and antiseptic. Even now, impotence is assailing him, and the fear of a senile old age. The earth has gathered her glory, and doom is raining decadence on it. God prances with his little mistress, and loves her huggly, having been prompted by a monkey gland operation, which has brought out all his infantile qualities, set his glee roaring anew, and rejuvenated the keen edge of his joyful faculties. Oh, how exhilarating. The world, below, is crashing. The cosmos is stopping, and orbits are silent. Man is seeking extinction, ruining his self-survival. But God giggles and cackles, sounding almost inhumanly effeminate; and Creation, which at one time had been his masterpiece, has suddenly gone berserkly abstract, dropping culture to its highest low ever maintained by corrupt achievement. Oh God, save us. But he's lazy, and we alone can do it. Yet we lack the means, and have an uncanny ability to fail. Successfully, we all fall out, and for prize must embrace the oblivion whose scorny smile freezes the tears as we pass. What an ungainly fate. God, being otherwise employed, is beyond helping us, and at most molests or hinders us. Well, we have lost. The game was played tragically, the work has bitten the hand of the doer; and man, which is an experiment, falls steadily beneath his God, who topples behind him, racing him in even odds to the next perch on the descending circle where wounded existence at once declines.

"God, I call you once more. Unless you help me, I'll disown you forever, and damn your obscene soul, you useless waste of an empty image, you obsolete symbol, you shadowy contempt of substance, you flattering and ungainly miracle against whom I am but a mirror exposing you, while you reflect me, and the world crashes between us both. If I leave you, we both go, and as you lack your servant, I'll miss my slave, for we both draw pictures of the other, which modernity distorts. I devalue you now, if I lose my life. Won't you interfere? Try, and wield your power. I'm weak, and depend on you. Or grant me the strength to dispense with your services, and I'll uncreate you, and begin the myth all over. Reality is so plain, I can never see it. You have damaged my eyes, and in their stead have described a church, whose Sunday praises afford you sweet lullaby. Wake up, so that I die. I want it clean. My own spirit would be pure, but for you. You are the disease and the crutch, unless, by amputating you, man grows whole again, and derives a new innocence from the sin of experience without guilt, thus elevating him to a simplicity which, by itself, controls the spinning of an alien earth. Remove the sun, and you are helpless. You are a common man, God. Stop putting on airs. I hate to be your underling, and detest your preaching. Why don't you die, and surrender the beauty and truth to my own mind where, learning the proper qualifications, I'll harbor them against the hour when slovenly decay comes biting at your work. You've had your fun, and been the most of a man, at his maximum least. We interpret you; please stop fooling, and thrust our life beneath our feet on firmer footing, so when we slip, the downfall shall be sublime. I call your bluff. I love but myself; can't you, with your legal mind, understand this vanity? Score things my way. Lead everything to me. Set it up, be fair, and let's have a ripping good happiness together, get starving drunk, and intoxicate the infirmament, like grand old pals, each as equal as the other, though your title is God, and mine, bless me, is one of your latest creature comforts, man. United, why, aren't we invincible? You bet. So closet me in you, and give my soul a super extra charge, just what I need, so what a bursting forth shall take place, more violent than spring, and sweeter than the scent of a winter pine."

The forest stirred. The sermon had hit home, and struck God.
The Sunday sunlight persisted. Eric raised his hand; the old preacher

asked, "What?"

Eric said, "You criticized God too much. What do you expect of Him? (I restore His capitalized pronoun.) On the one hand, you blame Him for being responsible for man's sad lot. Then you ask for divine intervention. You seek man's independence, yet you rely on the Great One to grant it him. And you reduce God to man's scale. Or elevate man, to where God would be. Your logic is tattered with inconsistency. You blasted nature, condemning it for corrupting man, whose purity you would want intact. Yet you believe in natural piety, and are in charge of a chapter of it. What do you want? Why not leave God alone? You're just sore that He neglects you. I wouldn't blame Him. You're a stuffy pedagogue, jealous of a power, for good or bad, which God owns and you'd like to have. And your humanizing of God, as a petty adulterer who duplicates your own motives and is plagued with impotence complex, is unfair. Where'd you get your information? You fabricated His image; it's not real. You're low, so you raze Him down. How dare you? Keep your place. He's too high for you to criticize. Your sermon was a flop. Do my friends agree?" And Eric searched the crowd for confirmation; he was hooted down, and the grave Sunday lecture, by popular consent, was recorded as nothing less than a positive affirmation of man's rising spirit. God had better be alerted, for man was overtaking Him.

As a holder of minority opinion, Eric was cast into underdog status. But no violence was inflicted on his person, in view of the leniency that Christ's pulpit disciple liked to be identified by. It was an excellent religious weapon, and would foster his ambition.

Had God turned up? No. Eric was tired of hearing talk about Him. A personal visit would be preferred, a celestial condescension for an interview. Then, Eric would ply Him with questions.

But men presumed to know Him, citing imagination as authority, having destroyed dogma and not gleaned a sanctioned source. The forest meeting dissipated into irregular, shifting, free-for-all talks, loosely conversational, on the man-like nature of the Comic Hero above, Whose villainy was notorious. The Lord was belittled, regarded disrespectfully as a joke. The preacher's influence toward diminishing His stature had roused disgruntled malcontents to agnostic malignings of their sole creator. Yet no lightning bolt severed those mockers, no thunder-call of wrath jolted sinners or disturbed heaven's serene countenance, the benign aspect of that day. Magic was out of date. Man was immune to threat. He debated where the Lord stood, and assigned Him to degrading servility. Man's ego was restored, now that nature was dealt with. Only science remained, to oppose man's dominance and resist his crusade on behalf of immortality as God's renowned replacement. Progress was sky-high, and the lid was off. The far limit swooped near, and God's domain was fair game. Metaphysics itself would be invaded.

Breaking up into split congregation, the Sunday prayer meeting dispersed. The hikers bundled up their knapsacks and wearily began to tread home. Reporters and clergymen, and others of a civilized cast, rustled through a path, obscured by natural trees, leading to a place alone a road where they'd parked their cars. They'd fly back in comfort.

The preacher, lion of the day, poked his way through the woods, led by a stick that supported him, lopped off from a sizable branch. He had chosen to accompany the hikers, as an exercise in humility, rubbing with the rabble. Eric fell in with him, to challenge the old fraud on some sore points in the theology-mangling lecture that had so upset Eric's equilibrium. From an unfriendly impulse, he heckled the other rudely, while they stumbled over dead leaves.

The dignitary's henchmen kept nearby, to protect their ward from slight or slur. Poor Eric spoke his piece to his equally bearded elder, not knowing how his words were being apprised as to their weight of balking dissent and other dangerous evidence of disloyalty, which would be met, at a signal from their persecuted savior, with some solid thumps of brutality from assorted bodyguards and dense but obedient thugs. Yet Eric yacked out his idiot's brand of ideology, heedlessly oblivious to the gentle fascist punishment that would correct his ill-advised pattern of speech. Both feet were well entrenched in his fumbling mouth, from which sore-infested orifice sported his silly vocabulary and sputtered his inane utterances dripping bile and recrimination, his critical rantings so definitely unwelcome to the victim of so unprecedented a verbal assault, whose blasted dignity was stretched to its utter boiling limit. Yet, in fairness, he held up a creaking hand, to hold off his embittered followers from belting this reprehensible flea Eric and battering him into a fine distinction of unconscious, where pulverized dreams would seep through his cracked skull and afford him delicate frenzy. Let Eric first talk, to merit each blow that punishment, to vindicate the pride of justice, held in fierce readiness of stroke. Then let those contrary ideas survive on their own, pouring from a bleeding vessel. The ghost, not the man, would be left in defense of already beaten-up principles, braving the stupendous right that might backed up in force of so armed a thought. Then, Eric would learn.

What had he, untaught yet, to say? Still harping on that enormous sermon held openly in the forest, Eric, matching the preacher stride for stride in their walk strewn with decayed nature, told him with voluble arrogance, "You shouldn't have raked up God's private past and made his amours public matter for scandal on the tawdry level of malicious gossip; His eminence is too lofty for you to fling stones at, and His name too hallowed for your taking it at vanity's worth, following your own petty scale. *You* sinned, not God; don't project. Blasphemy is not proper homage. Your personal survival is unimportant; God's scheme is too vast to include you. Yet you would be Him, and having gained your identity, obliterate the model. How you dishonor gratitude! Should civilization decline, must God pay the sacred penalty? To save your neck, you advocate that God should stoop to change places with you, assuming that mediation trumps up no truce. You beg God to help you be free from the need for His help. And how'd you pay Him for that? You preach an irresponsible doctrine that discounts basic ethics and forgets man's place. You want exemption from God's jurisdiction, as though, outside of His control, you could exist at all! Doubly you're a fool, and to be a knave compounds your crime. You hope that God topples down, to your immortal benefit as His permanent substitute. Dreamer! Yet, you woo Him at the end, and offer to support Him in return for patronage. You'd go partners, benevolently, with your Superior! You unholy cutthroat! You deceitful jackass! First you'd beat Him, but barring that, you'd join forces, on equal par! You're a crude faker. There, there's a moist spit on you, here follows another. May it fertilize your sanity!"

Eric was grabbed, and was in for a working over in the hands of the offended one's disciples, but slipped their grasp and threaded the woods in a shifting plunge to escape, darting at might and dash, pursued by a yelping pack. The hounds stalked him, as though he were a fleeing deer.

But he tore a match from his knapsack to flame to extinction the scent that fled behind him the more he ran for forward safety. A minor forest fire ensued, scorching the brush, but blown out by cold wind. Eric left no trail, ran at a steady rate of exhaustion, reached a main arterial road, and hitched a truck driver to ride him to town. But the vehicle blazed by, having spotted his beard. He looked like an eccentric, or a left wing radical, and his hiking rags did nothing to mar this impression. To be a hunted quarry, chased by the entourage of a maniac whose will was opposed to God and whose cunning wiled a revolutionary plot to usurp Kingdom's rule, was hardly a state to be envied for its security. Eric knelt down, and prayed. "Grant me one wish," he said, by the road's side, with cars whizzing by; "Come to me, ere I die, clad in Your Presence, so that, in my naked eye, I might behold Thy Form. Promise me just this sole boon. Amen, Thy Everlasting Grace."

Despite the inconsistent rhetoric and uneven terminology, God heard; only had no time to heed, burdened by important business that would brook no delay. He ignored the part (Eric's plea) to trim or expand the whole—the world itself, peopled by menaced men outdone by brother men in strife rank with hatred. The case was urgent; the world was declared an emergency area, and aid was rushed through the process of red tape in frantic haste; but bureaucratic bungling, in specially assigned intermediary agencies, officially mishandled the desperate priority of the world's plight. In consequence, ruin and chaos divided the globe, raping decency everywhere. God tried to restore order, with time's vulture spinning around. But insubordinate officials, deputized to administer His will, gummed up things further; the crumbling edifice of mankind was cored by a central flaw, where it was structurally rotten. Beams collapsed, supports toppled, sand slipped out of joints, the weak solidity was bared. God, held personally responsible as an inept executive, grew introspective, seeking primal causes. Under His closed eye, the ferocity of disaster, unchecked, in accelerated momentum, ran down to swift catastrophe. Man had only one recourse: to suffer. This he did, in all his plural fortitude.

His prayer done, Eric rose; but his act of devout genuflexion had been spotted by a speeding clergyman, who braked his car and pulled up. "Want a lift?" he asked.

Eric climbed in. "Where's your destination?" said the benign minister. "Heaven," replied Eric, literally bent on getting there. Though hell must be crossed, first.

"That's nice," mentioned the minister; "where you from? Been bummin' around? Time to steady down, partner." "I heard a lecture," said Eric. "Yeah? On what topic?" "God, I guess," said Eric, uncertainly. "Yeah? I done preached myself. My sermon dealt with God too. What a coincidence," muttered this taciturn servant of the Lord. "I'm headed halfway 'cross the country," he added; "joinin' me?" "Sure. Nothin' to lose," said Eric, soon asleep. He was moving across a belt of night. Black, the color of corruption, was in the winter sky. The host in motion had been a guest preacher, and was now returning to his own familiar parish, where resided his local destiny in its native colors. Eric, homeless, slept in huddled-up inertia that was no match for the progress of divine speed. They roared up the thoroughfare, and without passing one toll booth had entered Monday, letting Sunday settle on its ass of a past.

And traveled quite a while. It was daybreak when they arrived.

The minister (who called himself a bishop) ordered his wife to include breakfast for Eric too. The ambrosia was difficult for an unrepented sinner to choke down swallowed, so Eric fasted on, nodding at the table. Devoid of grace, he subsisted on no nutriment, but napped on his erect chair and dozed out a dream that showed himself greeted by God's hand, which he shook, though the Face couldn't be seen. Was death the only entrance, pondered this world-worn sample of cheated life not yet adorned by God's graceful visage, to the bright sight of that Immortal Being? "Bishop," Eric requested, as the clergical couple stopped chewing to listen, "where can I find a direct face-to-face contact to the instant recognition of God? Do you know a divinity-broker, a go-between to pander the passage of my extreme meeting with Him who made me from the heart of my beginning? This would be my introductory end to merely my life, to enter on the tide whose form is a whole continuum, a middle preceded and concluded by nothing but itself. My soul hates its underpinning of bones. It wants to merge beyond my identity into the flow that streams with All, the Scheme with a place for every particle. On such a Union, would I dissolve."

The bishop and his wife exchanged glances; it was their pronounced opinion that their bearded guest, author of that remarkable request, was altogether crazy, a fog-brain at loose in a whirl of lunacy without end. Such insanity must be stifled. It was their social duty to institutionalize him: an obligation immediately to be discharged, with no loss or delay at the cost of time. The bishop placed his phone call to local authorities (the rural low-life sheriff), who relayed the message to town, where the civic reformers would know what to do. But Eric had gathered his knapsack together and done the disappearing act. He wandered, to the far borders cornered in by four horizons like bedposts that hem in the drowning dreamer plunged in flight. He became an itinerant rustic, a hermit holy in wonder from hill to hill. Spring defrosted him, and he landed on nature's lap. Cozily, he hugged Mother Earth.

From man to mendicant, the cycles of his metamorphosis became complete. He begged alms at farms, was rushed at by bulls, pricked by nettles, quacked at by ducks, pitchforked by mocking hayseeds, distracted by weather, and hunted by his pursuit, somewhere, of the concrete semblance of God. His martyr-like transformation trained him to endure what had to be borne, stretched in elastic reception of what coded transmission the Lord would, primed in readiness, deem ripe to communicate. Eric Felldunger's attitude was protracted to a profound posture of waiting; his youth had stooped to clumsy malformed age; his bearded nest held a spoiled egg, rotten from bleached sun. Bent down, he listened to the earth.

What rumble would vibrate for him? What message, transmuted from the sky?

His humility was officially garbed in wretched rags. His flesh inched down to bony minimum.

His shoes consisted of his sole feet. His money pouch had been empty for weeks.

He plucked berries, milked cows, did chores. God eluded him, everywhere.

He searched. His wandering, in temporal space, drew his body to its close. Death would be a few steps away. But he was too tired to crawl them; he ate a cooked squirrel, and while the fire flickered he slumbered his soul to rest. His limbs were sorely sprawled.

Words flew all around. He woke, and would write them down.

For miles about, solitude was still. The day was heightened to heaven's length.

Hills moaned, from afar. Deep away, slowly in a valley, smoke-fur hung, frozen on waves of the merry air.

Eric had words to write, but no paper. His knapsack was ripped. Its contents, dismissed.

He took a twig (preferring it to a knife) and laboriously scrawled, on a section of God's dirt, in printed upright letters, engraved in brown earth for storms to dust over, these, his concluding thoughts (Behind him, the sun pranced down, guiding shadows from the slanting words, which he wrote kneeling, as though inscribing a deep prayer. A rooted tree stood by, and natural evidence of his land. From him to home, these mental words were made out in a faltering hand, received, like seeds to fertilize, by the soil's father-laden womb; struck richly to his first home, his carving recovered his heart's final ground; the unburdening, phrase by phrase, ground out, in leaking letters that pumped away his blood, his resignation to forego comprehension of God's miracle-enclosed mystery.):

A DIRGE OF PRAISE

"The seasons seem to move, and at weather's length they undo nature and do her again, in climate's slow rhythm. A tree obeys this process, and man sometimes learns, occasionally turns wise, discovers laws. The sea goes, unbroken, on.

"A bird has the sky to fly in, floating on his birth-gift. The sky performs a sun, heating the strands of grass. Light confirms vision, and brightens our path; by it, we read-explore the wilds of the printed page, where learning is stored. History has cultivated us, and we display a civilized nature. Inside, in the most painful, secret place, love guides us in a frenzy of frustration. We would be devoted, and bless, and light upon temporary objects. Beauty is a feat of being alone, suffering in the solitude of vision. How widely we would wish to share it!

"Insects crawl, and the remains of our ancestors are treasured in chemical underground while, in simple and compound elements, the ball we make love on whirls in mad space. At night, we forget it.

"How splendid that geography should divide countries! It makes traveling resplendent with variety, and we bring back trophies of interest. Home is where home is, in our temporary displacement. How well an airplane cuts the air, dividing dark from light! Engineers are cunning, in their scientific approach to nature. We live a little longer now, and bring a versatility to joys, recreations, and amusements, distracting life from death. Nature never has a perpetual seed.

"Real things have the most imaginary impact. A wound ever echoes, in a mind riddled with memory. When we gave pain, met love with scorn, and touched a vulnerable hurt, it resounded in on us. We have chambers of guilt, the bureaucracy of our conscience. There, we are imprisoned, at liberal salary, and many compensation premiums. How far are we going, when the going comes to pass? With whom, among the multitudes of other lonelinesses? It's a scared world we live in, a fear in depth of tones, wide-ranged colors. Peace is the goal of action, the holy residence of God. No wonder we place God at a distance!

"My breath, converting air to human essentials, lives further to an increase of thought; ideas are abroad. What is the best one? Somewhere, scattered among the many. We get it at remote. What does it say? It speaks, in so plain a silence that our deafness communicates by understanding. We would scream. How harmless that would be.

"Nature, I was once you. How I am graduated! Beyond recognition, almost. So deeply away, I may never again be found. In such strenuous absence, I plead with you to continue. Create, while the formula still works. Make beautiful things, to conjure with our ugliness. I am a frail spectator, so dim as a phantom, so lost in magic, so vanished at a trail where vast substance fades, that I fear in my deadly life the loss of all my thought. May a bird ever sing in a tree, at the bright meadow, in a corner of a remembered happiness; and this image shall revive me.

"Alive; and here. God, you comfort me, and by stages convert strangeness to a shallower familiar: at sacrifice of depth, but at least bearable.

"Then, teach me. I shall endure the agony of ignorance, and abjure coarser knowledge. Better to question, than to know, if questions tap at Your source, and knowing cracks a hollow surface, which rings consolation. When an answer is withheld, may I fill the gap with so waiting a patience that I'm a monument to humility; having no information, I'm ripe on a time basis, ready material for a flood to sweep, the motions of light. Nature is more than surface, and no image may enclose it. I'll go, and may the flowings run into far comings, speeds for space to find and motions to swallow, mysteries in the season of eternity. So final a belonging includes me, in that deepest of all events, God, that there, armed with a fatal finding loss, I'll be in the center of still travel, hurled on by wings of all of space, forms that rush understanding in on myself, and my discovery shall be discovered. I stand at the last, being understood, thus possessed by that I wanted, and now all need fails; success gained me off, and at the edge of knowing, the fall became complete. And in the sum that remains, I'm struck out, among the empty and the done."

Two archaeologists found Eric's body. They were disappointed; he was so recent a version of man, so post-historic, that no value as relics would accrue to his bones. But what's that?—nearby, in the dirt, they decoded the inscription, through the blur of earth's compression. This dying essay moved them.

One observed, "He accepted ignorance, as an act of obedience. To whom? God?"

The other lit a pipe, puffed brokenly, and emitted a voluntary cough, by way of reply. It was open to ambiguous interpretation.

In this manner, they conversed, commenting on that double spectacle that lay strewn beolw: a dead author, and his work. They stood, and decided what, if anything, was meant.

One cautiously apprised the other of the fact, "His interest in nature is undoubted; the world is praised for being excellently organized; but he subjected himself to ignorance, deliberately. There's a case, if you will, of humility with its reward in a share of eternity. Apparently, he was God-haunted."

The other said, "Your statement seems reasonable. Was this fellow enlightened, would you say?"

The discussion lasted a good long while. With the talk buzzing over him, Eric delighted in his new taste of death. When would boredom set in?

Lighthearted, absent from guilt, he peered about for God. Not a sign. Choked by this disappointment, having given his all for a goal that failed, Eric gagged on the bitter cheat of his defeat, and detected no benefit derived from his current habitude of death. In these circumstances, the problem was altered, for which a strange solution was adequate. The archaeologists picked him up, and brought him to town on a truck. The formalities of burial, an ancient rite, were next in his odyssey. His quest was far from satisfied. Having not encountered God, either in life or death, Eric was prepared to assume that, in some third condition, he would achieve his objective. Fortified by this hope, he lost his earthly remains, and suffers change in a sea of chemicals. What novel throb in the course of his adventure is yet to assault his already dispirited soul? Through a waste of flesh, his conscience is molding new substance. For some terrible sin, God is needed. The search was plagued in torment. Even now, garbed in non-existence, he who was Eric hopes, through contrived accident and casual innocence, to sense-perceive God's self, be it ever so absent. His path crossed many turns. Mathematically, was it impossible, chained by a series of chances, for God to say "Hello" once to Eric? Once? The ocean of his appetite shall have been barely whetted.

A term of sturdy friendship would then be his unflagging ideal. God would be hounded; Eric would crush Him to his will.

ACKNOWLEDGMENTS

The publisher thanks the following individuals for their generous financial support which helped to defray some of this book's production costs:

Alvin Krinst
Antoinette Grace Hui
Bob Plourde
Brian R. Boisvert
Cody Garrett
Colin Myers
Deborah and Peter
Geoffrey Moses
Gil Klein
HankD
Haya K.
Jessica DeMarco-Jacobson
Mark S. Mitchell
Maureen Crowley Heil
Michael O'Shaughnessy
Michael Skazick
Shane Jesse Christmass
Sidney McMahon
Steve Elsberry

ABOUT THE AUTHOR

Marvin Cohen is an American essayist, novelist, playwright, poet, humorist, and surrealist. He is the author of nine published books and several plays. His short fiction and essays have appeared in more than 80 publications, including *The New York Times, The Village Voice, The Nation, Harper's Bazaar, Vogue, Fiction, The Hudson Review, Quarterly Review of Literature, Transatlantic Review,* and New Directions annuals. His 1980 play *The Don Juan and the Non-Don Juan* was first performed at the New York Shakespeare Festival as part of the Poets at the Public Series. Staged readings of the play have featured actors Richard Dreyfuss, Keith Carradine, Wallace Shawn, Jill Eikenberry, Larry Pine, and Mimi Kennedy.

Born in Brooklyn in 1931, Cohen has described himself as one who has "risen from lower-class background to lower-class foreground." He studied art at Cooper Union but left college to focus on writing, supporting himself with a series of odd jobs including mink farmer and merchant seaman. He also taught creative writing at The New School, the City College of New York, C.W. Post of Long Island University, and Adelphi University. Cohen currently lives in New York City with his wife, a retired paperback editor.